Hunting Gideon

A novel by Jessica Draper

ZARAHEMLA BOOKS
Provo, Utah

ISBN-10 0-9787971-4-0
ISBN-13 978-0-9787971-4-0

Cover design by Paul Browning

Published by
Zarahemla Books
869 East 2680 North
Provo, UT 84604
info@zarahemlabooks.com
ZarahemlaBooks.com

"This is a novel for people who enjoy science fiction and fantasy—gamers, hackers, role-players, and anyone who remembers and loves *The Adventures of Buckaroo Banzai Across the 8th Dimension*. If virtual reality is your reality, if you can hike through cyberspace without supplemental oxygen, if you believe the future belongs to the geeks—this is the novel for you. If you've been waiting for an LDS novel that affirms your faith but doesn't assume you're a housewife with an eighth-grade reading level, then you'll love *Hunting Gideon*."

—Preston McConkie, editor and journalist

"Finally! A new, fresh flavor of LDS fiction—smart, funny, and high tech. With appealing characters and unexpected turns, this story of hunt and pursuit will leave you grinning, satisfied, and eager for non-special agent Sue Anne Jones's next adventure."

—Eleanor T. Thorne, Ph.D.

"*Hunting Gideon* is the best novel I've read in a long time. With fun, intelligent characters, this fast-paced, exciting adventure kept me turning pages. It is vividly written, and it immersed me right at the beginning and kept me enthralled clear through the electrifying conclusion. A must-read for anyone who enjoys smart, fun action-adventures."

—Julie Nelson, editor

I STALKED SILENTLY through the buzzing data corridors, my feline ears pricked for the slithering of worm's scales against file walls. I slipped around a well-worn electronic corner in the shadowy database and peered discreetly into the next volume—and pounced! As my claws slashed through the ether, the slick tendril reared back and curled on itself, flashing away down the dark channel toward the portal. I threw myself after it, all four sets of claws digging into the hallucinatory fabric of virtual reality for traction. As I ran, I tapped alerts into the system around me. Obediently, a firewall sprang to life, blocking the worm's path with a blast of light and heat. The worm desperately flexed against the locked files around it, flailing against the burning walls in blind, mindless-program panic.

I closed in, grinning sharply—I couldn't help it, with my teeth. "You'll make a lovely addition to my collection," I purred. I readied my worm safe, the sticky strings of code ready to envelop and immobilize the sneaky program. Once safely contained, it could not avoid my sharp claws; I'd dissect it, pull its master's name and address from its digital guts, then track him down and pin him to the wall.

The worm trembled and folded in on itself. Just as I pulled the worm hook from my belt to snag it, a blast of anti-light blazed across the scene. As the firewall sputtered and died under this flood of override codes, a glowing figure appeared out of the V-Net connection. Pass codes streamed from its wings; its thin, silver soul-string trailed from its sparkling hair, connecting it to its real-world operator. With a casual gesture it deleted the crystallized worm, then turned a brilliant smile on me. "Not this time, Sekhmet," it intoned triumphantly before diving into the wild tides of the V-Net once again. The firewall snapped back up the moment the interference ceased, almost singeing my whiskers.

"Rats!" I snarled.

The sound of my voice broke the mesmerizing spell of virtual-reality immersion. I was no longer Sekhmet, my avatar. She was the character I controlled in the world of Aireon's virtual-reality network; I had named her after the Egyptian cat-goddess of the underworld and designed her accordingly. I left Sekhmet's lithe self for the mundane, gravity-bound reality of my own flesh and bones. My long-neglected muscles complained, shoulders, legs, and back all registering their objections to moving after their extended stillness. *Ook.* However, there was nothing wrong with me that better posture wouldn't fix.

I sat up straight, slipping my fingers out of the datagloves, then stretched, arching my back and reaching for the ceiling with my own short-nailed hands rather than Sekhmet's long-fingered claws. I collapsed back into my usual slouchy posture, shaking my head to clear the wild vision from my mind's eye. Sekhmet's green, feline eyes shone at me from my monitor, a series of scrolling readouts beside her telling me what I already knew too well. Despite my best efforts at catching it, the invasive spy exie—hacker shorthand for *program*—that had tripped my WormAlert had disappeared from OmniMental Employment's databases. Someone who thought of himself or herself—I leaned toward *himself*, since most crackers are guys—as an angel had found a hole in the agency's security system and made a connection through the V-Net, sending a surprisingly sophisticated modified computer virus—a worm—on reconnaissance missions through OmniMental's corporate network.

And I, Sue Anne Jones of the FBI's National Infrastructure Protection Center—the NIPC, pronounced "nipsy," a typically silly federal name; Computer Crimes Division would have been much better—had now chalked up three unsuccessful showdowns with this worm's creator and still didn't know where in the world the slimy, virtual beasties came from—and more importantly, who really sent them. I'd have to find out, though. After all, that's what they paid me for.

All right, here we go with the necessary background. The Department of Justice and the FBI created the NIPC at FBI headquarters in February of 1998. Yeah, hard to believe it took them so long to create an agency to deal with computer crimes, but despite it seeming like we've always had the V-Net at our fingertips, there are actually people still working today who took a typing class rather than keyboarding in high school—back when an IBM Selectric was the neat new addition to the classroom equipment, the station everybody wanted. (I know that says as much about pitiful education funding as about the rapid advancement of computer technology, but still.) Eventually, of course, the schools upgraded, and a bit later than that the FBI did too.

NIPC, unlike most FBI investigative programs, isn't a strictly government operation. It's a combination of federal, state, local, and private organizations. That gives us a wide and fairly deep reach, but sometimes it makes for lines of reporting, responsibility, jurisdiction, and command that are as organized as a bowl of noodles and not nearly as tasty. It also makes us vulnerable to the lobbying and money influence that major corporations and monopolies just love to throw around back in Washington, D.C.

Here in the Portland field office, we only occasionally get that kind of high-powered blowback and even then just for the really major cases. Mainly we just try to carry out NIPC's mandated mission: "To detect, deter, assess, respond to, and investigate computer intrusions and unlawful acts, both physical and cyber, that target the nation's critical infrastructures (i.e., banking systems, air traffic control, and transportation)." That's a direct quote from the FBI V-Net site, so I figure it's a fair assessment. My personal contribution to this grand scheme of things is to discover, hunt, track, document, and generally throw a big old virtual wrench into the schemes of all the bent geeks, phone phreaks, info thieves, wire-fraud artists, data burglars, cyberterrorists, RAM racketeers, and other slime dogs who crawl the V-Net looking to make a fast couple million bucks off the hordes of innocent, worker-bee citizens who throng our digital highways and cyberhavens day in and day out.

As you can imagine, that covers a pretty wide range of activities. NIPC started out as a minor part of the White-Collar Crime Division, which has always been the FBI's biggest criminal-investigation program. "White collar" seems to include every kind of crime that doesn't require its practitioners to wear a hard hat or ski mask, basically — so I guess it made sense to cram computer crimes in there too.

These days we're also closely associated with the Domestic Terrorism Investigative Program, as the original happy hackers and phone phreaks have evolved — or devolved — from juvenile pranks and stolen phone time to electronic hostage-taking and mass destruction. We also deal with the Organized Crime/Drug Program (OCDP) fairly frequently — the Mob may not be all that organized, but they're not slow to take advantage of new technologies, which is a pain for the Special Agents on their tails.

I'm actually what the FBI terms a non-Special Agent employee — "professional support personnel," in the Bureau's jargon — which is as close to civilian as an FBI employee gets. We're the ones who do everything that doesn't require the intensive training that the Special Agents go through at Quantico. They're what you think of when somebody says "FBI"—the ones who have to fit the age, height, fitness, wardrobe, and humorlessness requirements. Okay, I made those last two up, but the Bureau is adamant about their field agents representing truth, justice, and the American ideal of five-percent body fat. I don't fit that mold at all—I'm reasonably fit, though not ripped—but I do pride myself on doing an excellent job of tracking down guys like WormMaster and siccing those specially trained, square-jawed, suit-wearing, sunglassed Special Agents on their sorry tails. This time, I had to admit that we were still a long way from that point. Dang!

My half-embarrassed chagrin faded quickly, though, evaporating in the remembered joy of the chase. Whoever WormMaster was, he surely knew how to write a squippy program. I'd catch him the next time he sent in his beastie; I'd nearly snatched him this time, despite his slick use of the administrator override account he shouldn't have had. Then again, OmniMental, bless their naive hearts, were practically poster children for everything *not* to do in this oh-so-wired age: easily guessed passwords they never changed, a revolving door of administrator permissions, total lack of encryption on their file servers, an amazing degree of carelessness about applying the latest virus guards or NetSys updates from Aireon. (No wonder Aireon was making a huge deal out of the new auto-deployment program it planned to roll out soon.) The amazing thing was not that a cracker had infiltrated OmniMental's databases but that no one had done it sooner.

Oddly enough—and luckily for OmniMental—WormMaster didn't seem interested in their financial transactions, even though thousands of dollars poured through their coffers every day. Instead, the worms hovered around the personnel databases, poking and prying. I had spotted this particular worm inside the e-mail servers, nuzzling its headless front end into the nonstop flow of electronic vitaes and résumés. However, I'd never actually seen its master within the company's confines; he preferred to lurk in the shallows of the V-Net connection, not quite committing himself to the full contact that would let me nab his avatar's built-in identification.

For all the occasional embarrassment and frustration, though, I enjoyed the chase and the challenge—and guys like these represented job security. Besides, spending a Saturday night dive-bombing around inside somebody else's computers surely beat the usual single-chick routine of kicking back on the couch with a brain-spew comedy on the vid and a bag of chocolate-chip cookies beside me on the couch. If only I looked more like Sekhmet, all cheetah sleek and exotically spotted, maybe I wouldn't be able to completely sympathize with Mae West's observation that "It's better to get looked over than overlooked." Fact is, my best feature is my hair, real auburn and waist-length. ("Sue Jones," the guys down at the office said. "You know, the one with the hair.")

Oh, well. I might be a medium-build, medium-sized computer geek in the unforgiving light of reality, but I made up for it by having an active fantasy life.

That vivid imagination certainly made my forays into the wilds of the V-Net and corporate computer systems much more interesting. The V-Net had grown from the old Internet, a decentralized network connecting millions of computers around the world, a system that in just minutes let a girl in Singapore trade photos with a guy in Johannesburg and decide they really weren't meant for each other. The Internet was just the beginning, though. Once you connect computers, you have to make it easy for people to use the connections to do things far beyond simple data exchanges. That's where Aireon came in, principal architects of the new V-Net. However, Aireon Technologies' exclusively patented virtual-reality interface, while great for games, everyday computing, shopping, and live interactions, failed miserably at conveying the kind of detailed information we at NIPC actually used to track and monitor the far-flung reaches of the V-Net.

Despite the amazing three-dimensional role-plays available out on the user sites that the news programs, movie producers, and everyday V-Netizens loved, hardcore hackers still depended on readouts, diagnostic tools, logic-bombs that stopped intruding programs, and too many lines of nasty-bad code that popped up in display windows over the three-dimensionally rendered images. Network troubleshooting, boring on the outside, was a lot more exciting inside my head, where I added the hot action to the basic visuals.

Loren—another non-Special Agent employee and fellow hacker and tracker—laughed at my purple-prose descriptions of our battles against the forces of evil, but he enjoyed them. Especially the bits where I described him as the Black Knight brought out of Darkness to serve the Light, even though he invariably snuffed and made a sarcastic comment about romantically repressed Mormon maidens. Pretty uppity for a Catholic-raised, orphan-boy anarchist, if you ask me.

Right then, however, I decided to put that overheated imagination on cool and devote my few remaining mental energies to figuring out the best visual aids to use in presenting the concept of the Holy Ghost to a class full of four-year-old Sunbeams. That would be challenging enough without *Ghastlie and the Ghouls*, the latest kid-oriented cartoon to populate the Saturday-morning Cartoon Network with critters you'd never want to bump into in real life. If I could just get the point across in preschooler terms, keep Tyler from jumping off his chair, and convince Jaylee that her skirt belonged around her knees rather than her ears, I'd consider it a successful Sunday.

I retired Sekhmet to her usual treetop perch in the woodland background filling my monitor and pulled on my other skin, the one I used in civilian life, to go resource hunting. I hadn't put a lot of effort into this avatar, primarily because I spent by far most of my time walking around on Sekhmet's clawed hind paws, but my personal avatar was certainly distinctive. In all my wanderings through the looking-glass universe of the V-Net, I'd never run into another ghost avatar—specifically, an online persona built entirely of transparent ether, with only a pair of eyes, gloves, and an occasional flashing grin to indicate a presence at all. It certainly got me noticed—when people did notice. I'd even unwittingly won Aireon's Original Avatars contest—plus the prize of a dozen or so free avatar upgrades—a few months back. Sometimes, as I laughingly told my sister Penny, less really is more.

The Lamanite maiden paging through the clip art and activity suggestions in the Sunbeam room of one of the best Primary-oriented V-Net sites instantly recognized the pair of large, green, disembodied eyes and the wide, sharp grin that floated onto her screen.

"Hey, Sue," she chirped. For such a dusky maid, she'd chosen a very light voice for herself; it sounded very young as it burbled out of the speakers. I had no idea what she looked or sounded like in real life or much of anything about her except that she too taught Sunbeams, frequented this V-Net library at odd hours on Saturday nights, and was a friendly soul.

"Hi, Becca," I returned. "You on Holy Ghost too?"

She laughed, her avatar's lovely face freezing in a smile instead of moving with the sound. One of the differences between hackers like me and regular people is that they don't get all uptight and intense about minor things like facial expressions. She'd simply licensed a ready-made avatar—Sacagawea or something—and hadn't done a lot of customization aside from hiking up the neckline and lowering the hem of the figure's buckskin gown. "Yes, indeed," she said. "Bet that's right up your alley!"

I gave her a bright smile of my own and let it go with a "Ha, ha" that probably sounded sincere coming out of her console speakers.

It was no surprise that I didn't find many visual aids dealing with the Holy Ghost, but several of the suggested activities looked like they had possibilities for my gaggle of goslings—especially the ones involving blindfolds. They'd quite liked my earlier lesson on lies, which included getting tied up in soft clothesline. Pity I couldn't work that into more lessons.

Nancy, the collector and compiler of all this Primary-oriented material, made everything available for free. Bless her heart, she'd used the virtual room that came along with her Aireon account to make life easier for us novice Sunbeamers, collecting all kinds of resources and decorating the electronic walls with pictures of supernaturally cheerful, well-behaved Primary classes.

My own V-Net room stood bare, completely empty aside from my stacks of sheet music and random scribbles of original guitar tunes. V-Net rooms had replaced the Internet's original websites; they were places where you could express your personality for everyone to see, lock up your secrets, or just let virtual dust gather. Thinking about that, I told myself I shouldn't dis Becca's off-the-shelf avatar; I guess it's all a matter of priorities.

"Thanks, Nancy—you're a lifesaver," I wrote on the message board for her to read when she came in the next day, then I retreated back into reality to fold a dishtowel for use as a blindfold, read the lesson, and get ready for Sunday's spiritually oriented circus.

By Monday morning I was ready to go back to work. Rolling out of bed too early in the morning and exercising is no fun, but it's less stressful than Primary. Breathe in, hold, spread arms slowly, fingers reaching, back straight. Beads of sweat blurred my vision for a moment, but wiping my face on my shoulder took care of that. I knew that aerobics was an old-fashioned exercise method, but I preferred it to the alternatives. ErgoNomics touted their full-body datasuit as the ultimate replacement for both datagloves and exercise equipment, helping—or forcing—users to act out every move their avatars made in cyberspace, but that didn't appeal to either my wallet or my sense of dignity. Besides, my computer console and monitor already dominated my small living room; installing the kind of human-sized gyroscope that full-body motion required would transform my apartment into the human equivalent of a really complicated hamster cage. Nah, I'd get my exercise in reality and deal with the occasional stiffness from sitting still too long while my fingers did all the work. Besides, going through the familiar moves let my mind rest too — or at least go skipping around random thoughts and memories.

I'd once sarcastically told Loren that I endured the aerobic workout because I enjoyed the cool-down stretches so much. He'd played it literally and asked if I often beat my head against a wall because it felt so good when I stopped. The only comeback to that was to inform him that people with fast metabolisms would die first in the Great Famines of the Apocalypse.

I was just kidding, of course — I could just as easily have attributed a hypothetical food shortage to Mount Hood finally blowing its top, but the quip led to a discussion of Armageddon, the Revelation of St. John the Divine, and the Mormon beliefs about them; I told him that most of us know better than to try to set a date on an event that even the angels in heaven do not know and that the entire purpose of Revelation was to show that despite Evil's best efforts, Good triumphed completely in the end.

Loren's always trying to understand how such a rational, intelligent woman — he means me — could believe the doctrines of such a bizarre sect. I just laugh and tell him we're a peculiar people. I also told him once that when he decides he really wants the answers to life, the universe, and everything — as well as the right questions to ask — to let me know. Then I backed off for the moment. If he wants a serious discussion, I'm more than happy to oblige him, but he's got what they used to call "issues" with the whole idea of God as a benevolent, all-powerful Father. Probably came of being an orphan and feeling abandoned in a selfish, cruel world — though that feeling didn't necessarily follow for all of us orphans.

Ook. I didn't want to think about that right then — my parents' absence still hurt, even though I knew they were okay and that I'd see them again sooner or later — so I turned my attention back to the vid screen and the too-early morning newscast.

"Sunshine Foods proudly announced a dramatic breakthrough in the field of consumables delivery today." Images of smiling corporate bigwigs replaced the morning newscaster's slick head and fashionably loud tie. They clustered in front of a fleet of huge transports, each brightly painted with Sunshine Foods' cartoon sun emblem — why does a sun need sunglasses? — posing for the cameras as the voiceover continued, "Using a revolutionary tracking and navigation system approved by the Federal Department of Transportation, Sunshine Foods will now be able to deliver their products to any outlet in the country in record time."

A quartet of scruffier-looking creatures lurked behind the marketeers as the CEO stepped to the microphone to reaffirm her pride and joy at Sunshine Foods' sole claim to these ground-breaking new patents. The guys in the back were geeks. Instantly recognizable. Probably the brains behind the robot big rigs standing patiently at the loading docks, where busy mechanical stevedores piled pallet after loaded pallet into their spacious guts. The last loader rolled back down the ramp, its metal arms empty. Behind it the jaws of the transport's double doors closed smoothly. Lights flickered along the edges of the huge trucks, the bass hum of the motors rumbled under the merely human voices jabbering at the camera, and the six-transport convoy rolled forward in perfect synchronicity. The camera operator, betraying his own technology-loving leanings, followed the boxy train for a few seconds longer than the producer probably liked, but I appreciated the extended view. Plenty of worried people chattered and speculated on the V-Net and off about the nightmare problems they saw lurking behind the glorious mask of ever-expanding automation of the world, but I always found it interesting and exciting.

Breathe out, curve arms, lunge slowly to the right, keeping the movement slow and smooth. Yes, I know you shouldn't do Tai Chi — not even my mutated version of it — while watching television; the California-blond sensei, Rick, who taught the Fitness and Meditation class I'd taken last year would have a massive coronary attack, despite his resting heart rate of forty-two and arteries of a four-year-old. Fact is, I've never been able to concentrate on something as profoundly dull as exercise without something else to distract me.

On screen the smiley faces babbled on, incapable of letting the pictures speak for themselves. The gist of the live-action press release, I decided, was that Sunshine Foods had just consolidated its position as sole grocery supplier to the Western portion of the United States and slipped out from under the thumb of the Teamsters' Union in one swell foop. From one monopoly to another. Now they staged this low-key propaganda rally to convince me that it was a great thing for me and my fellow consumers. I elected to reserve judgment. Automation I liked; the wholesale consolidation of everything from media companies to airlines to insurance agencies to grocery stores didn't thrill me.

Raise foot, straighten knee, bring arms down, pivot lightly, hold—two, three, four. If I could actually do this at Jackie Chan speeds, I'd be lethal.

The newscast touched on the latest allegations of corporate-cop brutality against protesters, subtly plugged Aireon Technologies' latest NetSys rollout announcement, burbled through the weather report—cloudy, chance of showers, the usual—and at last reached the human-interest segment they always used to wrap up the broadcast. This cute-animal story starred a hamster in England who jumped around on a touch screen to create rodent designs in time to the latest Brit-hit dance music. Its owner, Ms. Lydia Blankenthorpe, assured the viewing audience that the hamster contained the reincarnated soul of David Bowie, nee Jones. Much to the commentator's delight, she also made a habit of donning a VR helmet and body stocking to "dance" with the little beastie in real time, claiming to have found the love of her life in the hamster's online avatar, Adonis. "Adorable," smugged the heavily accented BBC narrator. "Avatar amore in Ayreshire."

And stretch, and stop. I mopped the last of the aerobic-bout perspiration from my face and waved my hand toward the vid's motion sensor. It blinked off, drowning Ms. Blankenthorpe's made-up face in pixilated darkness. "Why do some single femmes have to be such twits?" I asked the Sea Queen hanging in blue serenity on the living-room wall. The question dissolved, answerless, in a cloud of shower steam as the image of the WormMaster raised its angelic head in my mind. Whoever he was, he had a serious case of self-adoration to choose an avatar like that!

"So," Loren drawled in a perfectly knowing tone, "how was Primary?" (Ah, yes, the tall, skinny guy incorrectly lounging in his ergonomically correct office chair is my coworker, Loren Hunter. I introduce him as my assistant when I'm being obnoxious, but I really consider him more of a partner.) He didn't bother to straighten up from his languidly stretched pose across his cubicle, his legs looking even longer compared to the cramped space. He did hook the audio input away from one of his ears, though he kept a blue eye on the flickering newsfeed scrolling down one side of the main screen as he glanced at me. One of the last of the white knights — he twitched his chair aside just enough to let me squeeze by.

A paper airplane flew over the cubicle wall, bonking off my body and landing on the desk. I unfolded it, wrote "Hello back, Ed" under "Hail, auburn-maned Amazon!" and tossed it back over the partition. Ed always came in just before I did and prided himself on never saying a word to anybody in person — only electronically or through some kind of proxy, like paper. Weird guy, good programmer, absolutely fascinated with real life — as observed on his dozen or so video monitors, that is.

Other than the desks Ed, Loren, and I occupied, the rest of the cubicles dividing the big pod room sat bare, dark, and empty of everything but the drifts of dusty lint that all computer installations accumulate like New England hills collect snow. The physical population of our department varied widely by the day and week; nearly everybody else preferred to work from home and showed up only to file reports or get their evaluations from Dave. There had been a push for doing those online too, which Dave refused by telling the ones who suggested it that he had to make sure they were actual people, rather than obnoxious avatars who'd somehow gained self-awareness and independence — or were all actually the same person, using the V-Net to collect multiple paychecks from the generous, unsuspecting government.

Dave is Dave Connor, our local Special Agent in Charge. That's SAC in Bureau parlance; federal cops like acronyms almost as much as the military does. I teased Dave about getting a promotion so he could be our DAD instead — Deputy Assistant Director, the third in command of an entire FBI division. However, there are only thirteen FBI divisions, and even Deputy Assistant Directors are very big fish in the FBI lake, so that'd be quite a leap. He isn't even an Assistant Director in Charge (ADIC); only D.C., Los Angeles, New York, and Dallas have field offices big enough to merit that honor. So Dave supervises the epic victories and heartbreaking defeats of the two-dozen of us non-Special Agent types who sniff out, locate, and tattle on crackers of all kinds, and he has an Assistant Special Agent in Charge (ASAC), Special Agent Damien Stark, who runs the bunch of Captain America Special Agents who actually chase down the bad guys for us.

Pinky, one of our quasi-phantom coworkers, once started a petition asking Dave to declare everybody's homes as resident agencies, official satellite offices of the field office that could have as few as one and as many as several dozen employees. That designation, she claimed, would promote us all to Supervisory Senior Resident Agents, boosting our official government rating and raising our salaries. Dave didn't go for it. When she complained, he told her he'd happily transfer her to the Information Technology Center in Pocatello, Idaho. She told him that she'd quit better jobs than this, stomped out, and had another petition circulating the next week—this one pushing to add cable-connection fees to the list of reimbursable expenses. A girl had to have enough cash to buy bon-bons, after all. That petition died the same swift, silent death as the others; everybody—even Pinky—knew they had a good thing going already.

So, most of the cubicles stood dark and abandoned, except for the small island of habitation here by the windows. Ed dragged his reclusive tail into the office because he wanted to get away from his mother; I preferred to keep work at work and home at home whenever possible. Well, I told myself I did—my actual behavior put a huge lie to that excuse; I guess I came in because I'd rather have somebody real to talk to than stay locked away in my apartment, associating with electronic ghosts all day long. Loren just seemed to live at the office, though I knew that he paid rent on an apartment somewhere.

"Oh, Primary went fine, just fine," I informed Loren. "They came away knowing that there are two ghosts in the world that they don't have to be afraid of—Ghastlie McGhoul and the Holy Ghost. We had only three instances of table-to-chair-to-floor dive bombing, the underpants-comparison session went very well, and everybody enjoyed watching Tyler tear around the room blindfolded. They even sang at the top of their lungs—true, they did it between the official songs, but at least they sang. I'm clearly making some progress in one direction or another."

Loren looked sympathetic. "You know what your problem is? You invest too much emotional energy in trying to make them learn something. They're just four years old—all they care about is that you like them. You do that, you'll be surprised how much they pick up."

"Well," I sighed wearily, "they do know that they're supposed to fold their arms and walk reverently, even if they actually tear around like maniacs. If only you were so easy to train. Where are your manners? Here it is Monday morning, you haven't seen me for a full forty-eight hours, and what do you say? No 'Good morning, Sue,' or 'My, you're looking lovely today—the aerobics are really paying off.' Nah, all you want are the latest war stories from the Sunbeam front." Standing before my computer, I scanned down the list of incoming e-messages, affecting world-weary nonchalance.

That earned me a full-on grin, Loren's chipped front tooth off-setting the wickedly elegant arch of his eyebrows. "Hey, that's not all. I also want to hear all about how the WormMaster slipped out of your clutches—again."

I gave that the eye roll it deserved and scanned down the entries in my mailbox: a "Hi, Sue!" note from my sister Penny (she knew better than to try to write me at my "civilian" address), three pieces from Pinky detailing the latest juicy gossip (I got at least six messages from her every day, besides her infamous petitions, but I'd seen her in person only three times—twice at company parties), a follow-up reply to the question I'd sent to Shawnie in the Foreign Liaison Office in D.C. about a Mexican company selling cut-rate and cut-quality pharmaceuticals over the V-Net, two advertisements that somehow managed to come here instead of to my civilian address, an appointment from Dave scheduling our weekly department-wide teleconferencing meeting, and so on. All the usual stuff, until one item on the list caught my eye.

I groaned and said to Loren, "Why don't you get it from the horse's mouth instead?" I slid my fingers into the datagloves and flicked open the electronic envelope.

The message unfolded, revealing the angelic face of WormMaster's avatar. "So good to see you again, Sekhmet," it said, "from all angles." I slapped off the animated display, exchanging its full-motion audio-video for plain text—angels, however twisted, shouldn't leer like that. The rest of the short message echoed the WormMaster's usual cocky attitude: "But you better be more careful, kitty—you know what they say about curiosity killing the cat, and it would be a shame if something permanent happened to those lovely pixels."

"Mm—threats," Loren noted, reading the note over my shoulder. "You worried?"

I laughed. "No need. It's just the usual cracker jive. He pulled my avatar name off OmniMental's wide-open mail computer, and he's been treating me like a video-game opponent ever since. I just about caught one of his worms Saturday night, and I'll skin his name out of another one the next chance I get." I shrugged, opening my calendar for a look at the daily tasks that seemed to grow there like mushrooms overnight. "I'm more interested in the Sunshine Foods announcement this morning. You see that?"

He rolled his eyes. "Oh, yeah, the multiple cartwheels over their drone-ship fleet. Bully for them — until one of their new robo trucks delivers a shipment of Twinkies to a Whole Earth commune outside Frisco instead of the Los Alamos Missile Base. Nothing like offending granolas with hydrolyzed vegetable shortening and yellow number five while depriving bit-biters of their high-lipid lifeblood to expose the glitches in technical marvels." He opened his own task list with unnecessary force, growling, "They're a bunch of piranhas anyway. You see the jack-up they pulled on the prices they charge offline locations? As if rural types don't have enough stacked against them without having to pay extra shipping charges for groceries."

"There's that rabid social conscience, rearing its righteous head again," I clucked teasingly.

He thumped his forehead dramatically. "Oh, sorry — I forgot I should've dumped that when I joined the Bureau, along with my sense of humor and my taste in music."

"Speaking of which, what've you got pouring into your ears now?" I asked, settling into my chair at last. Dave often teased me about my princess-sensitive derriere being allergic to our cube-dweller chairs because I tended to stand up when I wasted valuable company time chatting with my coworkers (and him); I usually let the comments go with a smile and made a point of describing him as "such a Dave" when talking to people within his earshot. He had good hearing too, which made it all the more amusing.

The second I slipped Loren's audio hook over my ears, thumping bass and wailing guitar blasted into my brain, a deep baritone growling Halloween lyrics in German to a reverse-heart beat. "What *is* this?" I asked over the surprisingly catchy crashing and banging.

"You don't have to shout," Loren assured me, chuckling. "I'm not the one with Perforated Spleen blasting into my head."

"They seriously call themselves that?" I reluctantly surrendered the hook into Loren's long fingers. It would make a terrific soundtrack for my next duel with the WormMaster. "Not bad music for a serious gut trauma. Can I borrow it?"

"Sure. The band's actually called Entropy Twins." He waved to his monitor. "Found 'em blowing the roof off a V-Net hole based out in Montana. Not bad for a bunch of cow punchers, eh?"

"Eh," I agreed. Then I groaned, looking at my monitor again, with more attention this time. "Oh, jeez—looks like OmniMental's sent Dave another panic-button wail." I opened the e-mail marked *Urgent*. Its title proclaimed, GET A MOVE-ON WITH THE MENTAL CASES, a sentiment repeated sixteen times, in ever-growing fonts, through the body of the message and signed off with *Your impatient BOSS, Dave*.

"Thought you'd like that one," Loren said nonchalantly, indicating his own monitor. "I got it too. Looks like you'd better take Dave down a peg or two. He's getting uppity."

I moved to smack him lightly upside the head. "Think I don't know spoofing when I see it? Besides, Dave is too PR conscious to call them mental cases. What if they found out by some fluke?" I flicked my Truth-or-Die exie into the message, and the "From" line dissolved, *Edward D'Eath* replacing *David Connor* in a wash of solidifying mist. Eddie Death—just one of the many avatars Loren used for his personal V-Net business, and my personal favorite. "So, now you've got Eddie running scams for you," I noted sadly. "Why can't you pick an avatar for work and stick with it?"

"Call me a split personality," he suggested, then grinned wildly. "Cliché alert! I don't suffer from insanity, I enjoy every minute of it. Variety is the spice of life. Come up and see me some time. A loaf of bread, a jug of wine, and thou. . . . Oops—abort! Illegal access to personal-relations domain! Reboot system!" He closed his eyes, went utterly still, then perked back up, systems normal once more. "All right, so Dave didn't send that. But what are you going to do about that nasty bug crawling the files at OmniMental?"

"I'm going to make another one just like it," I told him. "Maybe three or four."

"Make more of them? You can't catch the one we've got. Have you started using one of those newfangled hemp-based shampoos?" He was giving me the big, disbelieving reaction I expected, but I could see the watchful interest spark in his eyes, behind the ragged curtain of glossy, black bangs. He wouldn't know a decent haircut if it walked up and bit him, but he did keep the unruly locks clean.

It was my turn to grin. "Nope, but I'm going to persuade a skinny, blue-eyed, cynical ex-cracker to use the copycat bug in Aireon's NetSys 11.3 to make a duplicate of that snoopy worm, and slap that puppy right into my worm box. Then our seraphic buddy WormMaster can delete his minion all he wants—I've got the sample I need to make a vaccination for his particular brand of virus. And then we'll put the beastie through our version of a bare-bulb interrogation and make it tell us who WormMaster really is."

"Ah, the good old copycat bug." Loren sighed nostalgically. "I'm really going to miss her when Aireon puts out NetSys 11.4 next month. We've had some good times, the old tabby and me."

"You'll just have to find something else—unless I beat you to it," I said, leaving myself open for his "know-it-all little girl" retort. He always performed better when I presented the task as a personal competition.

By the time Dave wandered by to check up on our progress, we barely muttered "hello," absorbed in bending the Aireon system's unintentionally powerful program-duplication feature to our ends. That was one of the characteristics of super-complex software programs; their wide-ranging features usually had unintended and unforeseen consequences.

"Got it!" Loren exclaimed smugly. "Let's see WormMaster squirm his way out of this one." The neatly written exie hovered innocently, a fuzzy kitten sleeping peacefully if incongruously in the undersea scene filling his monitor. An electronic fish swam up to the small cat, nuzzled her curiously—and instantly split into two identical, brilliantly colored fish. They regarded each other for a moment, pop-eyed and mouthing, before the kitten happily pounced on one of them and swallowed it down whole. She sat back, licking her chops as the original flashed away and vanished in the watery distance of the simulated kelp forest.

"Nice," I said admiringly. "Where's the handle?"

"Right here, the scruff of the neck. And here's the trigger," he explained, stroking the visual representation of the copy program through the datagloves. "You pet her, she purrs, and there you go, instant twins. One goes on its way, one goes down her hatch, and we make her hork it up later. Got Sekhmet ready to go? It's time to eat some worms."

Actually, it turned out to be time to wait around. My dad used to say that every hour of police work included forty-five minutes of boredom, ten minutes of paperwork, and five minutes of sheer terror. By my estimate he was off only on the proportion of paperwork, but that could just be the difference between the FBI and "real" cops. In this case, though, cyber criminals acted just like physical housebreakers, never pulling a job when it was convenient for the good guys. I figured my dad probably got a kick out of his daughter making a career out of combining his out-of-college summer police work with the video games he'd considered a complete waste of time but still played occasionally.

Loren and I logged in to OmniMental's system using the specially issued password that gave us unlimited access to their computers. Sekhmet's lithe, feline form appeared within OmniMental's brain-on-lightning icon on my monitor. So did the vicious-looking emerald-and-ebony monster Loren called Mama. ("After Grendel's mother, duh. Don't you read anything but comic books?" he had sighed when I first asked him about it. I actually did, it just surprised me that *he* did.) Aireon's interface was supposed to allow only one avatar per person for identification and billing purposes, and certainly only one at a time, but Loren blithely blew past that restriction, using one of the better-hidden programming holes to create as many virtual identities as he wanted, each with different capabilities. The multiple-avatar program Loren used really was an extremely slick hack and could've done serious damage to Aireon's monthly income — if you ghosted around the V-Net with an unregistered avatar, their usage monitors couldn't pick it up or bill you for it — but part of the reason the Powers That Be let him get away with it was that he didn't share it with anybody else, not even me. Even Dave didn't bug him about it any more, after knocking heads with him so many times on various other matters that Dave's skull practically had a set of dents in it.

The one side effect of Loren's off-brand identity habit was that any evidence he uncovered using an unregistered avatar wasn't admissible in court; therefore, he usually used his one legitimate Bureau persona: Special Agent Man, alias Sam, an exaggerated film-noir representation of Loren as a blue-cheeked, cigarette-smoking, trench-coated Philip Marlowe archetype. The same went for me, actually, and for everybody else in our team: we had to use our FBI-sanctioned avatars for all Bureau-sponsored business. That meant that Sekhmet or Sam had to "officially" discover any evidence of malfeasance — if I didn't spot it myself and Loren wasn't in character at the moment, he had to point it out to me so I could. His acceptance of that situation surprised me, but Loren seemed blithely free of the usual macho impulses; he got a bigger kick out of thumbing his nose at the rules than taking credit for some of his "kills." I didn't know whether to take his stated excuse — "I'm just helping them realize what a great hacker you are, partner. You caught *me*, didn't you?" — seriously or as a tease. However he meant it, he was extremely helpful and good at cracker tracking, and I enjoyed having a competent coinvestigator to watch my back and chew over possibilities with me.

The two of us prowled through the employment company's computers, sniffing for any trace of worm activity in the company's network. We startled an employee enjoying a round of Blast Raider on company time: Mama destroyed his railgun with a single swipe of one massive paw and snarled "GET BACK TO WORK" in such a bass register that the poor guy's speakers probably sub-woofered themselves into short-circuiting. We eavesdropped on an annoyingly perky audio-video e-mail message from Human Resources: "It's Fitness Week! Join Michelle and the rest of the Human Resources staff in the Garden Atrium for a lunchtime walk around the campus. Free cookies and drinks after the activity!" And we interrupted an administrator working in the databases. His avatar, a standard-issue superhero 'toon with *Byte Man* blazoned across its rippling pecs, shot "Who the heck are you?" at us in flaming font and a standard-issue baritone as he reached for his account disabler. He wasn't fast enough, of course. Mama caught him in a slowdown loop that temporarily blocked all his administrative privileges.

"Watch your language," Mama snarled in freezing letters. "There's a lady present."

"Two ladies, actually," I purred, and pulled my OmniMental hall pass from Sekhmet's carry pouch and presented it to Byte Man. It unscrolled, flashing green as he verified it.

"All right, you're legit," he grudgingly admitted, shooting glare daggers at Mama before sending Sekhmet a grin with a glint in it. "Lose the monster and come on back here alone, kitty?"

"Don't do it," I warned Loren aloud. Mama reluctantly returned the infinite loop to its place underneath her scaled chest skin. "We're here on duty, remember? He's a dork, but he's also a civilian. Let's just go." Suiting action to words, I favored Byte Man with Sekhmet's sharp-toothed smile and used him as a springboard for a gymnastic back flip. He crashed backward into the glittering database as we dove once again into the data stream.

"Let's just go," Mama mimicked, using Sekhmet's hissing accent in a deeper register. "He's just a civilian. Sure, so you can lay a spring-kick retreat on him, but I can't give him the electric constipation. Where's the fairness in this world?"

"Call it a case of the lady taking care of herself," I suggested airily. "But it was sweet of you to step in like that." Within the monitor, Sekhmet bestowed an affection peck on Mama's Tyrannosaur cheek before springing off down the corridor once again.

"Hey, we're all ladies here," Mama growled back, then showed her teeth, with a long, crimson forked tongue flashing out of the fanged mouth.

"Kinky."

The roar of the datastreams increased in depth, and the V-Net portal lay before us, the firewall flickering menacingly. Streams of encrypted packets flowed through in both directions, flashing their key permissions. Other packets, without the correct permissions, hit the firewall and disintegrated in puffs of random bits.

"He comes in here." I pointed to the portal. Just then, a particularly nasty piece of spam hit the firewall and exploded into a rainbow of hissing particles. "When he comes to get his recon worms, he uses a standard firewall opener, loaded with codes one of the worms probably stole from OmniMental. The worms themselves get in through message attachments, ducking under the virus protection. Then, they just crawl through the databases gathering up copies of the information he wants, scramble it so only he can read it, and wait for him to come get them."

"So we warn the mental cases not to accept attachments from anybody they don't know, and tell them which firewall access code's been compromised." Mama shrugged, black scales glistening green in the firewall's glow. "Problem solved."

"We warn them *after* we grab either him or one of his worms," I corrected. "That way, he's not out there ready to try again with some other security-lax outfit. Besides, the mail-sorting program's automated — we've got to catch a worm and take it apart so we can tell them what kinds of attachments not to accept."

"They could just set it to refuse any code-active pieces. It'd throw out any homemade nudie interactives, but how many people use those, anyway?" Mama smiled at me with a set of teeth any crocodile would envy. "Ah, you just like the chase, and you know it. Little Sekhmet's got a new catnip mouse."

I brushed off the slight twinge of guilt but couldn't really deny the truth of the comment. I did love the chase; that was why I'd applied to the FBI's computer-crime prevention wing in the first place. Yes, I wanted to help the white hats defeat the black hats, and I'd always had a fiery lust for justice — the fact that I really enjoyed this kind of mental kung fu just seemed like icing on the whole doing-good-for-society cake. "Maybe so. If he were getting into anything really sensitive, I'd have told them how to stop him already. But the worms haven't been hovering around the accounting program or the business-confidential areas or the advertising campaigns or the telecom services or even the employee files. Come on, I'll show you."

We loped away, taking a sharp ninety-degree upturn in the wild Escher space of the network. The tightly controlled confidential areas fell rapidly behind us, the walls opening into a huge space. Whirring packets filled the virtual air, pouring from a dozen spigots and flying into a vast collection of bins marked ACCOUNTING, PROGRAMMING, and so on. Others rose from the bins and fluttered into neat bundles to join the stream of outgoing messages flowing into the corridor that led to the V-Net connection. We stopped beside a bin marked TECHNICAL WRITING and watched the gracefully frantic activity.

"They look like bees flying out and returning to the hive." Mama caught one out of the air, breaking its seal. A holophoto bloomed into life, showing a smiling, middle-aged woman posed in a sunny studio. A prettily formatted résumé scrolled in beside her. "Judy Nakamura is an experienced digital artist and Web designer," the résumé's soundtrack informed us. Its professionally pleasant voice continued, enumerating Judy's strengths and experience, finally listing her V-Net ID and avatar name for further contact. When it finished, Mama let it go; it wrapped neatly into its original package and continued its trip to the DESIGN bin.

"So what does WormMaster want with a bunch of public-access résumés?" Mama asked, question marks swirling around the words to match the inquiring tone in her rumbling voice. "These don't even have real-time addresses or phone numbers. What's he doing, poaching résumés?"

"I don't know," I admitted, my tail twitching. "But OmniMental is the top employment agency for all kinds of tech pros in the U.S. If he's out to steal a client base or recruit high-drawer employees without having to pay the headhunters, this would be the place to hit. Whatever he's doing, though, this is where the worms get in. The worm hatches out of the résumé and goes rooting around, catching other résumés out of the air. I've watched them. Sometimes they grab one, read it, and let it go without doing anything; other times they copy it and eat the copy. They're picky too. I had one in my sights last night, and it stole only two résumés."

"Sounds more like a Trojan horse than a worm," Mama noted.

"Yeah, worms usually just multiply like slimy little rabbits before sending themselves out to infect other systems. These are more like electronic spies. OmniMental said somebody'd been opening their mail before they got to it. But maybe the worms can't e-mail out a résumé, let alone a bunch of them. So these beasties have to get down to the V-Net portal and establish a connection back to their master to transmit the stuff."

"Well, we can't set the copycat trap in here." Mama gestured around the teeming space. "Too many other things could stumble into it." That grin reappeared, needing only tiny birds hopping between the teeth to complete the Nile River image. "I don't figure the mental cases would like it filling their computers with endless copies of Judy Nakamura, no matter how accomplished an artist she may be. It is tempting, though."

"A network brought to its knees by a marauding army of sweet clones." I laughed at the thought. "Nah, let's hide the copycat next to my WormAlert monitor. That way, when a worm pops in, the cat can copy it right off. Then we can follow it out to grab the Worm-Master. Obnoxious things anyway," I muttered as we retreated to the monitoring station, "not to show up when we come all the way out here, and armed for hunting bears too." I patted the kitten, which obediently curled up beside my monitor, its large eyes as blue as Loren's. "Keep those pretty eyes open, Copycat, and catch us a worm."

We left her there, sleepily watching the fluttering packets as we logged off OmniMental's network. We would come back and collect her when the next worm set off my alarm. Loren had also added a homing instinct; if the cat caught a worm and we didn't appear, she'd e-mail herself home to us. "Kennel class," Loren assured me. "Not cargo."

I blinked, reorienting myself to the physical world, leaving Sekhmet curled up on a long limb of the extravagantly branched tree inside the forest scene I used on my monitor. My palms tickled slightly, as if I could feel the kitten's soft fur. Given my affection for all things feline, it wasn't surprising that Loren's latest creation made me wish my job gave me more time for a pet. Oh, well, I'd settle for our little Copycat. It had pleasant associations of its own.

In a way, the copycat bug had played matchmaker for Loren and me. My first big assignment involved a headlong run-in with the unknown computer genius raiding and corrupting the corporate system at Aireon. Aireon was Paul Stanton's answer to the ancient feud between the U.S. government and Microsoft and the source of the software that revolutionized the entire software industry. Stanton had made the antitrust threats against Microsoft a moot point, quietly revolutionizing the old Internet by making an operating system so elegant that you could simply download it from the V-Net itself and so complete that you didn't have to buy word processors and spreadsheets. Then, instead of selling his revolutionary operating system, Stanton gave it away, publishing the code for anybody to use and improve.

What he did not give away, however, was the virtual-reality surface. Whatever you saw when you turned on your monitor — that three-dimensional jungle, beach, circus tent; the lifelike avatars that let you wander the electronic world of the V-Net; the system so easy to use that anybody from four to a hundred and four could use it — that was the real genius of Paul Stanton and the key to Aireon's total domination of computers everywhere. The underlying programs were free for the taking, but if you wanted the elegant skin over the complicated, coded innards, you had to register through Aireon. Then, for a very reasonable monthly rate, you could harness the power of the V-Net with the ease of breathing. Everybody could breathe, and everybody signed up. Nobody else's offerings came close to competing, even though they ran on the same underlying foundation. In two years Stanton quietly bought up shares in all kinds of Internet businesses, entertainment conglomerates, and so on. He didn't own any of them; he just profited when they did well — which they did, in part because they adapted to take advantage of Aireon's NetSys program.

Loren claimed that Stanton craftily spread out his insidious influence so it didn't look like a monopoly, while in reality Stanton controlled absolutely everything about the V-Net — and thus everything in our electronically connected world. He even muttered darkly about Stanton covertly sponsoring the cyberterrorism that had demolished Aireon's most capable competitor. Sure, Aireon's encryption and security codes beat anything else available on the market, but Solare had come close to matching it before a master hacker named Sherris had broken its system wide open and scattered the bits to the four winds. Loren had his own reasons to be wary of Sherris, but his dislike of Stanton predated Sherris's attack on Solare.

I guess it was inevitable that Loren, a dedicated — if rather old-fashioned — authorityphobe who had found refuge from a series of orphanages and foster homes within the Wild West reaches of the old Internet, hated both Stanton and Aireon with a bitter passion. He claimed to detest them because they had made no secret of their eventual goal of world domination—personally, I thought it was probably because they represented stability, ease, comfort, and barbed wire across the wide-open spaces of possibility. Whatever the reason, Loren had devoted his considerable smarts and skills to finding and exploiting the holes, bugs, and hidden features in the complicated software that ran the worldwide V-Net itself. He had gotten briefly involved with Sherris's coven of crackers; they had happily used his expertise for their own nefarious ends, but he'd been more interested in giving Stanton a headache than getting rich smashing software companies that refused to pay the demanded ransoms or helping villains disappear into the electronic ether and resurface with sparkling-clean identities stolen from innocent V-Netizens.

Loren used the copycat bug to steal the latest improvements that Aireon had not published yet and promptly flooded the company's computers with overwhelming feedback from their own code. In the process, he'd shut down most of the V-Net users in the Northern Hemisphere and drawn the attention of the FBI and its latest, greenest recruit. I suspected that we caught Loren primarily because he took pity on me—and because he took serious exception to Sherris's Doom Generation crackers who used his skills to provide escape hatches for some very nasty criminals—but he'd earned his place in NIPC through sheer talent. Fortunately, once Dave realized—with plenty of special pleading from me—how much Loren could help us and vouched for him, the FBI stepped in and got the felony charges commuted on Loren's promise of good behavior.

Loren had been skeptical about joining the evil empire at first, seeing the FBI as simply another branch of the corrupt system that defended the whims of the rich by denying basic rights to those without the money or power to make themselves heard. I told him that it was our job to make sure that didn't happen; we were the advocates for the good guys against the criminals, rich, poor, foreign, or domestic. To back up my argument, I read the FBI mission statement to him: "The mission of the FBI is to uphold the law through the investigation of violations of federal criminal law; to protect the United States from foreign intelligence and terrorist activities; to provide leadership and law enforcement assistance to federal, state, local, and international agencies; and to perform these responsibilities in a manner that is responsive to the needs of the public and is faithful to the Constitution of the United States."

He'd come back with a quote of his own, assuring me that he

knew all about the "core values" that the FBI publicized—"rigorous obedience to the Constitution; respect for the dignity of all those we protect; compassion; fairness; and uncompromising personal and institutional integrity"—then asked if I could look him dead in the eye and tell him that the FBI actually lived up to them. I'd leaned forward, keeping my gaze steady without any effort at all, and told him that while I knew there were still some problems in the FBI, I certainly tried to live up to those ideals and that I wouldn't work for any outfit without standards at least as high as mine. He'd kept up the staring contest for a few seconds more, then broke it off with a laugh. "All right, already. No wonder they use Mormons as missionaries. They can tell you they believe all kinds of wild things and come across as totally sincere!"

"That's because we are," I assured him. "So you can believe it too."

Loren didn't admit to anything, but when Dave came in to offer him the *It-Takes-a-Thief* deal, he accepted it without giving anybody too many problems. He passed the rigorous application process with flying colors—again, after plenty of special pleading on my part, though the specter of federal prison worked its persuasive magic as well. He breezed through the written tests, managed to keep his sarcasm in check through the interviews, and passed the background checks, proving that his diplomas came from accredited schools. The drug tests came back negative, as did the polygraph—a tack in the shoe, Loren assured me, messed up the readings to no end, not that he'd needed to do anything of the sort, of course.

The mandated interviews with past employers, neighbors, teachers, associates, social workers, and practically everyone who'd known him went surprisingly fast, given Loren's social-services childhood. There weren't any former bosses; Loren had supported himself doing freelance contract work and selling useful—and usually funny—add-ons to Aireon's NetSys. In fact, it turned out that nobody had known him very well. Everyone Dave talked to painted the same picture of an intelligent loner kid who didn't work up to his potential, didn't make any close friends, never ended up a victim and usually acted as a ringleader, and was always popular with the girls without getting serious about it. He'd bounced around from home to home, too old for anybody to adopt and too moody and sarcastic to fit in well with the physically or mentally handicapped kids in the alternative group homes; he didn't have the calm, warmly parental personality best suited for big-brothering or babysitting special-needs children. Finally, the state had given up trying to place a whip-smart teenage boy with abandonment issues and an unbreakable but possibly useful addiction to computers, had taken advantage of the welfare reform rules that let religious organizations act as government agencies, and finally remanded him to the custody of a charitable Catholic alternative school/orphanage.

Sister Emmanuel, the ancient, straight-spined nun who had supervised Loren's high-school years, sighed and said, "Loren Hunter is a good boy and has great potential for doing good. Someday he will stop kicking against the pricks." She had then fixed Dave with a stern eye and commanded, "You see to it that he does." Dave had ended the interviews with that one and recommended Loren for immediate hiring. He didn't include Sister Emmanuel's assessment in his final report, of course; instead, he argued that if Loren weren't one of us, he would be a seriously menacing cyberterrorist, someone who presented a dire danger if not properly corralled and rehabilitated.

I solemnly agreed aloud and in writing with Dave's assessment, but I didn't truly believe it. Loren was indeed a menace, and he could be a rascal, but he cared too much about fairness and people in general to carry out the computer-triggered financial meltdown with which he'd threatened Stanton. We still periodically argued about whether Stanton was the anti-Christ — the latest ended with a semiconsensus that Stanton was either the Beast or the Dragon — but Loren had mostly kept his promise to quit his holy crusade against Aireon. However, he still loved to get his hands on the latest Aireon program versions — released or not — and torture them into submission.

Aside from teasing him about playing David to Stanton's Goliath, I didn't do anything directly to either help or hinder Loren's crusade, as long as it stayed strictly harmless. I didn't care one way or another about Paul Stanton — as far as I could see, he'd earned his wealth and power as honestly as could be expected, and he did put out an excellent product — but I had come to truly admire and like Loren, despite his irrationality on the subject of Aireon. Not that I'd ever tell him so — it might go to his head, and he was already cocky enough. Actually, I should say confident instead of cocky; cocky implies that he isn't as competent as he thinks he is, and the fact is that he's even better.

Loren adapted quickly from Sherris's game of selling stolen identities to capturing the identity thieves that infested the V-Net.

Identity theft is the most prevalent kind of crime we deal with at NIPC; for every dramatic case of a rogue programmer demanding millions of dollars in ransom for a company's deepest secrets, there are hundreds of small-time operators trawling the V-Net for unguarded personal information — social security numbers, Aireon account codes, credit card numbers, et cetera — that they can gather up and either use themselves or sell to other criminals. Unfortunately, these guys have the same facility for sniffing out the holes in standard encryption systems that pigs supposedly have for finding truffles in oak forests. Applying for loans over the V-Net is quick and convenient — especially when you're using somebody else's credit history and bank account. Blackmail has risen exponentially too; Loren had it right when he finally told one highly upset man that, in this day and age, if you didn't want something to become public knowledge eventually, you just shouldn't do it in the first place.

The ultimate goal of all the would-be V-Net service-provider companies was to find a way to keep Mrs. Brown's personal and financial information secure while still letting her do all her shopping from the comfort of her own living room. This is where Aireon's astounding five-year rise to ascendancy came in; its databases use the best encryption and security methods out there. Even with the best security, however, the combination of careless users and information-hungry crackers make for a wild ride — and that's where *we* come in. Sometimes we catch the thieves before they can use their illicitly gained knowledge; other times it's a matter of securing the barn as an example to others after the horses are long gone. Thus, the usual assignment for our department involves tracking down the crackers who used careless security, public-knowledge information, and confidence scams to gather information that lets them grab other people's' money, qualifications, mail, credit ratings, whatever is available.

I glanced over my shoulder at Loren, wrapped in a personal musical bubble as he searched and cross-checked hundreds of theft reports, looking for matches and patterns that would lead from victims to perpetrators. Despite my frustration with the WormMaster's elusiveness, I welcomed the chance to do something different for a change. Time to go hunting again.

Of course, I'd already checked the registry for any official record of the WormMaster's existence and come up empty. Aireon's comprehensive database of all its V-Net users — and the few users signed up with other online services that used Aireon's interfaces—contained no listing for the seraphic avatar who had so dramatically disappeared back into the wilds of the V-Net. Only amateur crackers used their registered personas for illegal operations, anyway; this guy was clearly in a much higher weight class, which meant the pursuit would be that much more difficult. That simply meant I had to fall back on the traditional methods of police work: looking for clues, building a profile of the suspect, gathering evidence from every possible source, haunting chat rooms and conference halls where hackers gathered and gossiped, waiting for him to make a mistake.

I slipped my hands into the datagloves and stepped into Sekhmet's paws. The Kaos Komputer Klub looked like a good place to start. Its members were mostly aging hackers still trying to hold onto a rapidly fading hipness factor, flaunting the decidedly objectionable initials of their club as a badge of social recklessness, along with a few newcomers who hung with the oldsters on the off chance they'd learn something useful. I didn't suspect one of them was the face behind the WormMaster's mask, but they eagerly collected and spread any cracker stories that came their way, if only to get on their nostalgia high horses and tell each other how much hackers' skills, style, and ethics had deteriorated since their heyday.

They'd decorated their V-Net room in Early Anarchy; the scene looked like a combination of college dorm, sci-fi bar, and punk-rock club, with avatars to match. I waved off an extravagantly tusked troll trying to sell me a set of stolen passwords and settled into a corner of the room to watch and listen. Among the whispered conversations and general discussions, a flame war broke out between the room's proprietor—Phreez, an ice-statue avatar presiding over the gathering from behind the digital bar—and a multiple-armed, green Martian named Tars Carter. Carter maintained that the Nice Day Gang's recent spree of marking sites with their hijacked smiley-face logo represented the true legacy of the Klub, while Phreez said they were nothing but a bunch of amateur cracker-wannabe boys who thought it was funny to tag sites but had no decent anarchist philosophy guiding their choice of victims. (They didn't have any decent track-hiding abilities either; Ed had the Nice Day boys trapped, wrapped, and capped before the day had ended.)

"Takes an aging anarchist to complain about not being organized," an English voice with an unmistakable orangutan accent noted.

I sent a sharp-toothed grin to the huge, shaggy ape who appeared beside me, his puffy cheek pads and gold-eyeglassed, ancient-infant's face smiling above the threadbare cardigan that draped his pot-bellied body and trailed only halfway down his long arms. "Hey, Rang. I hoped you'd be here."

Rang was a seasoned V-Net rat, a whiz-bang programmer who occasionally took on contracting assignments but seemed to prefer having time to ramble the electronic neighborhoods and parks. I wondered if his real-life counterpart was retired, but V-Netiquette forbade even asking for that kind of information. I didn't need to know about his real life anyway; it was enough that he felt kindly toward NIPC and had acted as a valuable informant in several cases. He also seemed to like me, which predisposed me to like him back. He wrinkled his face into the requisite lascivious leer. "Always ready to serve a lovely lady, my dear. Shall we go private?"

I accepted that excuse to hide our conversation from observers. A small, private room grew around us, probably touching off a ripple of "There go that cat chick and Rang again—what does she see in him?" with the expected bawdy jokes. I didn't worry too much about that; even though the V-Net could indeed be a "polyphony of polymorphous perversity"—in the words of one alliteratively talented but somewhat derivative Southern senator—I stayed right out of those areas, and I knew Rang did.

I tossed an image of the WormMaster's shining, celestial form into the air between us. "Thanks, Rang. You're great for my reputation. Seen this guy around?"

"And you, my dear, are wonderful for mine," Rang twinkled at me. "Mentor to such an elegant creature."

I probably was too, since nobody in the Klub knew I hung out there only because I worked for NIPC. "Tell me everything you know about an angel who plays with worms."

"Angels," Rang grunted, scratching at his cardigan as he examined the image. "Everybody's an angel these days—it's like that gargoyle trend, and the anime fad before that. Nope, never seen this joker before. Can't help you with the worm bit either. Sorry."

"But what?" I asked, watching him fiddling with his cardigan button and blow out his cheeks. The wide range of twitches and gestures made it obvious that whoever Rang really was, he put a lot of time and effort into building and inhabiting his avatar.

He pulled a rubbery leer. "You're a curious little wench, aren't you? It's nothing solid yet, but I've been catching threads here and there, talking about somebody recruiting only very top talent for some big project. Can't even tell if it's legit or not — maybe for one of those big churches, the Mormons or something — a couple of them mentioned preparing for Armageddon."

"Oh, please, not another doomsday cult," I groaned.

"Doesn't sound like it — more like a fancy hack," Rang assured me. He pulled a lovely pocket watch out of the knitted depths, squinted at it through his glasses, and announced, "Lovely to see you again, as always, my dear, but I must be going. Time for my morning tea."

He dropped the walls just as I said, "Thanks, Rang," and I planted a feline kiss on the wispy-haired top of his orangutan skull, much to the amusement of the Klub denizens. He knuckled his way out, whistling "God Save the Queen." I ignored the appreciative, speculative stares from the audience, thinking about what a cracker's version of preparing for Armageddon would be. Somehow, I didn't think it involved food storage.

"Ha!" Loren's triumphant exclamation broke my reverie and brought me back to the real world again. "Take that. Got you, you low-down identity thief!"

I shuffled off the datagloves and rolled back my chair, looking over his shoulder at the cross-matched entries on the comparison readout filling his monitor. This particular thief had been very busy. Sixteen credit card applications, a home-improvement loan for serious money, two driver's licenses, and an even dozen Social Security numbers, all mapped through a single avatar and anonymous account. "Mrs. Florinda Gardner?" I asked. "That's quite the alias for a virtual cat burglar."

"Yeah, looks like somebody fell for the old theory that nobody would suspect a sweet little old lady." Loren shrugged. "And our loser is —" The monitor flickered, processing through the hidden data that linked the stolen accounts to the thief's own stashes, and then the white-haired avatar dissolved into the person behind her. "Mario Schiavelli." Loren flicked the name disdainfully. "Get ready to beg for mercy, Mario."

"Ooh, send Stark," I suggested, laughing. "He'll love it."

Special Agent Damien Stark was Dave's Assistant Special Agent in Charge, all six-foot-four, two-hundred-twenty pounds of him. He took being an FBI agent seriously — very seriously. The very fact that the Bureau had not only accepted but recruited computer geeks — and worse, short, redheaded, Mormon, *female* computer geeks — had made him slightly crazy at first. Having to take his hit list from Loren, the scruffy, nearly ex-con, avowed anarchist, simply added salt to the paper cut our existence had inflicted on his Old West lawman ego. However, despite his distaste for admitting nonsuperheroes into the Bureau, Stark took computer crimes as seriously as he took the Bureau's efforts to stop them. Some of the other Special Agents made no secret of their disdain for anything that involved bytes instead of bullets—a common Bureau prejudice that earned Stark some ribbing from agents at other field offices. He invariably ended up defending us in his own backhanded fashion, pointing out that the chance to bust a thieving cracker made getting the evidence for the bust from another geek less annoying. Besides, we'd eventually worn him down by proving that we were competent and just as dedicated to upholding the Constitution as he was. Now he viewed us primarily as obnoxious younger siblings, rather than threats to the integrity of his beloved Bureau.

Loren smiled, but his expression had a much nastier edge to it. "I wonder how many stairs Mario will accidentally fall down on his way to the clink?"

That thought added some darker shadows to the comical scene playing in my head. Picturing Stark as a trench-coated super agent breaking down the door to a stuffy cyber-lair and surprising a flower-hatted, dress-wearing Mario sitting amid piles of ill-gotten gains ordered from luxury e-stores amused me. The thought of Stark slamming the identity thief into the walls and tossing him out the window—as had happened with an embezzler last year when his company's security specialists tracked him down—made me a little queasy. I shrugged off the nasty image. Stark made a very sharp point of getting tough on crime and criminals, but he was a good agent and a good cop. He wasn't a corporate thug who blithely disregarded inconvenient obstacles like civil liberties and laws against police brutality.

"None, of course," I assured Loren. "And don't look so disappointed. Anyway, I thought you loved humanity."

"Humanity, sure. It's just individual people I can't stand." He shot back the cliché without hesitating, then shrugged. "I know Stark won't pull anything too nasty. But as far as these slimy mirror grabbers go, I vote for justice, not mercy. Ol' Mario got selfish, he got stupid, he got caught—and now he ought to rot in jail for a da—dang long time."

Good catch, Loren, I thought, as he flicked open the e-mail to send

Mario's real-world identity and evidence of his crimes to Stark. "Preferably one with rats," he muttered.

"Well, maybe there'll be rats after all," I speculated as Loren and I left Mario's indictment hearing four days later. "He could be a terrible housekeeper."

The courtroom doors closed, leaving us in the teeming hallway along with the arresting officers, Special Agents Stark and Warren Ieyasu, the cyber-savvy junior agent who'd actually chased Mario down the stairs and tackled him in the basement. (Loren tried to collect on "our bet" about the stairs; I told him to keep dreaming.) Of course, life isn't fair, so Ieyasu rather than Mario ended up with the wrenched shoulder. I had gone along to the hearing as moral support and as an additional expert witness, should the judge need more convincing. As it turned out, he didn't.

Loren had testified first, summarizing the electronic trail the suspect had left from one plundered identity to the next. Mario was a great con man, convincing people to give him their confidential personal information, but he was only a fair hacker and had left fingerprints all over the files in question. Stark had then taken the stand, his flattop haircut and sharply pressed suit presenting an amusingly stereotypical contrast to Loren's rumpled denim look, and briskly led the court through the seemingly endless series of exhibits—computers, data, bank accounts, cash, and goods—confiscated from Mario's apartment. Mr. Schiavelli, on the advice of his lawyer, had opted to plead guilty to several fraud charges and accept four years of house arrest instead of trying to fight Loren's electronic evidence and Stark's tangible evidence. Better to admit to a comparatively simple crime and wear an anklet that tracked his every move and warned his parole officer if he left the prescribed safe zone than to try to fight the charges and end up in a federal prison.

Loren didn't have a chance to perk up at the thought that Mario's house might have rats after all. "Good job, Hunter," Stark boomed, slapping him jovially on the back. "Get a haircut."

"Get a life, Stark," Loren growled softly, not even pausing as he headed for the bulletproof doors and the parking lot beyond.

Stark laughed, falling easily into step with us, waving off the door guards with his FBI badge as his and Ieyasu's sidearms set off the metal detectors. (Loren and I had to defend ourselves with our wits alone—nonagents aren't issued guns.) "Take your own advice, kid. Tell you what—catch us another pathetic cyber loser, and I'll convince the boss to let you come on the bust. It'd do you some good to get out of that data cave once in awhile. See how the real FBI operates."

"Sounds fun," I broke in perkily, widening my eyes with the sheer excitement of the thought. "I've got another identity thief on the hook, just waiting for a last confirmation from one of our electronic snitches. When do we go?"

Ieyasu laughed. "As soon as you dump that Tai-Chi stuff and get into some Gracie jujitsu."

"You're just saying that 'cause I'm a girl." I scowled theatrically. "Gracie, Savat, Tai-Bo—all for wimps! Little do you know, foolish man, that I am mistress of Turkey Kung Fu!" My scowl changed into a pleasant smile and "thank you" as Ieyasu opened the van door for me while laughing at the mental picture of me as a ninja. I don't expect it, but I'm always ready to reward chivalry. I'm also more than willing to let the guys do the gun-waving and run down the suspects in real life. I like mental games, tracking crackers through the V-Net, where I hold most of the advantages, but when it comes to evaluating myself as a physical specimen, I'm a realist. I know I couldn't put enough menace in my voice to make *Freeze!* sound like anything more than a mild suggestion.

"Nah." Stark shook his head at Ieyasu's naiveté—silly man, thinking that I would use Gracie jujitsu even if I knew how. "Don't even think about it. It's not that she's a woman—nobody smart takes a Mormon into the field. When I first started out down on the Pima reservations in Arizona, we had a case with a bunch of bootleggers working the border towns. We needed somebody who knew Pima and Spanish, and the only guy in the office was this Mormon kid. So we pull him out of his suit and tie, get him grubbied up, and send him down with Alvarez." Stark strapped himself into the driver's seat, automatically checking the rest of us for seatbelts. After a brief staring contest in the rearview mirror, Loren buckled his belt.

"They walk into this tavern, right," Stark continued, pulling out into traffic. "The kid's staring around, eyes big as saucers, drawing all the dirt bags' attention, so Alvarez tells him to watch his toes instead. They walk up to the bar, and the Mormon bumps into the stools, he's so into watching his boots. The bartender asks what they want, and before Alvarez can say anything, this kid comes out with 'Sprite.'" He guffawed. "'Sprite' the bartender says. Alvarez steps in and says, 'Yeah, on the rocks.' So the Mormon busts out, 'I don't want rocks in my drink!' Alvarez had to get him out of there before he got both of them shot. They had to use the second-best guy for the job."

"That would be where you came in, right, Stark?" Ieyasu asked, laughing.

"Yeah," Stark growled at him. "Taught them not to send a Mormon to do a real agent's job."

They were all looking at me, waiting for a reaction. I looked back wide-eyed and said, "I don't get it. Why did they put rocks in his pop?" I managed to keep a straight face until Stark started to explain it to me, then dissolved into giggles.

He looked nonplused for a moment as Ieyasu high-fived me. "Good one!"

"Turn the other cheek, Warren," I told him solemnly. "That's my motto."

"It'd be a more effective strategy if you wore shorter skirts," Stark informed me. "Notice how these guys who have more than one wife always cover them up? Muslims, Mormons—covered head to toe. Must be worried about poachers or something."

"Eep!" I exclaimed. "I knew I forgot something this morning. Better close your eyes, Stark, until I can get my chador back on."

The conversation carried on, jabs about Mormons on their side, innocent-sarcastic non sequiturs on mine. I didn't actually mind their teasing, and they weren't hostile about it. Fact is, the FBI and CIA both do a lot of recruiting at universities, and Brigham Young University—yes, my alma mater—was one of their main targets. Mormons, however out of place they look in lowlife bars, make great agents: patriotic, honest, hard working, well educated, linguistically diverse, and utterly dependable. Of course, the CIA and FBI had both learned not to send Latter-day Saints to certain assignments: anything having to do with pornography, for instance, or missions that involved the shady areas of international diplomacy. Having strong morals and an ingrained sense of right and wrong sometimes got in the way when the CIA wanted an agent to indulge in dubious practices for "higher causes." One of these days they'd learn that the ends never justify the means, no matter how lofty the goals. I preferred the FBI—sure, there were a few fringy characters, and sometimes overzealous or even malicious agents subverted the Bureau's ideals, but overall I felt that the Bureau encouraged us to color inside the lines.

"Ah, but having a Mormon around has its advantages," Loren

pointed out casually as we at last came in sight of the discreetly professional building that housed the NIPC field office. The primary command center is in Washington, D.C., of course, but it's always best to cover all the bases, which is why the FBI made sure they had a field office in every state and several territories. The Portland area got its own center primarily because it was centrally located way back when; now that Aireon's corporate offices were located in the city, we jokingly called ourselves the "other Washington," because we were clearly the center of the wired world. Home sweet home.

When Loren got three puzzled looks, he explained his observation. "Look at it logically, people. Sure, Mormons are completely oblivious to a lot of the gritty stuff, they're totally easy to spot, and they're beyond innocent, but they're also so absolutely straight arrow that they're good at catching crooks." He ruffled my hair. "Why, just look at our little Susie—all she's got to do is think 'What would I do?' then do the opposite. Nails 'em every time."

"True, true." I smiled sweetly, kicking my door open as Stark eased the van into the designated loading zone in front of headquarters. "Still, I sometimes envy reprobates like you guys. It must be nice to know exactly how the criminal mind works without having to reverse everything." I waved thanks to Stark as he and Ieyasu pulled away, then ran into the building before Loren could even threaten to noogie me. He took the bait and charged after me.

We crashed through the door, skidded around the corner, and almost flattened Dave. "Whoa," Loren exclaimed, then recovered. "Darn. Almost had him. Boss dies before noon, you get the rest of the day off. It's in the rules."

Dave's expression cooled the flip response on my lips. "What's happened?" I asked.

"Have you guys seen the news?" he asked tightly.

"No," Loren said. "We've been down at the courthouse putting Mario under house arrest, and then we had Radio Stark going constantly on the ride back."

"What—" I began again.

"Just show us," Loren told Dave, catching our arms and hauling us into the conference room, where a small crowd had assembled. Everybody in that day, from the three interns to Stark and Ieyasu's alternates O'Malley and Reimschussel to Ed, who hunched in a corner with his sweatshirt hood up as a barrier to unwanted personal contact, stood watching as the video monitor treated them to the sight of a worn-looking woman bravely holding back tears. The spires and flats of the Southwest desert spread behind her.

"We're just so happy," she said, indicating an equally weathered man dabbing his eyes with a handkerchief. "It's like a miracle, after such a hard year."

The picture panned to show jubilant people rapidly unloading flats of groceries from the yawning cavern of a huge transport. The camera came to rest on a reporter, her sleek, urban hair and clothes in sharp contrast to the crowd bustling behind her.

"A miracle for the small community of Flat Mountain," she said, "but who is this mysterious Gideon? Is this the generosity of an anonymous philanthropist or a case of a technology terrorist gone wild? Mike, we'll keep you updated on the story as it develops."

The scene switched back to the studio, where the anchor flashed his deliberately trustworthy smile. "Thank you, Trisha. What an interesting turn of events, Michelle."

His partner smiled dazzlingly. "It is indeed, Mike. Very controversial. Let's find out what our viewers think. Tell us your opinion. Is Gideon a high-tech thief, or is Sunshine Foods getting what it deserves? Vote now, and we'll show the results in real time!"

The station's logo and wavering bar chart replaced Mike and Michelle's attentive faces on the vid screen. For the first few seconds, at least, it looked like the mob in the coliseum was giving Sunshine Foods a vigorous thumbs-down. That'd last until the corporation got wind of the poll and deployed their employees to ring in their own more friendly votes.

Loren didn't wait to see the tide turn; he grabbed Dave and pulled him out of the room. "Okay, enough with Tweedledum and Tweedledumber and their flock of button-clicking sheep. We don't have to wait through five minutes of corporate-sponsor Aireon commercials for the instant recap. What really happened, and what does it have to do with us?"

Dave waved us into his office and closed the door. He flopped into his chair and slid a printout across the desk to us. I picked it up and scanned through it as Dave explained. "Sunshine Foods just called us. Last night their brand-new auto-pilot trucks delivered eighteen loads of groceries to several small towns. The trucks pulled up to the general stores and popped open the cargo bays without waiting for payment transfer or entry codes. Then, instead of printing out an invoice, they spat *that* out." He gestured to the printout.

Dearest children,

Sunshine Foods, wolves in sheep's clothing, unworthy shepherds, have ground the faces of the poor, sacrificing the comfort and even lives of those who should be their brothers and sisters on the altar of their greed. Now, their reign of avarice and indifference is at an end.

As I live, saith the Lord God, surely because my flock became meat to every beast, because there was no shepherd, neither did my shepherds search for my flock, but the shepherds fed themselves and fed not my flock; Therefore, O ye shepherd, hear the word of the Lord; Thus saith the Lord God, Behold, I am against the shepherds; and I will require my flock at their hand, and cause them to cease from feeding the flock; neither shall the shepherds feed themselves any more, for I will deliver my flock from their mouths, that they may not be meat for them.

The pure shall rise from under the uncaring heel of the oppressors! For the Lamb which is in the midst of the throne shall feed them, and shall lead them unto living fountains of waters: and God shall wipe away all tears from their eyes. Because of their meekness, a defender has arisen to be their advocate in the courts of the mighty. The tools of the unrighteous rulers shall be turned against them, unless they repent of their wickedness and renounce their greed. Let this stand as a sign and a warning to Sunshine Foods and to others who set filthy lucre above their duty to their fellow man.

In love and admonition, Gideon

"It gets even worse," Dave began.

"Ooh, ooh, let me guess," Loren interrupted. "He sent that same message along to the News Twins on the All-News Network, plus the names of the towns and the stores where the robot trucks would appear, so their intrepid roving reporters could be on the scene the minute the 'miracle' happened, right?"

"Right," Dave sighed. "Now Sunshine's in deep yogurt. If they grab the groceries back or charge these poor ranchers the going rate for the area, they look like the Big Bad Wolf eating the little pigs' breakfast. If they don't get the shipment back or take payment on it—"

"They catch a fraction of a percentage less profit than they would've otherwise," Loren sneered. "Poor fat cats. Do you have any idea how much that company charges to deliver simple necessities like milk and flour out to these small towns? The shipping markup is over five hundred percent in some cases. It's obscene. This Gideon guy may be a thief, but in this case he's stealing from a bunch of crooks. Sounds more like a responsible protester to me."

"Thief, protester, whatever—talk about a God complex!" I exclaimed, looking up from the page, amazed at the sheer brass of the guy. "Hasn't he ever heard 'Vengeance is mine, saith the Lord'?" Rang's comment about Armageddon replayed in my head. Oh, no, not another wired kook plying his own version of cyber religion!

"Probably," Loren observed, as he snagged the paper from me and read the missive carefully. "He's plenty familiar with the Old Testament prophets and Revelation, so you'd think he would have." Sister Emmanuel's Catholic orphanage/intellectual boot camp had lasted the longest of Loren's temporary havens. The brothers in charge of teaching philosophy and theology hadn't managed to convert him or persuade him to take vows, but they'd succeeded remarkably in pounding scripture into his amazingly sticky memory. Sometimes I thought they'd succeeded too well; he could pull out every nasty-sounding misinterpretation of God's word in the scriptures, then blow off my Book of Mormon–based explanations of what the *real* story said. At least he remembered them too and occasionally shot them back at me. I told him he was a born Jesuit just to let him know that he couldn't intimidate me with all his tricksy memorization while I had to use the Topical Guide occasionally.

At the moment, however, he chose to put the scriptorian mantle onto me. "So, I get why you want little Susie here," he said with a shrug, tossing the printout back to Dave. "But what does it have to do with me?"

"And why do we want little Susie?" I shot back.

"Perfect match," Loren drawled. "You've heard 'set a thief to catch a thief,' right? From our very own Dave, in fact. Well, this is set a religious fanatic to catch a religious fanatic."

I made a show of looking around for something to throw at him. "Sounds more like you're the one they want. Set a nutty social reformer to catch a nutty social reformer."

"We want both of you," Dave broke in before the witfest could escalate. "As of now, Sue, you're off the OmniMental case and onto Sunshine Foods. They've got their network administrator waiting for you right now. Grab whatever you need and get on the way."

"Off the OmniMental case?" I yipped. "But they deserve to have their trespasser caught—it takes guts for a company to even admit it's been hacked. I've got to stay until we've got the guy himself pinned. He's a slick cracker, Dave, somebody who could make a lot more trouble if we just let him go free—" I sputtered to a halt under Dave's impatiently reasonable expression. "Are you going to give it to Ed or somebody else?"

"No," Dave said flatly. "You told me that you figured out how they can keep your WormMaster buddy out. Right?"

"He's not my buddy, but yeah," I reluctantly admitted. "I know how he's getting in, and they can block it."

Dave nodded. "Good. Tell OmniMental what they need to do, and let it go. We've got much bigger problems. The executives at Sunshine are expecting you ASAP. Get going."

"Hey, look at it this way," Loren suggested as I emerged from the ladies' room. (My all-too-brief career in the FBI had already taught me that you have to grab pit stops while you can.) "You get to go on an active-duty assignment after all. That oughta show Stark."

"Dang, and here I forgot to practice my stork-stance moves this morning," I laughed. "But I'll make sure I remember to order my Sprite on the rocks."

We climbed into my car. I preferred my own ride to any of the Bureau's vehicles; they tended to suffer from the sad effects of diffusion of vehicular responsibility: trash in the side pockets, stains on the upholstery, drink cups in the backseat, sprung suspensions from Ieyasu's latest wild chase. I landed in the driver's seat as usual, Loren arranging his lanky self on the passenger side and flipping open his portable console even before he fastened the safety belt.

Stark had tried to tease Loren about his lack of manly driving ability, which didn't really work; Loren shot back with some nasty comments about Stark's lack of mental agility and confusion of body hair and grunting with sexual prowess, which only escalated the whole thing into an outright argument. Despite hearing that one should never get involved in a dog fight, I'd taken my courage in both hands and jumped in with a comment about how I valued my life too much to entrust it to a guy whose two driving speeds were dead-snake crawl or mach-seven wild mouse. That and Dave's appearance in the meeting broke up the verbal brawl.

Later, Loren had sweetly complimented me on my ability to butt in where I wasn't needed. He maintained that driving bored him and wasted his valuable time, so he preferred to let somebody else handle it. I suspected that he didn't like dealing with the other drivers on the road. Whatever the reason, I was satisfied with the arrangement; the rule in my car is that the driver controls the radio.

I tuned in to the latest Celtic-industrial offering from Boadicea's Girdle and pulled out of the lot, the directions to Sunshine Foods' headquarters scrolling up the dash screen. It settled into a map that showed us as a dot along a brightly colored string that wove through the shadowy lines of streets I didn't need to take. Of course, I remembered what I'd forgotten only when we'd already traveled too far to easily turn back. "Awk!" I exclaimed. "I didn't send the port codes to OmniMental!"

"Took care of it," Loren assured me, intent on his portable monitor, fingers busy inside the unit's mini-datagloves.

"Thanks," I said, dodging a bunch of high school girls in a birthday convertible, then gave him a sidelong look. "Did you do it as you or as me?"

He smirked at the monitor. "As you, of course. You're assigned as the primary contact. Don't worry about it—I made sure I sounded just like you, no swear words or anything. You know I don't impersonate you unless I'm actually with you. Whoa!"

I knew that last exclamation had nothing to do with sounding like me. "What?"

"First of all, Aireon's got nothing on anybody named Gideon that fits the data profile we've got—or they say they don't. But I just got an earful from Abdu, the sysop down at Sunshine. I told him we were coming and asked him for the specs on the guidance system for the trucks."

"And he didn't send it, right?" I sped up to pass a line of traditional Sunshine Foods trucks. How did the drivers feel about the new drone fleet? Maybe one of them was Gideon, using scripture and virtual espionage instead of wooden shoes to sabotage the latest version of the infernal mills.

"Nope, just cussed me out for even suggesting that he send something so sensitive over an unsecured link." Loren chuckled. "Good thing I had the audio off. Guy's got quite the vocabulary, but at least he's not a total idiot on the security side. Well, not so far, anyway. Let's see how well he's got his computers locked down. Never can tell whether the back door's locked just from trying the front."

A newscast replaced the latest Slovenian dance hit, the deejay having altogether too much fun at Sunshine Foods' expense as he recapped the botched delivery story. "Guess those trucks showed up where the Sunshine doesn't, if you know what I mean," he said snidely, to the high hilarity of his sidekick.

"Ugh," I said, changing the channel. Asian dub filled the car, quirky but much less annoying. "Well, Baron, have you slipped behind their defenses yet?" I asked Loren.

"Baron?" He didn't look at me, absorbed in whatever his monitor showed him.

"Baron von Richtoffen. German nobleman, pilot during World War I, famous for flying behind enemy lines to harass other pilots?" Still nothing. "Should I have used the Swamp Fox instead?"

"You should've remembered that most people aren't nutty enough to double-major in history and computer science," he told me, at last looking up. His eyes shone brilliant blue in the oblique light reflected from a passing refrigerated truck—it simply wasn't fair that *he* got the lovely long eyelashes. "Even your Swamp Fox would have a hard time creeping behind these walls. They've got their drone program locked up tight." He ran down the list, ticking off each possible avenue of attack point by point. Sunshine Foods' dispatch and guidance system was nigh impervious, cut off from any outside influence coming in from normal—and, knowing Loren's methods, *abnormal*—channels.

"Nice," I said approvingly. Whoever Gideon was, he hadn't taken advantage of careless security arrangements. It looked like an elegant job, carried out with flair. Deep inside my imagination Sekhmet's tail twitched excitedly.

"Not nice at all," Loren growled back. "Gideon didn't give them half what they deserved. Listen to this." Loren explained that apparently a few of Sunshine's accounting records and e-mail archives lay outside the impenetrable wall that guarded the drone trucks' programming channels. He read off a list of wholesale and retail prices, delivery-charge schedules for various towns throughout the West, stock prices, and memoranda from people whose names meant nothing to me. The contents of the memos, however, sounded all too familiar, citing lack of competition as an opportunity to raise prices, advocating headcount reductions to improve stock prices, laying out plans to switch to cheaper suppliers while charging customers the same prices for lower-quality goods, even explaining ideas for convincing mothers to feed their babies more expensive formulas instead of nursing.

"Babylon," Loren spat. "There is no god but Gold, and Greed is his profit."

I smiled at the acid pun but couldn't help agreeing with his evaluation. "Just remember that Babylon gets torn apart by her own allies at the end, and all of them end up in the pit."

"Ah, the old argument that the bad guys will get what they deserve, but always some time later, after they've had free run to stomp on everybody as much as they like." He glared out the windshield. "How can you believe that any god who lets them lie and cheat and steal now is really going to punish them later? The meek will inherit what's left of the earth, all right — the day after the ruling class takes off for the next planet."

"He doesn't *let* them lie and cheat and steal, any more than he lets you catch them doing it and make them sorry they did," I said. "That's the whole point of life — we're here to choose what we're going to do and to take the consequences. You can't punish somebody before they do something nasty, just like you can't reward somebody for being good when they never had a chance to be bad."

"Did you learn that in Sunbeams or in Home, Family, and Social Engineering?" he asked sarcastically.

"Sunbeams," I told him lightly, but I seriously meant it. "Like I tell my kids, we have to do what Jesus taught us — learn what's right, keep ourselves on the right track, do all the good things we can, help each other through the tough times, throw a monkey wrench into the bad guys' schemes whenever the chance comes up, and trust that it'll all come out right in the end. Otherwise, I tell them they'll end up like you, ticked off at the injustice in the world and giving themselves ulcers over it instead of knowing that everything's in good hands and all you need is to do your bit."

He gave me a pitying look. "You do have an amazing imagination. It must be nice to wrap yourself up in cotton-candy insulation instead of facing reality. Why don't you go all the way and decide that all you've got to do is call on Jesus and he'll save you? That way, you don't even have to peel that little boy off the ceiling every Sunday morning."

"For the same reason you don't — because it doesn't work that way. We're saved by grace after all we can do — though sometimes it probably looks like we're saved in *spite* of all we do." I pulled neatly into a visitor space in front of Sunshine Foods' industrial-looking headquarters and popped open my door. I slid out, then bent down to grin at Loren. "And by the way, you're not fooling me one bit — if you truly didn't believe in God, you wouldn't get so mad at him!" I moved to meet the welcoming party hustling out of the wide glass doors, giving him no chance to mount a formal rebuttal.

He didn't come back at me with an applicable bit of scripture, but he did mutter a bit of Shakespeare: "You always end with a jade's trick. I know you of old."

Sunshine Foods' Chief Operations Officer, Ms. Alison, met us with a tight smile that did not get any warmer after hurried introductions. The smile was definitely for the benefit of the hopeful reporters lurking along the fence line with zoom lenses rather than for us; nothing else about her, from precisely tailored suit to perfectly controlled hair, suggested easy amiability. She promptly ushered us into the huge reception hall, where the security man verified our FBI credentials via our holo IDs. I obediently surrendered my fingers to the reading plate and gazed into the retinal scanner, then stared around the room as Loren took his turn. The company's smiling, sunglassed Sol logo dominated the space, painted on the walls and etched into the widows, its cheerfulness in stark contrast to the expressions on the faces around us.

"She's madder at Gideon than you are at God," I whispered to Loren as he moved away from the desk to join me, pocketing his ID. Under the eyes of the reporters, he settled for poking me.

"I cannot emphasize enough how important it is to have this matter resolved immediately and successfully," Ms. Alison said, handing Loren a packet. "First, sign the confidentiality agreements, which are binding. The temporary badges give you access to all areas of the company. All employees have been instructed to give you any information you need. However, we ask that you do not unnecessarily interrupt normal operations. This is Mr. Abdu, Chief Systems Administrator. He will be your contact for the duration of the investigation. I expect your initial report in three days."

"We'll keep you informed as appropriate, according to FBI and National Infrastructure Protection Center guidelines," Loren informed her coolly. "Now, may we get on with the investigation?"

I was glad he knew what to say; the woman's arrogance made me want to yell, "You're not the boss of me!" and throw the pen at her. (I'd really been in Sunbeams too long.) Instead, I hid a smile and signed the confidentiality agreement as she replied in a slightly deflated tone, "Certainly. We expect quick results."

We surrendered the agreements to Ms. Alison's silent, hovering secretary. Abdu didn't try to impress us with managerial attitude — he didn't need to. He had the caterpillar eyebrows and casually rumpled look that clearly communicated his place in the hierarchy. As network administrator, no doubt he knew that he stood at the top of the real corporate food chain, no matter what the organization charts showed. Right now, however, the chain was experiencing some nasty tremors, and he must have known that the peak predator usually suffers worst when something disrupts the local ecology.

"The drone program's not part of the corp net," he informed us darkly. "It's on its own track, walled off from my computers. Only time it touches us is to use the satellite link. I've had my people running diags and audits on our dumps, and we sent the right destinations and prices down to Jackson. Whoever this Gideon joker is, he didn't get in there through my system. Problem's not on my side."

"We know that," Loren told him. "From inside your network, the firewall's tight as Ms. Alison's—um, expression."

Abdu grunted assent and pointed with one large, hairy paw to a door marked Pɪᴛᴛ. He opened the door and yelled, "Jackson! Get over here!" An indistinct answering shout came from the crowded dimness inside. "It's Jackson's problem," he told us with some satisfaction. "You see if he can explain the glitch." He turned on his heel and stalked away.

"Abdu, you might want to check the replication password on your backup net-link computer," Loren called after him. "Especially since it has admin privileges for the root dir of the SunHQ domain. There's some interesting stuff in the volume's trash drive."

The network administrator trailed a stream of blue language behind him as he shifted from a self-satisfied strut to a flat run. He rounded the corner and disappeared. Somewhere in the distance, a door slammed, cutting off the diminishing sound of his footsteps.

Loren shook his head reprovingly. "Hear that? Same kind of nasty words he used in that e-mail he sent me. Fella's got a bad conscience for sure." He smacked his forehead. "Oh, I'm sorry—you probably didn't understand any of that. Do you need a translation?"

"No, thanks," I assured him. "I think I got the gist."

"Hi," a male voice said.

We turned to see a Hawaiian-shirted apparition in the Pɪᴛᴛ doorway, blinking through thick corrective lenses at the corridor's comparatively brilliant light.

I recognized him as one of the giddily grinning geeks I'd seen clustered in the background of the news segment on the drone trucks' launch. "Hi," I said, smiling and extending my ID. "I'm Sue Jones, and this is Loren Hunter. We're here to investigate the transport diversion."

"Whoa, FBI!"

Another member of the design team appeared out of the darkness, probably drawn by the unaccustomed light. He leaned forward confidentially over Jackson's floral shoulder. "It wasn't our security that fell down. You're going to want to talk to Abominable Abdu about holes in his satellite uplink."

Ah, I thought. *The pointing fingers indicating everybody and anybody else.*

"Come on in," Jackson invited.

We stepped into the Pitt. Open cubicles lined the walls and overflowed into the crowded central area. Consoles, towers, and monitors loomed through the dimness; it looked like the inhabitants had removed two of the three fluorescent rods in each lighting fixture. Aside from the data screens, most of the room's illumination came from a string of Christmas bulbs and a large lighted terrarium containing sand, miniature cacti, and a plate-sized tarantula. The arachnid's mandibles and front legs waved gently, the movement echoed by the mobiles made of data disks and soft-drink containers that hung and spun from the ceiling. Sunshine's corporate posters, defaced with comments and additions in marker, covered the walls. A package of Sunshine-brand turkey jerky sat atop a satellite uplink array.

"It's a bivouac, man. They sleep here,'" Loren whispered to me.

"That's a quote, right?" I asked.

"Yup. *The Adventures of Buckaroo Banzai Across the Eighth Dimension.* Great old show. They've seen it too."

"You'll have to show it to me," I said. "Later."

The introductions were as confused as the decor. I gathered that this was the design team for the drone fleet, that there were four of them, and that at various times they called each other Stu, Teddy, Weasel, Geek-boy, Eeeww, John-boy, Michael One, and Michael Two. Obviously, we had more names than bodies. I decided to assume that Eeeww applied to the spider and figure out the rest of the names from the material Ms. Alison had given us. I discreetly flipped open the folder, scanning photos and personnel information.

Stu—Stuart Michael Jackson, design team leader, Level 5 programmer, and so forth—waved his hands for emphasis as he assured us, "No way anybody could've cracked our security arrangements. We designed that system like Fort Knox, only even better. The whole team had all-night cracker sessions, trying to bust the system. No dice at all. Gideon got in through the system network and used their satellite codes to send new orders to the trucks." Nods all around at that; they clearly had perfect confidence in their system and very little in Abdu's.

Loren looked innocently helpful. "Yeah, I've already found some holes in the corp net. Still, you don't mind, do you?" With a magician's wrist flick, he gestured toward the primary system entrance glowing from Stu's data screen, and a data disk appeared between his long fingers.

"No, that's great, go for it," Stu said. The other three glanced at each other, then scattered back to their own terminals. Obviously, we were going to have company in cyberspace. I slid my hands into Stu's datagloves and activated the electronic access way, neatly landing on Sekhmet's clawed feet. Loren clanked into being beside me as Gilliam, his black-knight avatar. Smooth, impenetrable walls rose on either side of us, gently buzzing with the sizzle of commands shooting back and forth, guiding mechanical behemoths along the real highways miles away from this command center. The drone transports' control system was an electronic fortress, every portal guarded.

"Username!" the authentication bot growled through the speakers. Stu and his team had envisioned it as a robotic sphinx, the rippling muscles on its stainless-steel flanks contrasting with the mercury-smooth Nefertiti face.

"Carmelita21," Stu whispered to me. "That's the system-kernel username. She handles all the automatic functions after we program the routines."

I smiled as I passed that on to the steel sphinx. Stu certainly had security on the brain — who could overhear him here?

A few seconds later, the guardian accepted the cartouche containing the encrypted username. "Password!" the sphinx demanded.

Stu gently removed my hands from the datagloves, giving them back to me with a hint of blush under the thin stubble on his cheeks, and he slipped in his own hands. I politely glanced away, meeting Loren's raised-eyebrow gaze and giving him a half-shrug. Yes, we would need the password later, but for now I didn't see the harm in letting Stu keep it secret. The sphinx chewed the password, approved the taste, and moved clankingly aside. It folded neatly beside the portal, waiting for the next applicant.

"What happens if someone gives the wrong password?" Loren asked.

One of the programmers—Stu had called him John-boy, but his face corresponded to Sean Williams's datasheet—eagerly leaned forward. "This!" he said. His avatar, a baseball player whose gigantic arms dwarfed his tobacco-chewing head, stepped forward. The sphinx sprang up and issued its bass challenge. In response, the slugger batted a pair of cartouches in its direction. It caught the first and swallowed it without protest. When its teeth crashed together on the second, however, its face instantly transformed from lovely queen to snarling demon. It leapt lightning quick, bearing the steroid-pumped baseball player to the ground. I winced and glanced away as crimson spattered the scene amid whoops and applause from the design team. Why did guys always have to put in the gory effects?

"Yeah, very scary visuals. So what does it actually do?" I asked, pulling them back on track before they could wander off into a discussion about the real color of a suddenly exposed liver.

"It captures the user info for the avatar, records the session in the security dump, and closes the connection," Loren informed me.

"How did you figure that out?" John-boy demanded.

Loren shrugged, indicating the readouts he displayed on his own borrowed monitor. "I pulled a command window. Your sphinx interface looks pretty, but the readout here is more interesting."

I shifted over, glancing at the underlying reality behind the slick Aireon surface. Sure enough, the sphinx's orders showed clearly on the screen. The usernames and passwords we had used did not appear—the security precautions were effective—but the commands that captured the user's information, stored it, and cut off the connection glowed softly from the black window.

"You didn't disable the command window?" I asked, surprised.

"No," Stu shrugged. The others traded embarrassed glances. "It doesn't show anything we didn't want somebody to know, and it's display only—you can't actually do anything through it. Besides, we don't work on command line stuff. It's boring."

"Still, a smart cracker can use the info to figure out how to slide around your logging systems, if nothing else," I told him. "Speaking of which, I'll need copies of all the logs."

"It's not us," Stu repeated, annoyed that I had caught him in low-level carelessness. "It's gotta be Abdu's satellite link." He relented under my steady gaze and winning smile. "Okay, okay." He moved away to download the files, and I seized control of the datagloves, plunging back into the virtual world of the drones' control system.

Loren had, of course, gone on without me, but I tracked him through the maze. Underneath the Aireon visuals, the control software itself was straightforward, elegant, and very nicely done. I rapidly realized that the guys had spent a good half of their time creating the impressive visuals—aside from the metallic sphinxes that appeared with paranoid regularity throughout the corridors, each drone had its own brightly painted avatar, the uplinks showered as rainbow fountains toward the virtual sky and routes sparkled like bedewed spider webs, complete with huge guardian spiders. Loren and I—more literally, our avatars—moved through the system, opening data windows to examine the code. The design team shadowed our moves, their avatars appearing suddenly around corners or hovering over us as we investigated their world. I didn't pay any attention to them or to their real-world users, whispering conspiratorially across the room. I figured they were simply interested in watching the FBI in action, wondering what we'd do, and glad of the distraction from their normal work. I should've known better.

Flash! A logic bomb disguised as a flaming baseball sizzled past my head, ready to render Sekhmet blind, deaf, and helpless. I dodged, flipping acrobatically backward with a practiced flick of the datagloves. Another bomb splattered against Gilliam's breastplate, sparkling like ectoplasmic slime against the black metal. It utterly failed, however, to faze him; Loren had built protection features into him, as well as giving the knight the appearance of armor. That was part of the appeal of Aireon's avatars; you could buy or program hundreds of different capabilities into your digital self.

Gilliam laughed, the hollow bass tones rolling like thunder. "Fools! You dare challenge me? So be it!" He drew his broadsword from the scabbard across his back and charged the offending baseball player. The armor features prevented him from using distance attacks like logic bombs—another twist in Aireon's interface software. Its built-in limitations kept clever programmers from building dangerously overcompetent avatars.

A robed, wild-eyed figure leapt to intercept the black knight, activating a light blade. The two swordsmen met with a terrific—and rather illogical—crash. The swords screamed and clanged as the men battled across the corridor. A muscle-bound, shaggy Sasquatch lurked in the background, waiting for its opportunity to leap into the fray, and on the other side of the corridor the baseball player limbered his bat, hoping for an opening. When it came he pelted another logic bomb—at the Sasquatch. The duel dissolved into a general brawl, everyone indiscriminately firing logic bombs, swinging blades, and roaring. The inevitable gore splattered across the scene.

I leapt to the top of the smooth, gray wall, my tail whipping in annoyance. I enjoyed virtual games, but I preferred the puzzle-solving, narrative sort, not the shoot-'em-ups. Programmers! Always finding ways to mess around instead of just getting the job done, dropping everything to compare their avatars' abilities against all comers. The sounds of the battle rapidly faded as I sprinted away— though Stu and his cronies had lavished attention even to that detail. The crashing and cursing didn't instantly cut out the moment I left the scene; instead, it followed for a few seconds, until it got lost in the hum and rumble of the system's constant electronic activity.

These guys definitely had way too much time on their hands. They clustered tightly behind me, fingers working madly in the datagloves, their own voices mingling with their avatars' voices as they boasted, groaned, and roared challenges at each other.

Secure in my disdain for mate-winning mortal combat, I moved on, keeping my attention on the command window scrolling the cold-bit reality underneath the gaudy surface as I explored the system, searching for obvious back doors or cracks in the security arrangements. Nothing irregular appeared—well, in the command window; plenty of odd things flashed by in the Aireon visual interface—as I investigated the permissions lists, satellite uplink, and terminal communications, using the Carmelita21 identity to answer the security challenges that leapt at me around every corner.

Stu and the boys had the drones' programming sealed up very tightly against any unauthorized intrusion from outside. That left inside. I made my way toward the all-important center of the maze, peripherally aware that I had lost even Stu to Loren's showboating black knight.

The command room looked like tightly written code in the display window and like an intricately detailed starship's bridge in our visually shared imagination. The main vid screen glowed darkly, illuminated by the 3-D headshot of a pouty-faced blonde beauty queen Stu and the boys had chosen to represent the core of the program, Carmelita21 herself. Apart from that fabulous-space-babe note, however, the designers apparently preferred alien decor to human. The place reeked of battle-hardened warrior races — or it looked like it should. I snuffed just to clear the imaginary odor out of my head. The place had everything: cavelike ceiling with indirect lighting; crossed swords with too many curves and points as wall decorations; heavy metal filigree over every surface; throne-like captain's chair occupied by a bespectacled nerd wearing flood pants, pocket protector, and an old-fashioned Roman-style crested helmet . . .

Wait a minute. *One of these things is not like the others*, sang a little voice in my brain. The display window showed no sign of an active daemon, and no soul string trailed from the nerd's head to indicate a remote connection; this must be another of the team members' avatars.

I crept forward, slinking toward the skinny form whose virtual hands danced over the animated consoles, until I stood behind him. "Whatcha doin'?" I asked in Sekhmet's purring voice and italic font.

The nerd whirled instantly to his feet to face me, his strangely blank face suddenly creasing into a manic mask. "Curiosity," he said in a bass register more appropriate for a super villain, "killed the cat." Then he disappeared in a puff of opalescent smoke and sparkle.

I dove for the console, tripping the key-trap log at the same time. The faux readouts told me nothing; they were all in a curly, blade-like alien script that probably only Stu and his buddies could read. The face glowing from the computer screens put me off; I didn't want to ask a blond Amazon with silicone-plumped lips what the nerd had been doing. The log that opened at my command in another window told me that I had encountered a ghost, a utility exie done up in pixilated human form, rather than a standard avatar, which represented an actual user currently connected to the system. The nerd-ghost had seen my avatar's ID and promptly shut itself down, removing its instructions from the computer's memory.

Hmm. That was a very fancy ghost — some people didn't even bother to build in facial expressions for their avatars. Ghosts didn't often have vocal capacities either. Warning bells rang in the back of my head, like error messages from my gut instincts. I scanned up through the command history, looking for any evidence of the commands the nerd had issued before he clicked his own exit button.

The dull innocence of the few entries left surprised me. Certainly nothing to warrant the nerd's sudden disappearance or the Evil Empire tone of the comment about curiosity.

The command room yielded nothing else of note under my careful reconnaissance through the data windows. I finally asked Carmelita21 for a list of the users currently connected to the system. Her voice was as kittenish as I'd dreaded as she singsonged, "Connected users are Stuart Jackson as Tharg, Michael Yee as Obi-Solo D'Kwan, Chris O'Neil as Casey Bones, Cornell Arkan as Squatch, Sue Jones as Sekhmet, Grandmaster Merlyn as Gilliam, and Carmelita21 as Carmelita21." Cute. Stu had given her an avatar of her own. I shook my head at Loren's inveterate playacting; the guy couldn't resist jiggering Aireon's rules about avatars and proper IDs every way he could, even when spoofing his identity didn't have any real purpose other than showing that he'd found a hole in Aireon's software.

She simply said "No information available" when I asked about the nerd-ghost. I expected that; he had erased himself from her memory. Besides, Carmelita21 was busy. According to the data window, the computer's fictional identity was busily updating the programs on the twenty-four drone ships currently parked outside Sunshine distribution centers here — and in Nevada over the Sunshine satellite link. That probably explained why she hadn't greeted me as I entered the bridge.

I continued my circuit of the maze, avoiding Loren and his playmates as best as I could. Without diving deep into either the logs or the code itself, however, I had run out of leads. I let my mind grow quiet, shifting the puzzle into my subconscious for now, and found myself idly interacting with the virtual world the programmers had created to cloak their digital secrets.

Poking desultorily at an irregularity in the faux metal plating on the top of the wall, I suddenly found myself falling but landed neatly on my clawed hind feet. A high, vaulted ceiling curved above me, its ribbing flowing down into columns that defined a series of pointed arches around the walls. In each niche a holo portrait glowed.

It appeared that I had found an Easter egg, a piece of hidden code that the programmers slipped in for fun. As if this entire funhouse setup wasn't sufficient testimony to their sense of humor, they'd included a credits room as well for the original creators.

The muscle-bound baseball player Casey Bones slouched casually in his niche, bat over his shoulder, bulging cheek hinting at a nasty tobacco habit. A plaque pronouncing his mighty contributions to the effort — most of them clumsily risqué double entendres — decorated the wall beside him. The fighting monk D'Kwan stood to graceful attention, hands folded in an attitude of prayer — or the beginning of the mantis form of some exotic martial-arts style. His plaque was slightly less ribald, but most of the references escaped me; the few I caught seemed to rely on the reader's knowledge of kung-fu movies. Squatch the Sasquatch, hairy knuckles resting firmly against the floor, glared from underneath fuzzy, granite brow ridges and his list of accomplishments — *Squashed bugs, eated 'em* — were appropriately primitive as well.

A half-dozen more portraits decorated the walls, echoing the standard theme of aliens, superheroes, and elaborate visual puns. But I had not seen some of these avatars in person, and their plaques read more like obituaries. I *had* seen one of their ghosts, however: the nerd, who stood out just as awkwardly here as he had in the control room.

All those avatars paled before the figure that occupied the primary niche, however. Her amazingly exaggerated curves defied not only gravity but the tensile strength of the gauzy shift that more clung to than hid the details of her anatomy. Big eyes, pouting lips, more lush, flowing hair than humanly possible — I had already heard her speak, so I knew not to ask anything; I'd just hear more computerese uttered in a voice more suited to a fourth-grader than a grown — or overgrown — woman. She didn't have a plaque to list her contributions to the effort. She didn't need one. Muses never do.

"So we meet again, Carmelita21," I said aloud.

"Um, *ja.*" Stu appeared on my screen. He'd chosen a huge, heavily muscled, fat, sloppy Viking type as his avatar, a half-chewed chicken leg holstered beside a notched throwing axe at his belt. This apparition answered to the designation Tharg the Unhygienic, according to the plaque beside his portrait's head. The nickname was altogether too appropriate. While the mobile avatar lacked some of the sharp definition of the motionless version, once again I found myself suppressing the urge to sneeze away an imaginary odor.

"All right. You, I get. Her, I definitely get. Them, I can see," I told him. "But what's up with the virtual taxidermy specimens" — waving my hand toward the R.I.P. portraits — "and that?" I indicated the last figure in the gallery, my acquaintance from the command room, the nerd in all his geeky, stereotypical glory, the unmoving portrait even embellishing the image with a few pimples marring the thin face under the gilded Roman helmet. I waved around at the rest of the room. "Skinny fourteen-year-old computer nerds don't exactly go with the gym-boy theme here."

"Oh, they're guys who used to be on the project but got pulled off or left for other jobs or whatever. And that's just Davis—G.D. Davis, you know," Tharg informed me, ripping a chunk off the chicken leg with oversized, yellowed teeth. "He was our last gopher, an intern who came in for the middle part of the design project. He's gone back to school, left about a month ago. Talk about a klutzball—he wrote the worst code you ever saw."

"It didn't work?" I asked, surprised that such an incompetent could grab an internship working for a major corporation on a double-major project.

"Oh, sure, it worked," Tharg informed me, belching and spitting a bone into the far recesses of the portrait gallery. *Thanks, Stu.* "But it was bad—klugey, verbose, inelegant. System hog deluxe. His name was G. Donald, he wouldn't tell us what the G. stood for—"

"Probably something really stupid like Germaine or something," Michael One offered, joining us. He was Michael Yee, according to the folder Ms. Alison provided.

Surely it couldn't be that obvious, I thought to myself.

"Yeah," Stu agreed. "We got to calling him G.D. 'cause of all the times old Abdu chewed him out for crashing the entire system." He laughed uproariously.

"Quite an achievement, that," Gilliam's dark-chocolate voice observed. "Not getting Abdu to swear at him, but crashing the corp net, given the walls between the two systems." Ah, Loren had finally deigned to join the investigation.

"Interesting," I muttered. "So there was a connection at some point."

Stu affected not to have heard; Tharg didn't react to anything said offline.

"He must've been pretty good at diagnostics," I said aloud, disengaging my hands from the borrowed datagloves and popping Sekhmet's identity out of the computer's drive to indicate that our digital tête-à-tête was over. I stood up and stretched, which caught Stu's real-world attention. This guy needed a wife, for all kinds of reasons. "I ran into one of his ghosts up in the control kernel, running test routines. Very fancy one too, with vocal subroutines and facial expressions built into its interactivity."

"Yeah?" Stu considered, then shrugged. "Well, it wasn't like he didn't do anything right. Tests and echoes were kind of his specialty, even if they usually made our system run better by sabotaging Abdu's coffeemaker. Had some good ideas, but couldn't write a straight piece of code to save his skin. We got all his code cleaned up and everything working fine after he left—I guess we missed the ghosts 'cause they worked all right. Anyway, old G.D.'s name should've been Johnson, not Davis." He laughed like a loon. The other programmers, dislodged from their own communion with the virtual beyond, echoed the merriment.

"You haven't heard of B.S. Johnson? Gotta read Terry Pratchett, guys," John-boy informed us, seeing our politely blank stares of incomprehension.

"And see *Buckaroo Banzai*. Thanks for the recommendations, as well as the tour and the data," I told them, tossing the data disks containing the program code and log files from one hand to the other and then stowing them in my shoulder bag.

"And the battle," Loren added. "Haven't had that good a workout since last time I visited a kindergarten. We'll let you know when we've solved your little problem."

We left amid the customary verbal belly-butting, each side boasting that they'd track Gideon down before the other. Loren, as usual, got in the last jab, timing his comment to coincide with the elevator door closing. "Loser has to kiss Ms. Alison, Stu, so don't forget your lip gloss."

"Sneaky," I told him. "Totally junior high, but sneaky."

"Just showing off what I'm learning from you," he assured me, catching the door as it opened on the smiley-face-decorated lobby. Fortunately, Ms. Alison was in a meeting and did not get the chance to hound us out. We handed in our visitors' badges at the desk and emerged into the drizzle.

"So, what did you discover while I selflessly distracted the circling jackals from your search?" Loren asked.

"Oh, is that what you were doing?" I asked, grinning back at him as I dug the keys out of my purse and unlocked the car doors with the awkwardness that always afflicts my fingers in the rain. "I discovered that it looks like they've got the system locked tight against any outsiders hacking in, either from the V-Net or from Abdu's network. There could be a crack, but if it's there, it's hidden really well. The only time the link opens is when Carmelita21 uses it to establish contact with the trucks." I slid into the driver's seat and buckled my seat belt with a snap. "To me it smells like an inside job."

"So which of those guys have you pinned as our born-again terrorist?" Loren asked.

"I'm not sure. None of them seem like the type. I half suspect G.D. Davis, with his ghost lurking around and all, even though he's long gone. It bugs me that the ghost reacted to me, even told me that curiosity killed the cat. From what Stu said, though, he wasn't that slick a programmer, and Gideon strikes me as the prodigy type." I shrugged and tapped my temple. "It's in the basement perking away, waiting for inspiration to strike. In the meantime, I figure we might as well send Stark out to track down Mr. Davis. Who've you got your eye on? You spent most of the meeting trading thunderbolts, which has to tell you something about them."

Loren didn't answer immediately, staring thoughtfully at the runnels of rain sliding between the windshield wipers' semieffective swipes. Finally he sat back, singing along to a snatch of chorus from the song playing on the radio. "'Just don't hurt me, don't just hurt me.' Girl's got a real ambivalence problem. And speaking of problems, I think Stu's problem is coming from outside. It's not one of those guys. They're way too into this whole thing—it's their baby. They wouldn't do anything to hurt or compromise the system. They love it to bits. It may be an inside job, but it's not coming out of the Pitt now." His fingers tapped on the dashboard, the syncopated rhythm no doubt echoing the thoughts ping-ponging around his head.

"Maybe not anymore, but it may have once," I suggested. "There were a lot of bodies in that morgue besides G.D. Davis. And, like you say, plenty of people have reason to go after Sunshine." The synthetic heartbeat of the latest Haitian raga harmonized with the rain against the car, underscoring the relative silence.

Loren turned down the music to call Dave. He neatly summarized what we'd found at Sunshine and read off the list of previous employees somebody needed to talk to. "No," he said, answering a question I didn't hear but could guess at, "the only really suspicious one is G.D. Davis. . . . Don't know. I'll ask." He gave me a narrow look. "Dave wants to know if G.D.'s one of your relations."

"Tell Dave he's such a Dave," I suggested.

"She says yes, he's her prodigal younger sister, but she doesn't want to talk about it." I harrumphed; he blew me a kiss. "Yeah, we probably ought to send somebody over to pick the guy up. He's a student out at Jobs U, did some contract work for them and left a real ghost in the machine. We'll know more as soon as we go through the stuff Jackson gave us." He listened for a few moments, then said, "Right. We'll let him know. Yes, we'll get right on it. Yes, I'm sure Sunshine's been yipping and hollering at you all day. We met Ms. Alison ourselves—yeah, a gorgon in a chignon. Oh, and Dave? We're going to be pulling some serious overtime on this one, so if anything happens tonight and Sue gets excommunicated over it, it's all your fault for not providing a chaperone." He clicked off the receiver and gave me a broad smile. "Good news—Dave'll spring for dinner to make it up to you."

"So sweet of him," I laughed. "A pizza for my immortal soul. My price is a bit higher than that."

Loren nodded. "Sure is. We ought to be able to squeeze a box of donuts out of the deal too."

HQ was as dark and quiet as ever when we returned with the inevitable pizza box, three Chinese cartons, a dozen donuts, a half-gallon of milk—and a bag of baby carrots, which Loren teased me about, as usual.

"It's not the carrots in particular," he said, waving his chopsticks for emphasis. "It's the carrots in conjunction with the rest of it. Smacks of a half-hearted gesture toward assuaging a guilty conscience, pacifying the little health-teacher, mommy voice in the back of your head bemoaning the evils of junk food, the current sad state of young people's general health, and the lazy habit of not changing your sheets every week."

I didn't bother to defend my pitiful attempt at nutrition. I just crunched a carrot, took a long swig of milk, and smirked at him under my milk mustache. "All right, my dear Watson, which do you want—code or logs?"

He picked a slice of pepperoni off the pizza with his chopsticks. "Only one way to do this fairly, Murtaugh," he said solemnly. He picked up my unopened pack of chopsticks—I could use them if I had to, but I'm not a showoff like some people—extracted one, and broke it not quite in half. He palmed the unbroken ends, hid them behind his back for a moment, then extended his fist.

I bit my lip dramatically, extended a slightly shaking hand, pulled it back, then finally took a deep breath and seized one of the broken bits. Loren opened his hand, and we compared the two. "Dang, looks like I lost," I said. "It's the code for me, then."

"Oh, no, the code's the long stick," Loren assured me. "You win the unparalleled joy of tracking Gideon through the wilds of Stu's log files."

"While you undertake the mind-numbing drudgery of unraveling the fascinating code underlying Carmelita's improbable curves." I waved a donut threateningly in his direction. "You owe me big for this one, Hunter."

He caught my hand as I reached for the disk containing the logs and kissed the back of it gallantly. "Of course. Forever."

I wrinkled my nose at him and didn't shiver—obviously, that is. I just hoped the exchange had as much of an effect on him as it did on me.

The log files certainly had an effect—but the effect was brain-deadening, not frighteningly exhilarating. After the first hour I leaned back, stretched, and bravely resisted the call of the last donut. Loren had his feet up, fingers in datagloves, headphones on, tunes playing and the raw code from Sunshine's drone-fleet system filling the data windows of his screen and reflecting in his blue eyes. I, on the other hand, had the endless audit tracks for the drones. Boring as they were, I had to admit that it was a fair division of labor; in our partnership, Loren got the digger's role while I took the tracker's part. Usually my bit turned out more exciting than his. This time it didn't.

I felt a momentary flash of disappointment that I wasn't riding along with Stark, speeding through the darkness, guns loaded, eyes narrow under our snap-brim hats, a sight to strike terror into the heart of übernerd G.D. Davis when we pounded on his garret door at 2:30 A.M. Ms. Alison's folder hadn't included any information about the ex-intern, but a quick search of Sunshine's human resources records had turned up his application: G. Donald Davis, as Stu had said, registered at Steve Jobs University as a master's student in advanced computational systems, with an impressive résumé of projects to his name. I had only glanced through his transcripts—solid A's in number-related academic subjects, a few B's in the literary fields, a single D-plus in, of all things, fencing. Obviously, Stark wouldn't have to worry about getting stabbed through the heart when he confronted G.D.

That showdown would take place first thing in the morning. I'd sent the entire packet, along with G.D.'s listed mailing address, to Stark. Dave had, as promised, called the agent and officially assigned him to pick up G.D. Davis when we notified him of the necessity. Earlier this evening he'd agreed to do it, after grumbling about it being on the far side of his assigned territory. After he'd flicked through G.D.'s file, he glowered through the teleconference window and informed me that he wouldn't get on it until tomorrow. As much as Stark disapproved of crackers, he growled that he wasn't going to drag himself out of his house to start a long trip out to the Jobs U campus at this hour unless there was a bomb involved.

Come to think of it, going on this hunt with Stark would have involved a lot more driving and listening to him talk than doing exciting stuff, anyway.

My phone went off, breaking that nightmare scenario. "Hello, Sue Jones here."

"Sue, you're at work. Good." A quick check of the caller ID readout and postage-stamp video feed in the corner of my screen confirmed what I already knew: Shawnie was calling me from D.C. I turned on my own video and smiled politely for the camera.

Shawnie — or Special Agent Shawndell Lincoln, as she invariably answered the phone — worked for the head of NIPC in the FBI's headquarters office in Washington, D.C. (FBIHQ, in standard Bureau acronymese.) She wasn't a DAD herself, of course, though she acted as if she thought that job wouldn't sufficiently challenge her talents; she was an acting liaison between the powers that be and us underlings in the Portland field office. We officially coordinated with the foreign liaison offices through her, but she usually ended up needling us in political matters as well. Plugged right in to the political scene, that girl, and always trying to social-climb herself and/or the Bureau up the Washington ladder. She also had a condescending attitude — probably unintentional — toward the people manning field offices in general, with an extra layer of a sophisticate's disdain for us poor non-Special Agent types. Where Stark still thought of us as jumped-up computer geeks unworthy of badges but all right in our own places, Shawnie couldn't shake her mostly unconscious conviction that we were butterfingered incompetents who took the jobs we had only after washing out of the more selective Special Agent recruitment process.

Love your enemies, I reminded myself firmly — not that Shawnie's an enemy, exactly. *Do good to those that despitefully use you and persecute you. We're all on the same team. Be polite to arrogant Washington Bureau-crats. Turn the other cheek.* Well, I almost succeeded.

"Hi, Shawnie. Yes, I'm at work. We had a bit of a thing out here," I said, as if she didn't know.

She gave it right back. "Yes, that's what I'm calling you about. I've talked to Dave, your supervisor, and he told me that you were handling the Sunshine hijacking case."

Yes, I know Dave, Shawnie. "That's right. Have you solved it already?" I asked brightly.

She laughed. "No, that's up to you. I've told Dave, and now I'm just calling to let you know that Mr. Zevon, owner and founder of Sunshine Foods, is very concerned that the FBI and NIPC clear up this problem as quickly as possible. Mr. Zevon is a very friendly man, Sue, with a lot of good friends in the Senate. It's very important that the FBI and NIPC live up to their sterling reputations in this matter."

"Or Zevon's going to have his golf partners cut our funding for next year," Loren suggested.

"What?" Shawnie asked, trying to look past me.

"Loren says hi," I told her. "Thanks for the heads up, Shawnie. We'll be sure to make the home team proud."

"I told Dave you would," she informed me, smiling politely. "Well, don't let me keep you. Get to work, now."

I stared at the LINE FREE message, trying not to think things about Shawnie or about an irritated fat cat giving the Bureau fits because somebody in his organization very publicly messed up. I knew that Dave had gotten the message loud and clear, which meant that he'd be around tomorrow to ask me how things were going and give me some "encouragement" to get it solved faster. Yeah. Pressure and obnoxious people — two of my least favorite things in the world.

Loren gave me a sympathetic look but couldn't keep a straight face as he said, "Boy, am I glad that Dave doesn't totally trust me."

"Don't worry, dear, you'll get to lead a politically charged chase too, one of these days."

"Oh, I just can't wait," he assured me. "Maybe if I do really well with analyzing this competent but totally boring program, that day will come even sooner." Despite that looming possibility, he diligently dug back into our copy of Stu's system.

Well, I could sit there and worry about it, I told myself, or I could take it for the distraction it was and get on with more important things. Ah, never mind — I felt enough pressure to catch Gideon for myself, without adding Dave to it. Best to content myself with chasing G.D.'s ghost through the logs.

Going through the log files was like figuring out the tracks in a thin snowfall over a country lane. Dozens of different digital footprints filled the records, trails running in every direction, overlapping, fuzzy in spots with age or errors. I picked out Stu's lumbering marks, John-boy's scampering footsteps, all the traces of the design team's everyday activities. Carmelita21's tracks—I pictured them as the marks of stiletto-heeled, marabou-topped mules—showed up regularly, sending instructions and updates to the robot trucks. G.D. Davis's ghosts, three of them, also left sneaker-prints through the virtual snow, trailing hither and yon on errands, doing the chores Carmelita21 delegated to them. It surprised me to see how much she depended on them; most of the nonessential information gathering went through the ghosts. They couldn't directly touch the drones or the satellite uplink, but they handled just about everything else, including receiving inventory lists and itineraries from the bean counters attached to the corp net.

The total lack of unidentified contacts also surprised me; not a single anonymous user had attempted entry from the V-Net side. Everyone who had gained access to the system was either a current or former member of the design team, and even the outsiders devoured by the sphinxes showed up as familiar entries. Abdu's username appeared several times, poking at the transport system's security from the corp net. Several others had tried the same closed portal; all of them, according to Ms. Alison's employee packet, were system administrators reporting to Abdu. Lots of interest on the corp side in what Stu and the boys were doing, and probably some sour grapes as well, judging from Abdu's attitude. He and his minions had never actually gained entry, however, thanks to the monster-enforced authentication.

Identifying the players only confirmed my suspicion that Gideon was an insider, not an interloping alien. At the same time, though, I had to agree with Loren—I couldn't see Stu, Michael, Chris, or Cornell as Bible-quoting social-reform techno-terrorists. G.D. Davis and his fellow ex-team members looked much more likely.

"We've definitely got an inside job here, sir." I leaned back, stretching as hard as I could. "I can't find even a single unidentified track coming through that V-Net portal."

"You know what I always say, Murtaugh—shoot first, ask questions later." Loren stretched too, spider-tickling one of my outstretched hands.

I ended my stretch a little abruptly and sat up. "Which means what, in this case?"

"Nothing. I just like to say it." He smiled at me. "From what I've seen in their code, there is one chance it's not an inside job, if the loophole I'm thinking of really does exist inside Aireon's operating system code. If they haven't closed it, Gideon could've used the multiplexer to piggyback a signal the other direction when Carmelita21 called the satellite. I could pound through a baker's dozen of reference books, but you're looking blurry, and if I have to read one more line of code I'm going to blitz. What we need is a drive in the country." He sat up and keyed a connection from his console, opening his avatar zoo at the same time.

"Ooh, a vacation. Where are we going?" I scooted my chair over for a better view.

"Get it from the horse's mouth, I always say. Let's go visit Stanton's library. Incognito, of course." He chose the avatar he wanted, activating the alias program he used to get around Aireon's registration requirements with pirated codes already registered to other users, specifically the IDs of various hackers Loren had caught trying to hack into the NIPC computers. He figured that when Aireon came after them for unauthorized use of their avatars, or hacking, or whatever they were up to at the moment, they only got what they deserved.

Loren's choice of digital character glowed into being covered head to toe in slick, black, studded leather, standing with spike-heeled boots planted firmly apart. She shook her flame-red mane of hair back from her stunningly sculptured face, flicked her riding crop, and greeted Loren with an imperious, "What's the magic word, boy?"

I poked Loren. "Um, not to put too fine a point on it, but what in the world is *that?*"

Loren raised an eyebrow at me. "What? She's my command-and-control specialist. I think she's got a nice girl-next-cube quality. Don't you?"

Red hair. I got it. I didn't let on, though. (Did he really see me as a long-legged, gorgeous thing like that? Oh, cut it out.) "And she's going to find this possible backward-masking feature for you?"

"You bet. Hi, Trixie," Loren said as he typed his password. "Let's have some fun."

She snatched it out of the ether, tore it open with her teeth, and spat it out with a shrug. "Make it quick. I've got better things to do than play with you."

Another gesture of the datagloves, and she dove through a V-Net portal. She landed in the wide marble foyer of Aireon's open-source code library. The sweet-looking old lady at the reference desk nodded politely. "Welcome to Aireon's online library. Remember that all code contained in this library is free to the public and cannot be included in copyrighted applications. If you need assistance, click the call buttons at the end of each aisle. Please sign the guestbook to continue."

Trixie stalked past her, smacked the heavy ledger with her crop to sign it, and strode through the double doors into the library itself.

"Okay, mistress, go find what we're looking for," Loren said, feeding the information into his leather-clad search engine. Her heels clicked along the floor, sounding loud and metallic as the stacks whirred past.

"That's interesting," I said. "That you can hear her walk."

Loren nodded. "Yeah, these guys put in all kinds of bells and whistles. Hyperrealism is one of their big selling points for the Aireon interface, and they like to rub other developers' noses in it. Ed's programmed his avatar to get a hacking cough going whenever he's in here. You can hear it all over the room."

"Poor Scratch," I groaned. Ed made a point of incorporating every annoying characteristic possible into his online representation, just for the heck of it. Thank heavens that nobody had really come up with a way to generate virtual smells!

"This what you're looking for?" Trixie asked like she couldn't care less if you paid her, and she tossed a disk down onto a table.

It sunk into the mahogany surface, which shimmered and lit with a text window. Loren zoomed in so the documentation filled the screen. We scanned through it, reading over columns of variables, commands, and more, all part of the structure underlying NetSys. Notes accompanied each item, recording original programmers' names, explaining the intent of the code, and listing bugs found and fixed for each feature.

"There it is," Loren said. "Or rather, there's where it was." A section of the text glowed as he copied it locally. "Looks like they've tied up the piggyback problem. Hmm—Stoneface fixed it. Guy's good, gotta give him that."

"You know him?" I asked.

"Not in the biblical sense." Loren laughed at my groan. "I've never actually met him, just chatted with his avatar down in the Niffelheim Group's salon. I think he's actually a Pentagon antiterrorism specialist, but he's got a lot of juice in hacker circles, and he writes diamond-hard code."

"And he's fixed our problem, so we're back to an inside job again," I summed up.

"Mm-hmm." Loren seemed less than eager to get back to sifting Stu's drone-program code. "So, while we're here, you wanna see if we can get a preview peek at NetSys 11.4?"

"That's not due out for another couple of weeks," I reminded him. "And it's not open-source code, either. Loren, you're not supposed to try to hack into Aireon's proprietary code, and they're not going to use the same user permissions as for their open-source library."

"Just makes it more of a challenge," Loren assured me. "More fun. Don't worry—we won't get caught. Go get it, Trixie."

"I've never seen anybody so eager to see Paul Stanton's naked . . ." I let my voice trail off, waiting for the reaction; sure enough, Loren shot me a look. " Code," I finished, then added, "Have you ever heard of unhealthy obsessions?"

"They're the opposite of healthy ones?" he asked innocently, sending Trixie on her way again. "You've got to see this."

Trixie passed stack after stack of neatly shelved data disks, which gave way to shelves of perfect-bound books. "Older versions," Loren told me—unnecessarily, because the spines read NET-SYS 11.1. Occasionally, off in the distance, we caught sight of someone else browsing through the shelves or reading a disk from the bright surface of a table. Some of the avatars looked even stranger than Trixie in their current surroundings—though I will admit that the guy who came up with the octopus avatar as a research assistant had a good idea.

Somebody in the Aireon documentation department clearly had a sense of humor, because the books changed from standard manuals to old three-ring binders to iron-and-leather-bound treatises before the shelves themselves altered. Rack after rack of scrolls surrounded Trixie—NetSys 3, according to the Hebrewish characters engraved on their handles. These gave way in turn to rows and rows of incised clay tablets. Trixie at last came to a halt before a huge stone engraved on all sides with precise columns of tiny carved words and figures. The heading on the top of the monolith read NETSYS 1.1.

"In the beginning was the code," I intoned.

"And the code was buggy," Loren added, laughing. "Hence all the upgrades we've passed. Even I've got to admit, though, it's an elegant beginning for the engine that runs the entire V-Net today."

"You sent me all the way down here to look at a stupid rock?" Trixie demanded after she received no new instructions for several moments, which Loren and I devoted to staring at the oddly appropriate representation of Paul Stanton's revolutionary code base.

"High maintenance, isn't she?" I asked. "Creating a real girl for yourself?"

"It's part of the learning-program characteristics that make her such a good search engine and code breaker," Loren told me. I could've sworn his ears looked a touch redder than they had a minute ago, but he didn't give me a chance to inspect them. "She can't help being self-referential." Addressing Trixie, he said, "No, my impatient imp, I sent you there to show *Sue* a stupid rock."

"Thanks ever so," I said. "Now what? Back to our actual, like, *jobs?*"

Loren caught my chair, preventing me from scooting back into my own cubicle. "No. We're going to the developers' download area. Remember how I asked if you wanted a preview of NetSys 11.4?" He held up a hand to ward off my incipient reminder that we weren't supposed to be playing hacker. "Hush. Listen carefully."

We listened to the high-heel sounds of Trixie's prowling progress. She left the stone-tablet area at warp speed, the shelves blurring around her, and entered a cross between a standard reading room and one of those old automat-style food courts. A grizzly bear in a deerstalker cap and cape coat downloading a piece of avatar add-on code from one of the vending machines stared as Trixie went past. Loren's quick fingers flashed a command down the line; Trixie shot the ursine avatar a look that would've melted through a silicon chip. "Keep it for Goldilocks, Teddy," she advised in her honey-and-glass-shards voice. The bear had the good sense not to say anything; it just popped the add-on into its impressively fanged mouth and shuffled out of the frame.

His departure left Trixie alone in the room; she casually stalked from one machine to the next, prodding them with her riding crop. Each brightly painted cabinet front advertised a different product — codes, features, tools, some free for the taking, others available for varying amounts of money.

"What exactly are we listening for?" I asked.

"Error messages," Loren said softly. "This is the interface for Aireon's entire software downloading operation. Right now it's just dispensing bits and pieces; each of these machines represents a different publicly available code. Next week the whole thing will change as they download NetSys 11.4 onto all computers. They've already got the delivery system set up — they used it for part of their

NetSys 11.3 upgrade—so if we know where to look, we might be able to figure out where the new stuff is. Once we do that, Trixie may be able to slide us behind the door."

I knew we shouldn't be doing this, but I didn't renew my objections. I didn't think we'd succeed, for one thing, and for the other—well, let's just say that if every good cop is a bounder underneath, every good anti-cracker is a hacker at the core. I didn't mind getting a sneak preview of Aireon's latest and greatest interface improvements before anybody else did.

I kept my mouth shut and tuned into the heel clicks, buzzes, and chimes I'd shut out as mere background noise. Each time Trixie hit a vending machine, I heard a ghostly *ding*, the sound that usually meant the computers behind the machines were open and ready for business. At the end of the row on the next wall, however, the crop hit the metallic door of a heavy vendor with a subdued buzz. UN-AVAILABLE, its mirror face flashed in red letters.

"Got it," Loren whispered.

Trixie tucked the crop under her arm, leaning forward with one talon-gloved hand spread flat on the machine's front. Waves like heat mirages spread from her fingers; the buzz grew in volume. It changed pitch too, rising up the scale as it got louder.

"That is a restricted program."

The pleasant, neutral voice made me jump. The librarian from the reception desk stood beside the entrance to the download area. Loren just pulled a face and gave Trixie another batch of instructions.

"Please desist," the librarian continued, moving toward Trixie. "If you do not, your avatar and computer may suffer permanent damage." As it came closer, the librarian looked less like a neatly dressed, middle-aged woman and more like something you glimpse out of the corner of your eye when you're browsing the basement stacks alone.

This phantom didn't disappear when Trixie whirled to face it, however; it stood there with its toothy skull glowing through its face. When Trixie snapped her crop at it, the librarian ghost roared and lunged, clawed hands outstretched. I jumped in my seat and stifled a scream. The ghost cut right through Trixie, studded leather and all. Bright-crimson avatar blood splattered the unavailable vending machine.

"Fletch!" Loren growled, his fingers flying in the datagloves as he pulled Trixie away from the growling guardian's sharp grip. The download area abruptly vanished as he cut the connection, leaving Trixie lying in a pool of red hair and redder gore against the gray-cell background of Loren's monitor.

"Say the magic word, boy," she whispered, then went limp.

Cleaner bots, tiny troubleshooting utilities, swarmed out of the walls and over the avatar, retreating as quickly as they'd come and leaving nothing behind.

I whistled softly. "I could've done without the whole slasher-game motif, but they're sure taking security seriously." I leaned over to look at Loren, trying to judge his expression behind the long bangs curtaining his bowed head. "She going to be all right?"

He looked up, flipping his hair out of the way with a practiced head jerk. "Sue! She's an avatar. She'll be fine—recode the com mand database, dump the corruption, restore the heuristic program from backups, and she's as sassy as ever. Don't worry about the ID trace—RaeDawn Ben Jacob'll be getting a nasty letter from Aireon about the penalties for trespassing. We got off scot-free." He snuffed. "But we won't be seeing if Copycat still works in NetSys 11.4 tonight. Da—darn their hides for the paranoid geeks they are."

"It isn't paranoia if somebody's actually out to get you," I reminded him. "And you're definitely out to get Paul Stanton."

"He deserves it. Anywhere else you want to go?" he asked hopefully.

I grabbed the back of his chair and turned him firmly toward his desk, shoving him closer and using Third Law dynamics to fuel my roll back to my own desk. "Nowhere but back into the wonderful world of Sunshine. Come on—let's figure out who's been messing with their drone trucks' heads or steering wheels or whatever. At least we know it's definitely somebody on the inside now."

Loren sighed deeply, put upon, but he obediently resized the windowful of Stu's code and settled his headphones over his ears.

I waited until I was sure he wasn't going to do anything interesting before I turned back to my own console. Now that I had identified who had interacted with the system and gotten a rush of adrenaline from Loren's near-death experience to fuel a few more hours of mental efforts, I turned to establishing the timing. Patterns slowly emerged from the chaos; I programmed my console to eliminate the routine transmissions and transactions, then to map the remaining entries. Galaxies of colored dots filled the dataspace inside the screen, each dot representing a connection, a data transfer, a change in the drones' guidance system. I rotated the array; changed the display parameters; eliminated internal communications, external communications, programs; restored the outside links; added the ghost programs' activities; drew in the authentication monsters' admittance records.

By the time—2:30 A.M.—I finally admitted that my brain had absorbed as much as my seat could endure—having the data points dance to ancient disco hits was a big hint that I'd reached the end of my productivity rope—webs of colored lights moved and flashed behind my eyes. I peered through them as I unfolded my poor stiffened body from the chair, said, "Gotta go home and crash" to the back of Loren's head, and drove home.

I'm pretty sure he told me to drive carefully and called me sweetheart, but he denied that last bit later.

The patterns shone like star-bright bird tracks in the black snow of the void behind my dreams. This was worse than the comparatively primitive puzzle game I'd gotten addicted to when I was four years old! The data points even fell and scattered across my eyelids as I said my morning prayers. I apologized, taking a deep breath and quieting the monkey mind chattering away in the back of my head. After a few minutes of concerted effort to give the proper attention to my prayers, the apology turned into a gleeful "Thank you!"

I catapulted to my feet and zipped through my workout, mostly ignoring the newscaster's recap of Gideon's guerilla grocery delivery as I looked at my new idea from all angles. It still looked plausible, if a little thin. It certainly looked better than Sunshine Foods at the moment. According to the latest report, they had generously decided to donate the stolen semi-loads of groceries, and to prove that they were the good guys after all, they would donate another eighteen trucks of food to various worthy and kid-related causes throughout the region. Ms. Alison announced those decisions for the cameras, using a smile she hadn't bothered to try on Loren and me. It probably wouldn't have worked on us, anyway; it certainly didn't work on the reporters.

Instead of following the Sunshine Foods clips with flattering shots of improbably scrubbed urchins happily feasting on snack cakes delivered free to their shelter, the reporters put on their frowny faces and gave the outraged but simple-minded public a much-simplified version of the same regional price-scale information that Loren had given me. It didn't sound any fairer coming from Mike and Michelle; no wonder Gideon had included it along with his messiah-complex message to the press. They loved it and thus loved him too for saving them from a slow news period, and they did all they could to hype the possibilities. Mike signed off with dire hints about a repeat Robin Hood performance from Gideon.

"Sorry to disappoint you, Mike, but Gideon's grocery-jacking days are just about over," I told the vid, clicking it off. "You and Michelle will just have to content yourselves with the journalistic equivalent of a one-night stand." I ran out to my car with a spring in my step and a grin on my face, despite the too-early hour and the last drops of shower water dripping from my hair.

"Hey, Loren!" I called exuberantly, grabbing the back of his chair and giving it a vigorous shake—which was juvenile, but probably more appropriate than my first impulse, which was to kiss the top of his head. "Do red herrings leave tracks in snow?"

"More like floppy marks," he said, illustrating with one hand as he pushed himself away from his console. "Why?"

I threw myself into my chair, sending it rolling across the floor protector to thump into my desk. "Total inspiration, my dear Watson. I think I've found some herring tracks." The display woke under my fingers, Sekhmet uncurling from her arboreal perch and stretching. My lights sprang into life in their window, the rotating pattern matching the spots that had danced behind my eyes all night.

"See? I spent most of my time chasing G.D.'s ghosts all over the place because they were the strangest thing in the logs. Most of the time they just did all these little maintenance tasks, cleaning buffers and straightening the furniture. Occasionally, though, they'd go into this funky little routine of checking the satellite connections, like that one was doing when I busted in on him in the control room. He'd do that every time Carmelita21 issued the updated instructions to the trucks, even if the instructions were just 'Keep waiting, boys, we haven't gotten the go-ahead yet.' That looked really suspicious, so I kept trying to figure out how you could use a ghost like that to break into the satellite links and get to the trucks—"

"But you can't," Loren finished for me. "Unless the ghost isn't really a ghost." He gestured to the display window on his own screen. "And one of them isn't. It's a cut-down avatar that knows how to erase its keystrokes from the command history." He smiled. "It's a nice one too, very neatly programmed to pack three times the usual capability into the same-size program as a ghost."

"Which one is it?" I asked.

Loren gave me the ID string, and I threw it into my screen and told the computer to eliminate all data points except the ones for Carmelita21 and this super-ghost. The pattern shivered, splattered, and recrystallized—in exactly the simple array I had seen that morning. *Thank you again!* I thought heavenward.

"Looks like good old G.D. was a real expert on red herrings," I said, "fooling Stu and everybody else into thinking they could instantly tell his programs by their klutziness, while he left an agent behind, perfectly disguised by its own elegance."

"Eh, it's easy to fool somebody as arrogant as Stu—he didn't even bother to disable the command window."

"He's also infatuated with Carmelita21," I said. "Listen, Loren, the ghosts aren't the thing. They're just tools, and part of their job is to pick up the delivery lists and feed them through to the system. So they get the new program from Gideon, then Carmelita21's the one who actually sends the altered instructions to the trucks. The satellite link goes straight through her—nobody else has access to it. Even the password for her user account is hidden in such deep encryption that if Stu gets hit by a truck, nobody's going to be able to get into her. It's not that Gideon hacked into the satellite link—he managed to get to Carmelita21 by hacking into the ghosts—"

"—through a back door." Loren again finished the thought, and now it was his turn to dive to his console for some inspired data crunching. "Right there!" He triumphantly indicated a few lines embedded into the harmless-looking identification for G.D.'s ghosts. "I wondered why G.D. put a phone-home routine in there. His ghost called him by opening a standard V-Net line while Carmelita21 was using the link, got the instructions, then fed her the altered itineraries when it updated the general inventory lists and checked the satellite uplink. And Stu never caught it, because he never thought to look for G.D.'s code in the cleanest part of the system."

"And what do you bet the strange name G. Donald wouldn't tell anybody is Gideon?"

If we'd been basketball players, we might have tried a high five or a hearty slap on the behind. We settled for a mutual rebel whoop.

I checked my watch and smiled at him. "Carmelita21's next update is at six o'clock. We can catch G.D.'s little nerd general in action before he can erase his tracks. Shall we bring Stu in for the kill?"

"Go right ahead," Loren said. "I'll get us there."

"Mr. Jackson," I purred when Stu sleepily answered the phone, "this is your wakeup call. GET ONLINE RIGHT NOW! Your darling Carmelita21 has a boyfriend on the side, and his initials are G.D. Davis."

Stu sputtered, but it took only a few seconds for his disheveled head to appear in the conference corner of my screen. "Miss Jones?" He blinked owlishly out at me as Tharg took shape in the glade below Sekhmet's tree. "Did you say something about Carmelita? What's going on?"

He snapped awake when Loren sent annotated code scrolling over the link between us to display on his screen. G.D.'s back door stood out in high relief, as did the instructions the ghosts fed into Carmelita21. I muted the sound feed from Stu's bedroom; Abdu wasn't the only Sunshine administrator who knew his way around a colorful metaphor.

"There it goes," Loren told me, as the timer on his console went off. "Carmelita's established her satellite link. The back door's open."

I activated my link tracer and dialed in to the back door, using the ghost's user ID and password to pass the sphinx sentries as Stu watched openmouthed on the monitor. Sekhmet landed right in the control room, once again behind the skinny form of G.D.'s specialized ghost. Packets flew past me, down the open conduit into the vast web of the V-Net. The tracer arrowed after them, marking their path through the strands as it went. The ghost spun around, just as he had before, and once again that look of surprise crossed his face.

"Curiosity killed the cat," he said. I expected that. But I did not expect him to pull a feathered dart from the crest of his helmet and throw it at me. Despite my practiced reflexes, the dart struck my arm. Digital infection spread from that point through the link, a virus wriggling toward my own computer at light—or at least *link*—speed.

I hissed between my teeth, yanking the hijacked connection between my console and Stu's computer. Sekhmet stumbled back into the forest and froze, lying still amid the ferns. Antivirus exies swarmed out of the undergrowth, checking my avatar and my console for destructive digital diseases. I shoved away from the desk and zoomed across the few feet into Loren's cubicle.

"Trace is gone," Loren said aloud. Over his shoulder Tharg charged into the control room, grabbing the ghost around the neck with one huge hand. Ah, good—Stu had managed to use the back door into his own darling Carmelita21's boudoir as well.

Instead of struggling, however, the nerd simply nodded. "Gotcha," it said and disappeared.

Tharg cussed nearly as well as Stu did. I watched both the programmer and his avatar—one in pixilated life, one across a video conferencing link—rip the ghosts' code out of Carmelita21's program. With the last blow of Tharg's axe, the graphical representation of the control room abruptly blinked out. Stu had slammed the back door.

Loren dinged for Stu's attention; the programmer's face returned to the camera atop his console. "We're sending the rest, log file entries and code to watch for," Loren told Stu. "And we'll pick up G.D. Davis. Good luck with the ghost busting." Stu nodded and got as far as "Tha—" before Loren added, "Be more thorough this time," and disconnected.

"You just really are kind of obnoxious, aren't you?" I smacked his shoulder.

"Just disappointed," he told me with a sigh. "We caught Gideon before he had a chance to bankrupt the company."

"Well, you'll be able to express your admiration in person, when Stark brings in Gideon Donald," I said. "I just hope he wasn't connected to the link when Stu started ripping it all up, or he knows something's up."

"He wasn't," Loren told me. "No soul string trailing from the ghost into the connection, just the message packets. That's an unreliable communication, not a virtual connection. He's going to know it in another couple of hours, though, when Carmelita21 is supposed to run her next update and he doesn't get a 'Hi, I'm still here' message from his ghost."

"Carmelita21's not going to be running standard updates for a while. Not until Stu replaces those ghosts with his own code." I sighed. "So I guess we've got time to start writing up the report."

"Nah, we can't start writing it yet—we don't know the ending. How about breakfast?" he suggested. "If you're not fasting, of course."

"That's Sundays or special occasions," I told him, simplifying matters somewhat for my Gentile audience. "And you, my procrastinating friend, are buying."

"Glad to."

Easy for him to say, and easy on his wallet too—the last spasm of employee morale boosting included the installation of a coffee-vending machine, jiggered to dispense its very low-grade product for free. Handily, the health-nut disdain of caffeine prompted the manufacturer to put in fake cocoa as well as bad coffee, so both Loren and I had something to sip and grimace at. He topped off his liquid breakfast with a couple of cold toaster pastries out of the fat-and-sugar vending machine, then kindly hooked an apple out of the snack carousel for me. We wandered back to our cubicles carrying our subsidized breakfasts.

I flicked out my pocket knife and sliced the apple in half, neatly substituting one section for the pastry Loren wasn't nibbling. Talk about a compulsive reader—he was already buried in the latest article on a new tech V-Net site. Some people couldn't help it; when their jaws moved, their eyes locked onto anything printed. Loren was the type who'd read a cereal box down to the nutrition information. Even one for an adult cereal like SuperVitaBran.

"Look at this," he told me, motioning to the diagrams and paragraphs on the screen. I leaned over my shoulder and had to correct my initial impression—this wasn't mastication-induced boredom; it was sheer lust.

"Wetware," he said, almost reverently. "The next big thing on the horizon, the coming revolution. Computers that use enzymes instead of magnetic storage. Protein's folded this way, it's a one. Other way, it's a zero. Total binary capability in the smallest possible space, next to atoms. Fast as life itself. Impervious to magnetic fields, power fluxes—"

"Great," I whispered, mimicking his awestruck tone. "Computers that can literally get viruses."

"What?" He gave me an exasperated look.

"Viruses," I repeated. "You know, nasty little packets of mindless protein that specialize in messing up living cells' enzymes and DNA? Mad cow disease, my boy—prions. Tiny, half-evolved viruses that specialize in refolding enzymes into totally useless shapes." I patted his back bracingly. "Don't look so grief-stricken. You couldn't afford one of those monsters anyway."

Loren huffed. "What, on my salary? Chump change for guys like me and Stanton." A crooked smile lit his face. "Besides, I'm not going to get one for myself. I'm going to convince Dave to get the latest model for the department."

"Oh, right—for the department," I echoed knowingly, leaning back with my hands behind my head and stretching my legs under his desk. My toes hit something heavy and yielding, and I leaned down to investigate. "I wondered why you were here so early," I said, pulling his heavy duffel bag partly into the light. "You stayed here overnight, didn't you? Did you lose your apartment again?"

"I know exactly where it is." He shrugged, embarrassed beneath his casual sarcasm.

"Who was it this time?" I asked, shoving his worldly possessions back into their place.

"Sophie," he admitted, gazing deeply into his coffee cup to avoid meeting my eyes. Sophie was the latest entry in Loren's never-ending string of damsels in distress, the sobbing young ladies he rescued from a dizzying variety of stupid domestic situations — all of them, in my cynical view, eminently avoidable and springing entirely from the girls' bad taste in men. He dried their tears, listened to their woes, and basically gave them the emotional shirt off his back. They invariably thanked him, said he was their very best friend, and claimed he'd restored their faith in humanity. This time it seemed that the Good Samaritan act had gone way beyond the usual couple hundred dollars' worth of "bus fare" to get them back on their feet — or to their mothers or hometowns or a big city where they could really find a good job.

"Mm?" I prompted. I would have felt wildly jealous of Sophie and her ilk if they weren't completely stupid — and if Loren's involvement ever went beyond emotional and financial. It never did, though; I teased him about having a knight-errant, courtly love fixation, but I was just as happy that his insane idealism and Catholic upbringing — or maybe innate common sense — prevented him from falling into bed with any of those chickies, at least as far as I knew.

"Sophie, Michel, and Brandyn," Loren clarified. Adding her kids into the equation explained a lot. "The county welfare people got her a job as a V-Net psychic — before the higher-ups decided that wasn't a legitimate area to place their workfare moms. Anyway, turns out she can cover rent or day care but not both, and I had a few months left on my lease, so what the h — heck?" This time he leaned back, gesturing grandly around the cubicle warren. "What more do I need than what I've got right here? We've got a company membership at the gym across the street, so I have access to a shower. There's a couch and fridge in the break room. I can stay here perfectly happily for years."

A note flew over the partition and fell onto the desk, folded into an origami swan. Loren unfolded it, then turned to show it to me. "There goes the neighborhood."

"Thanks, Ed," he called through the wall. "Glad to be here." He lowered his voice. "Anyway, thanks to Dave, the terms of my parole forbid me from having any unmonitored computers of my own, and all my music and electronic equipment is here. So what would I do at home anyway?"

"Polish your chivalry trophies?" I suggested, with no sarcasm involved. "Talk about heroic and pitiful at the same time. You need somebody to take you home, look after you."

He gave me a flirty look and waggled his eyebrows, lifting his apple piece in a mock toast. "Well, you are the most sensible person I know. Are you suggesting I move in with you?"

I pulled a prim expression. "Now, Mr. Hunter, you know I can't have you do that. My shotgun-toting, Mormon-redneck husband will be returning from visiting one of his other wives in Henefer any day now, and I'd hate to have anything nasty happen to you." I didn't mention that the idea of having him around permanently actually sounded about evenly terrible and wonderful.

"Right," Loren said, his sarcastic shell snapping into place. "Hate to mess up your direct line to heaven. You seriously expect me to believe you had a vision about Carmelita21 and G.D.?"

"Inspiration, not a vision. Revelation can also just remind you of what you already know or prompt you to pay attention to something in front of you, you know. All you have to do is ask." I kept my tone light but didn't look away from his eyes.

He nodded wisely. "Ah, yes. 'Seek, and ye shall find; knock, and it shall be opened unto you.'"

"Well, kind of. More like a subtle little poke at the back of my brain. It doesn't happen all the time, but it doesn't hurt to enlist the heavy hitters, right?" I knocked back the last dregs of the imitation cocoa and grimaced.

Loren pulled a face too, but not for the same reason. "Oh, yes, Jesus—that really good friend of yours, the one you call every day, the one who never says anything back."

"Hey, he does," I assured him, sympathetic to the loneliness that I suspected lurked under his flip attitude. "Of course, unlike with your Catholic saints, I've never heard voices or seen angels or pillars of light descending over my head. I don't have angels on my shoulders or a dedicated line to heaven." I shrugged. "But I do believe he hears and answers in his own way, because things go right too often to believe otherwise."

"How could I have missed it?" Loren exclaimed, smacking his forehead. "It's been God on your side from the beginning—that's how you caught me! And again just now, when you figured out what G.D.'s ghosts were doing. That's gotta be divine intervention."

I waved my hands, denying the charge. "I wish, but I wouldn't go that far. Some people claim the Spirit tells them what color of socks they should wear. That doesn't happen with me—as you well know. I do everything I can, think things out, make sure I'm prepared, give it my all. Look, I'm not claiming special favors—but I do know that prayer can help me think things through, and it helps to think somebody's listening and caring about me." I thumped his chest. "And about you, even if you don't believe it." I leaned back, swallowing the crack that had crept into my voice on the last sentence. I always start sounding choked up when I talk about really important things. It surprised me how much I wanted him to know this, to believe it.

"Nice to have somebody there to help you, even if he is just an imaginary friend," Loren said with a smile that didn't quite make it to his eyes. "It's a lot harder to have to do it yourself."

Clearly it was time to lighten the mood; I hadn't meant to poke him in a soft spot. "Hey, like the book says, trust not in the arm of the flesh—even when you're being diligent about doing Tai Chi and aerobics every morning." I flexed both arms and smiled at him. "Besides, you don't have to do it alone. You've got me, you know, and we've both got friends up there and down here. We're a good team, too. See? Between you and me in cyberspace and Stark pounding on G.D.'s door in real time, we've got him pinned down cold."

"Careful, there," Loren warned. "Doesn't the book also say that pride goeth before a fall?"

Right on cue, the phone rang. "Next time you pixel-pushers send me after a geek felon, get your address right!" Stark snapped through the speakers, without waiting for me to say anything. "There's no G.D. Davis here—it's a sorority dorm and has been since it was built."

"You're kidding," I gasped.

"Do I *sound* like I'm kidding?" Stark almost bellowed. "Waste my time driving all the way out here because you think you've got a leash on this guy—"

"And find that he's skunked us," Loren interrupted.

"Sorry, Stark," I said. "We did pull up his taproots at Sunshine."

After Stark hung up, Loren said, "He didn't sound consoled.

You'd think he wouldn't be so ticked off about making a surprise visit to a sorority dorm."

"No accounting for taste," I agreed, but then I sobered. "Sounds like our Gideon D. Davis is a lot more slippery than I expected. And don't you say anything about being glad he got away with it."

He raised his hands, all innocence. "Farthest thing from my mind. Don't worry about Brother Davis. If we don't track him down, I'm sure we'll run into him again."

"Somehow that doesn't cheer me up," I told him.

"Like I said, don't worry about it. The more he shows up, the better to catch him, my dear. Remember, we've got a line to the great beyond." He gestured to the ceiling and pulled a pious expression that lasted just long enough for me to roll my eyes at him. He brushed his hands together briskly, all practicality. "Meanwhile, best way to keep from getting anxious is to stay busy. You ought to jump right on that report for Dave and Ms. Alison."

"I ought to? You're on this team too, mister."

"Yeah, but I don't like typing, and you're so good at it." He was good at the big-blue-eyes expression. I wondered if it worked on the nuns back in the orphanage. Probably.

"Blatantly genderist remark—anybody in a skirt makes a good secretary," I said.

"It's true, though," he said, losing the innocence in a grin.

He did end up helping me, as I knew he would; he can't stand to let somebody else tell a story without filling in details or questioning their conclusions. Between both of us—yes, I did the typing—we put together a full report thoroughly detailing the ghost code and logs, all topped off with a tight executive summary for Dave. We had to present it in person to Dave, of course, along with Stark's much less professional but equally concise summary of his morning's travels.

"Right," Dave said, rubbing his eyes. "Good job cutting the connection, even if Stark didn't bag the guy. I'll handle Sunshine and their Ms. Alison pit bull. Loren, get that system vetted out with every one of Gideon's routines highlighted and documented. Sue, get on tracking down G.D. Davis, wherever he is. They're going to want his head on a platter, and we don't want copycats out there playing Gideon all over the place, hoping to get on the evening news."

We watched Dave stride out, straightening his tie, ready to act as the public face of NIPC for this area. Yes, he occasionally got more than his share of credit, but he had to take most of the heat too — plus, he had to wear a tie and worry about his hairline.

"I'm glad I don't have his job," I said softly. Loren just nodded.

Two hours later I had doubts about being glad for my job. My initial adrenaline gradually wore off as I wandered through the V-Net's webs. I chased G.D. Davis's shadow through the university first. He was registered, as expected, but not one of the three professors whose e-mailed recommendations appeared in his transcript had ever heard of him. His transcript, down to the poor grade in fencing, belonged to Catherine Al-Faludi, who had likewise never heard of Gideon Donald Davis. She was considerably less than enthusiastic about the idea of a semifamous cracker hijacking her sterling academic record, but she did take the opportunity to question me about career possibilities in the NIPC division of the FBI. My glowing description of the joys of tracking crooks through the digital labyrinth caught her attention — until the subject of finances, background checks, and work hours came up, that is. At that point the conversation pulled a G.D. Davis and evaporated.

Checking his lease history echoed the developing theme. According to the online records, he had occupied one room of a four-person flat in Greenwood Apartments for three undergraduate years. According to the inhabitants of the apartment in question, specifically a young male specimen who identified himself as Sage — "You know, like the plant in all those old Westerns" — a guy named Brownie currently lived there and had for two years straight. Sage's own tenure did not extend into the far-gone era that preceded Brownie's moving in, but his fast and incoherent survey of the other bodies draped around the big-screen vid resulted in the consensus that either Kraig or Joaquin had lived there before, depending on which of them had the blue hair. At any rate, Gideon did not live there now and apparently never had.

I said a quick, semi-irreverent prayer expressing my gratitude at not having to actually visit the place in person.

As Sekhmet, I prowled through all the traces Gideon had left through the far-too-trackful wastes of the V-Net, finding nothing but the same sad story. Graduate school clubs, credit cards, social security number, birth records — they all dissolved in my claws like dry ice on a hot stove. He had built himself a life history that perfectly resembled a real life in every way, except that it didn't exist from behind.

"Aarrggghhhh," I said, or an exclamation to that effect — gutturals are so difficult to spell.

"Tough chase?" Loren asked. He's very quick with the sympathy when he's deadly bored with what he's doing too.

"Tough? Try impossible!" I gestured violently at the readout on my screen. "This guy's life is like a movie set — looks fine from the outside, nothing but scaffolding from the back. It's just gone — every bit of it, it's just gone!"

"Erased?" Loren asked. That got his full attention, no doubt snapping a chill down his spine, remembering Sherris and his brief career as one of her professional erasers. He'd sold her out to us when he found out exactly what she was doing and for whom she was doing it, but we'd never brought her in.

"No, he didn't just erase his identity. I don't think he ever even existed." I sighed. "Which means we've got somebody out there who'd been planning to hit Sunshine for at least a year."

"And developed an entire messianic spiel, built around one company?" Loren tapped his fingers against his lips thoughtfully. "No. I'll bet Gideon's got more up his sleeve than a few hot snack cakes."

An express message appeared on my screen, which opened to reveal a very fat and sassy little Copycat. She pounced out of the envelope, landed on one of Sekhmet's branches, and burped an iridescent worm into my worm trap.

"Well, at least kitty's had a good day," I said. "She's earned a good night's sleep. And so have I."

"Please, Tyler, get down!" I whispered frantically, aware of the Primary president's glare boring into the side of my head. "We don't have lightblade battles in the chapel!"

The water had reached the top step of the stage on which the Primary had assembled for their annual program, but that was less of a problem than the fact that Tyler wouldn't climb down from the podium. He struck a heroic pose, blade raised to the high ceiling. "Look at me! Look at what I can do!"

I lunged forward and grabbed Tyler off the podium, the parents in the ward chuckling politely, the lot of them still smiling and watching the Primary program attentively as the link-tide of sparkling, virtual water rose toward their chins.

The worms suddenly broke through the surface of the water. Their glittering scales coruscated with data bits, their rapacious mouths gaped wide open, ready to suck my Sunbeam class down into their endless electronic gullets. Soul strings trailed from their narrowing rear ends, gathering into a twisted, glowing rein that rested firmly in the WormMaster's long-fingered hands. The cybermonsters reared toward the stage, threshing in the tide.

I hissed a feline warning, growing Sekhmet's claws, sleek fur sprouting over my skin as my dress and shoes disappeared.

"Sister Jones!" the Primary president gasped. "That is hardly appropriate language for a Primary teacher!"

She was probably right — cat-speak is ninety percent swear words, nine percent sensuous endearments, and one percent neutral. "Sorry," I told her shortly and sprang onto the podium myself, tail whipping behind me as I pulled a logic bomb out of my bandolier and readied my worm trap with my other hand.

Behind the writhing bodies and churning foam, the WormMaster smiled as angelically as the fallen son of heaven he was. He beckoned seductively to me, the crackling energy discharges glowing in his sapphire-blue eyes, promising in elegantly silent sonnets to give me all my dreams.

I spat at him and tossed a logic bomb into the mouth of the nearest worm. It reared back, lightning flashing along its flanks, raising its maw to the dome of the sky. Its pain pulsed, its cry an unnaturally regular, horribly annoying ringing that rose above the thunder of the walls collapsing into the tidal waves. The pulsing and the pounding went on and on, filling my ears as the water filled my mouth, ears, lungs . . . .

Gasping, I lifted my face away from my pillow and fumbled for the phone. It skittered off the night table and hit the floor; I lurched after it and fell to the carpet myself. I grabbed the uncooperative instrument, poking at the RECEIVE button to stop the ringing as I stumbled toward the front door. "What?" I barked into the phone, flinging open the door at the same time.

"Wake up, Miss Jones," Loren said into my ear. He smiled at me as well, standing in the hall with the security light glinting off his hair, his own phone at his ear. He'd clearly been up longer, judging by his reflexes — he caught the door before I could slam it. "What, no 'good morning, glad to see you'?"

"It's too early to be a good morning," I growled. "Too early to be pounding on peoples' doors, scaring them out of a sound sleep." I took a deep breath, my heartbeat gradually slowing.

"You could at least invite me in," he suggested. "Especially since I didn't just open the door and let myself in. I don't think you want me standing out here where all your neighbors can peer curiously out their doors" — he waved pleasantly down the hall; a quick slam followed — "and see what kind of disreputable people you associate with —"

"I sure don't," I agreed, pulling him in and shutting the door. "Last thing I need is a reputation like that." Mrs. Halasi would love this one; she bugged me enough already about living like a professional escort, with my odd hours and never bringing anybody home. She'd assured me that she totally believed my protestations of innocence, but she'd also semidiscreetly checked my belt for a beeper.

It suddenly occurred to me that we were still talking into the phones. I laughed, punched the END button, and waved the phone at him. "I must be zonked, yapping on this thing when you're standing in front of me. Why didn't you hang up, for heaven's sake?"

"What do I care for heaven?" he asked, teasing. "Besides, I didn't want to hang up on you."

"Very sweet of you. Could almost be considerate in other circumstances — you know, if you hadn't rousted me out of my bed so abruptly." I brushed ineffectually at my hair, which I knew must have come straggling out of its braid during the night. I felt a rush of gratitude to my mother, who'd given me a nice striped-flannel pajama set for a long-ago birthday. I didn't look glamorous — yeah, right, like I ever did — but I was certainly decently covered. No reason at all for the blush that kept threatening to climb over my ears.

"Sorry about that," Loren told me, his smile fading. "Better me than Dave." He paused. "You're with StarWest Bank, right?"

I grunted. "Like anybody's really got a choice, unless you choose your mattress instead."

"They're all in Stanton's pocket anyway," Loren told me. "Check your bank account."

I didn't bother to ask "Bank account?" or any other inane thing; I practically sprinted to my terminal, typing in my password the moment it awoke. As I connected to my financial account, I asked, "You let yourself in the security entrance?"

"You gave me a key, remember?" Loren said absently, staring over my shoulder as the bank's logo faded into my personal-user page. "To pick up your mail and water those two pitiful plants when you visited your family a couple of months ago."

"Ah, yes — the key I never did get back," I began, then stopped, the sheer number of digits scrolling across the screen halting the sentence as effectively as a hand over my mouth.

Loren nodded, satisfied. "I thought so."

"You thought so?" I gasped. $1,025,346.18 glowed from the AVAILABLE BALANCE line.

"Well, couldn't be sure, because you've never given me your banking password," he told me. "But from what I saw in your e-mail, I figured we'd find something like this."

The message, sporting the anonymous, haloed face of a medieval saint icon instead of the usual avatar portrait for the sender, got right to the point: *Dear Sister, we understand your need to foil what you see as a violation of the commandment forbidding thievery. Your zeal on behalf of the right is commendable, but in this case misdirected. Do not fear to break free of the devils who are your master, even as Mary of Magdala. As our gift shows, we bear you no malice. Our sheep hear our voice and respond to our call. In holy fellowship and love, Gideon.*

"Mary of Magdala!" I exclaimed. "First he compares me to a woman possessed by seven demons, then he tries to buy me off!"

"Obviously he doesn't know you very well," Loren observed, amused. "Or he would've used Saul of Tarsus instead. Something about kicking against the pricks."

"Gideon." I let the tone inform Loren exactly who I thought was a prick at the moment. "He didn't wait long to resurface, did he?"

"Nope," Loren said. "It looks like our boy's on a very aggressive schedule for furthering his personal cyber-Armageddon." He reached past me and flicked on the newsfeed.

"Electronic terrorist Gideon strikes again!" the audio headline blared. Loren muted the sound, rendering the overnight reporter voiceless as the closed captioning scrolled by. "Another incident of apparent cyberterrorism is being attributed to Gideon, the hacker who has claimed responsibility for hijacking the Sunshine Foods drone fleet. He may have struck again, this time at the central offices of financial giant StarWest Bank Corp." The body of the article laid out the specifics: thousands of millions of dollars in profits that Gideon claimed came from insider-trading schemes, illegal holdbacks, and hidden fees had vanished from shareholders' and bank officers' accounts overnight, redistributed among the accounts of the bank's customers.

Because these Pharisees have shut their hand from their poor brothers, withheld their wealth from the poor, and hardened their hearts against the cries of the widows and the fatherless, their gold is taken from them, Gideon's missive to the media thundered. *The Lord maketh poor, and maketh rich: he bringeth low, and lifteth up. He raiseth up the poor out of the dust, and lifteth up the beggar from the dunghill, to set them among princes, and to make them inherit the throne of glory. StarWest Bank Corp has now been shown the error of its ways. He that by usury and unjust gain increaseth his substance, the righteous shall gather it for him that will pity the poor. Let them learn this small lesson, and let all pay heed to our timely warning: He will keep the feet of his saints, and the wicked shall be silent in darkness; for by strength shall no man prevail. The adversaries of the Lord shall be broken to pieces; out of heaven shall the thunder come upon them; the Lord shall judge the ends of the earth.*

"Armageddon is right," I said, resisting the urge to bang my head on the desk. "I just hate it when crazies and criminals start quoting scripture! This kind of thing always makes the rest of us who really believe look like wild-eyed crackpots or outright hypocrites. I don't even want to know what Mike and Michelle are going to say about this."

"No," Loren agreed. "You don't."

A more personal concern reared its head through my general chagrin on the part of Mormons—and other religious people—at Gideon's abuse of scripture and the media's milking it for a gullible public. Gideon knew where I had my account—he knew my personal e-mail account, the electronic identity of the FBI tracker assigned to his case. The FBI, and especially NIPC, never let anyone know who was assigned to which case—too much chance of retribution.

"He knows who I am," I said softly, ominous music cues rising in my imagination. "How does he know who I am?"

"He doesn't know who you are, who Sue Anne Jones is," Loren told me confidently. "He knows that Sekhmet is your avatar, so he knows your NIPC e-mail address. The only way he'd know who you personally are is if he managed to break Aireon's encryption codes and pull out your private account information from their databases, which he obviously didn't, because that's impossible. And I speak from experience there."

"So he knows about Sekhmet, because his ghost got my ID packet in Sunshine's computer," I said, following his line of reasoning. "And that told him my public e-contact info. And he figured that I'd have my money in StarWest—"

"Because, like you said, what other choice do you have?" Loren finished. "He spread the wealth all over the place, especially to people with less than $50,000 in their accounts."

I waved a hand dismissively. "Of course, we'll probably find out he absconded with a big wodge of it, to fund further good works or a nice condo in Szechuan. Meanwhile, it's an even bet I ended up with a good chunk of change, and it's fun to taunt the opposition."

"Such disparaging words for such an obviously altruistic terrorist." Loren laughed and patted my back bracingly. "Anyway, you don't have to worry about an up-close-and-personal confrontation any time soon. Get up, get dressed, and let's go check out the Star-West offices—as soon as you write your thank-you note, that is."

I snuffed at him. "Thank-you note. Uh-huh. If this gets me into trouble with Internal Affairs on suspicion of a bribery rap, I'll give him a thank you he won't soon forget. You think this is just funny as all get-out, don't you?"

He tried to suppress a smile and failed. "The guy's got style, I've got to give him that. And the bank deserves it as much as Sunshine did."

"You're incorrigible," I said, but I couldn't help returning the smile. "Gideon's got a serious God complex, and he's going to get a serious wake-up call too." The REPLY option glowed greenly available on Gideon's message to me; he obviously wanted a reaction. *Gideon*, I clicked out, *you're supposed to give away your own stuff, not somebody else's. Check out Luke 18:22, and stop this nonsense.*

"'Now,'" Loren quoted, reading over my shoulder, "'when Jesus heard these things, he said unto him, Yet lackest thou one thing: sell all that thou has, and distribute unto the poor, and thou shalt have treasure in heaven: and come, follow me.' You're not going to spell it out for him?"

"He's such a spiritual guy, he can dig it out for himself," I said. "Getting into the scriptures on somebody else's agenda might do him some good."

My phone rang; Loren scooped it up and said, "Jones *demesne*, houseboy speaking. Yes, she's up. Yes, we're on our way. No, we don't need Stark there immediately. Right. Oh, Dave—have fun out there. Give Michelle a big ol' kiss for us, would you? Okay, Mike then."

He put down the phone and gave me a shocked look. "Dave hung up on me!"

"Good," I said, tossing down my datagloves and heading for the bathroom. "And by the way, we're not married, you know."

"Who, you and Gideon, or you and Dave?" Loren blinked.

"You and me," I informed him. "You get into my e-mail, you answer my phone—"

"Ah, we might as well be, devoted partners as we are," he interrupted. "There's not too much potpourri around here. I could get used to this place. 'Course, you'd have to move that throwback bookcase to make room for my keyboards and music gear next to your guitar, but—"

This time it was my turn to interrupt him. I turned at the bathroom door and gave him my best shot at a sultry expression. "Loren, you know what you call a musician whose girlfriend breaks up with him?"

His expression said he knew better, but he fed me the line. "No, what?"

"Homeless."

A few wet and soapy—and solo—minutes later, we thumped down the stairs toward my car. Bless his heart, he'd braved public transit at this time of night, just to see my face when I discovered that I was an instant millionaire.

"So, what's your take on Gideon's financial redistribution technique?" Loren asked me.

"Inside job," I said confidently. "It's gotta be, just like the Sunshine thing. Our little G.D. Davis managed to get himself a job at StarWest and put a trapdoor into their system. I know you know how tough it is to get into a bank's money from the outside."

"Who, *moi?*" he asked, missing innocence by a mile. He sure could nail mischievous every time, though. "All right—I concede that point. Even pulling off a single bogus transfer is hard, and this one involves breaking into not only the main banks, but a whole slew of individual accounts. So he's managed to jigger the access rules *and* break into their database. Otherwise he wouldn't know the balances so he could give extra money to the church mice and leave the fat cats in the cold."

I grinned, not as sharply as Sekhmet but with the same hunter's excitement. "StarWest doesn't have an automated update, either—everything that happens down there happens in real time. He had to be there to run his little program. I'm looking forward to meeting ol' G.D."

"If he even works at the local bank office," Loren reminded me. "That's why computer crimes are federal affairs, you know—he could've set off his charitable campaign from Missoula just as easily."

"Ah, don't burst my thriller-vid bubble," I told him, wishing the Peter Gunn theme would come on the radio right then. Instead, a public service announcement was reminding everyone that Aire-on's latest V-Net sys upgrade would appear magically on their computers soon, as the company used their automatic rollout program to provide an even more intense virtual-reality experience for everyone who paid Aireon's nominal monthly fee. Then, yet another announcer babbled on about the advantages of registering as a free agent with OmniMental temps. Yes, appropriately coincidental, but not nearly as musically satisfying.

"As you can see," Mr. Gray chattered nervously, watching us like a hawk—actually, more like a small, slightly molting owl, but you get the idea—as we prepared to check the network security arrangements at the local—and thus the national—StarWest Bank, "our network arrangements are completely secure. I thought that was what you people did—keep honest businesses like StarWest Bank from being victimized by hackers lurking on the V-Net. You really must catch this malefactor quickly!"

Loren and I exchanged a glance. Ah, the lilting leitmotif of our professional lives, dancing across our ears once again! We both put down the pens we'd used to sign the inevitable nondisclosure forms. Loren leaned back in his borrowed chair—it squeaked sadly, but he didn't react—and fixed Mr. Gray with a cold cop eye. "Hackers lurking on the V-Net, huh? Stranger danger, dark figures creeping around your databases, unknown enemies conducting industrial espionage—"

The bank manager's eyes got wider with every dire image. He jumped when Loren sat upright abruptly.

"Fact is," Loren told him accusingly, eyes narrowed, "ninety percent of computer crimes occur *inside* corporate firewalls. Employees, Mr. Gray, not unknown hackers, account for the vast majority of the damage done to corporate networks. And do you know why, Mr. Gray?"

The bank manager took a nervous step backward as Loren rose to his full six-foot-four height and leaned menacingly into Mr. Gray's personal space. The two corporate guards flanking Mr. Gray upped the macho quotient in their expressions; the smaller one actually let his hand drift toward his sidearm.

"Two words: intermittent conditioning," Loren informed him. "You and your bosses created an entire generation of employees who feel no loyalty because they've never seen it—all they know is that you start dumping headcount the minute the stockholders want new yachts. Military terrorists used to use that technique on prisoners of war, to break their spirits. Line everybody up at dawn, pull one guy out of the line, put a gun to his head, pull the trigger. The trick is that sometimes the gun was loaded, sometimes it wasn't. Sometimes, *bang*—brains all over the wall. Sometimes, click, nothing, guy goes back in line."

Mr. Gray swallowed hard. "But—"

Loren cut him off, his voice dropping to an intense whisper. "See, that's the clever part. If somebody always got killed, the rest of the prisoners could adapt. It's the not knowing that gets to you. Lose your life, or lose your job—you never know when it's going to get you. You never know when a pink slip's going to pop up on your monitor, when your password's going to stop working, when you're going to be signing up with some headhunter outfit just to keep toaster pastries on the table."

We paused silently, immersed in that dark vision, until Loren leaned back and shrugged nonchalantly. "So, no wonder the occasional wage slave goes nuts and torches the barn when you try to sell him down the river. That's where you boys come in, right?" He slugged one of the guards on the shoulder, then rubbed his hands together. "Enough chitchat. Where's the mainframe?"

Mr. Gray tried valiantly to correct Loren's obvious misperception—"It is a sophisticated, state-of-the-art, multiple-path, integrated processing system, not an antique mainframe!"—but his indignant sputters died in the face of Loren's pasted-on smile and metronome nods. It was all I could do not to start laughing like a loon.

"Sad surroundings for a sophisticated, state-of-the-art, multiple-path, integrated processing system," I said. The programmers' cubicles here were even colder and darker and dingier than our own gray-box, mouse-maze environment at NIPC. Of course, the presence of a couple of armed guards probably contributed to the nasty atmosphere. They regarded us suspiciously but without real comprehension as we dove into the bank's computer system.

Loren and I slotted our data disks into the bank's primary computer, sending our avatars into a melancholy, straight-lined series of corridors and cells. The virtual scene closed around us, perfectly institutionally gray, just like our surroundings in the real world although, thankfully, less dusty. No perky-breasted sphinxes or fang-toothed blondes around here, that was for sure. A few years ago, it would have surprised me that they had a VR interface at all, but Aireon had made graphical representations so common and available that even hard-line text-interface geeks like the router guys had given in and gotten used to programming through the electronic dream world. Judging by the completely uncustomized walls around us, however, the bank clearly took the no-nonsense attitude they promoted to the rest of the financial world right here at home. They spent their money on mahogany and marble for the foyers and executive offices, not on nice furniture for the drones' cubicles or even not-so-expensive graphical upgrades for the interior of their computer system.

Sekhmet looked decidedly odd in those generic surroundings, but Loren's digital alter ego stuck out like—well, like a tree in a prison yard.

"What in the world are you?" I asked him, staring.

A small, four-branched walking tree glowed back at me. Digital wind rustled its green leaves. It waved a twisted root in a friendly manner.

"New avatar," Loren said unnecessarily. "I put it together last night, around an avatar add-on that seeks out cracks and data leaks in security systems. Seemed like a useful tool, with Gideon running around out there. Guess I ought to call it Lom, under the circumstances."

"What, for Lombardy poplar?" I asked.

"Nah. L.O.M, for love of money. You know, the *root* of all evil, us working for a greedy bank, financial matters?" He snickered as I groaned.

In deference to Mr. Gray's fervent insistence that Gideon had gained access to the system from the outside, I sent Sekhmet to the boundaries of the bank's system. The firewalls roared and glowed, standard Aireon representations that the bank's imagination-challenged programmers could not have changed even if they wanted. The display window showed every transaction, scrolling along without a single unusual entry—StarWest had thoroughly automated their external transactions, not granting outside access to even a single human. The bank's computers spoke only to other computers and accepted no transmissions not explicitly scheduled beforehand. Sekhmet pulled the logs for last night's transactions, sniffing for clues among the tracks they recorded. Not a single suspicious record popped out.

"Looks like they're tight—conform right down the line to the federal guidelines for financial institution security systems," I said aloud. "Gideon didn't get in from outside."

"*Quelle surprise*," Loren muttered sarcastically as records scrolled past his nose on the other monitor. Lom had sunk its roots deep into the bank's computer infrastructure, the questing tendrils searching for openings, intentional or not.

As we suspected, the internal network had only so-so security. The more Sekhmet dove around their files, the more holes I found, and a good programmer could exploit plenty of them. Some were obvious, simply oversights and laziness on the part of the network administrators. It's easy and natural to trust the people you work with. In this case, though, convenience had turned around and bitten them right in the —

My train of thought abruptly derailed. Deep in the computer's memory, a few out-of-place lines of code scrolled before my eyes. I scanned them, the shock of recognition tingling my hunter's instincts. Two programs, one that used a back door to open the Star-West funds-transfer program and one that gathered and changed account information. Both elegantly written, spare as oak branches against a January sky and just as lovely, in their own — unfortunately, sick and twisted — way.

"Loren, look at this. We've found G.D. Davis again."

He took one look at the code and leaped Lom into that section of the computer's memory. Sekhmet backed out of the connection, letting the hyperactive tree take over. Lom's branches quivered as its roots dug deep, surrounding Gideon's programs, gently detaching them from their nest among the bank's own programs. The database raider glowed softly, a gem in the virtually real world of Aireon's interface. Lom snipped each connection, closing Gideon's back door. As the last silver strand parted, however, the gem burst into glowing life.

Lom took the brunt of the force, its branches rippling and leaves frying in the backwash that also erased the program. Loren jumped and nearly swore: "Filth!" He flew into action, fingers blurring in the datagloves, trying to resuscitate Lom and recreate the self-destructed program. Line after line of code flowed through the display window, accompanied audibly by Loren's equally steady stream of imaginatively altered expletives: "Rat-catching, stuck-up son of a —" Et cetera.

In this case, I couldn't quite tell if his stream of invective was directed at Gideon or himself. Finally he shoved himself away from the terminal, viciously snapping his data disk out of the computer's drive. He waved it at me fiercely. "I am so sorry. My fault. Thumbs for fingers—" He took a deep breath. "I'm going to take this back, put it through the wringer, and recreate that program out of its bits. And I promise to give you a free pass if you ever do anything that stupid."

I sniffed. "Oh, like I'd do something so dumb." I did throw in a smile, however; he was much more furious at himself than I felt I could be at him. I was just glad that Lom had triggered the self-destruct, instead of Sekhmet.

Plus, I had to be proud of him for his all-but-completely-successful display of linguistic creativity. The first week we'd worked together, I'd given him a whole substitution list for the standard set of swear words. Unfortunately, giving him dirty looks and making snarky comments about profanity being a crutch for the linguistically impaired had done nothing to encourage him to use the list. Loren's conversion from sailor language had happened when Stark blew up at something he thought we'd done wrong and cussed a blue streak at us. After he stormed off, I leaned over and said, "Boy, he sounded a lot like you there." That worked very well; Loren didn't want to come across as anything like Stark.

He gave me a smile back, almost as sharp as Sekhmet's. "What time is it, seven-thirty already? How about we go tell Gideon in person how much we appreciate his work?"

"Tell him?" I asked, then leapt for the terminal Loren had used. Sure enough, the name *Gideon* glowed from the list of employees, his hire date marking him as a fresh catch—he'd joined the StarWest family only three months ago. "But this says Gideon Smith, not G. Donald Davis, and that well-fed blond guy doesn't look anything like the skinny nerd boy in Sunshine's file."

Loren tossed the disk into the air, caught it, and stowed it in his shirt pocket. "What, you think he'd use his own name? He's cocky, but he's not that far out. Besides, anybody can fake an ID shot." He shrugged, half-admitting the improbability of that scenario. "All right, call it a hunch. Let's go stake out his office and give him a friendly greeting when he drags in his sorry carcass. I'll bet you he'll act all innocent outside, but he'll be smug as a cat on the inside."

I gave him a skeptical look but I had the same hunch. How many guys out there have the name *Gideon*? Besides, if he was the wrong one, he'd have an interesting story to tell his family this evening, all about how he got busted by the FBI—mistakenly, of course.

Calling Gideon Smith's workspace an office stretched the definition of the term past the breaking point. The security guards, visibly perking up at the potential for mayhem involved in physically apprehending an employee, led us to a half-partitioned cubicle tucked away in a dim corner of the vast operations room. The few early birds among the bank's drones gazed at us in mild surprise as we passed, most of them clutching cups of whatever beverage they believed they needed to kick their sleepy systems into gear.

"Looks like nothing at all," I said, surveying the pink-walled, gray-floored computer container of an office. "Didn't even bother to bring pictures of his family or anything."

Loren settled into the empty chair, flicked on the monitor, and overrode the USER LOGIN screen with the supervisor password Mr. Gray had reluctantly given us. Gideon's apathetic attitude toward personalizing his environment glowed from the screen as well. The default Aireon interface greeting appeared, *"Good morning, Gsmith,"* unaltered and unpersonalized even with a full name instead of his system username.

"Not a good sign," I said. He obviously hadn't intended to stay long.

Loren simply nodded, rapidly scanning through Gsmith's files, pulling a list of the projects he had worked on since he was hired. According to the notation in his employee file, he had come to Star-West during a massive crunch time provoked by the final transition from various hold-out European currencies to the euro. His initials popped up repeatedly in currency-translation routines, signing off code for changing deutschmarks into euros into dollars; that had been his first assignment. Clearly he'd done well, because his duties had expanded. His initials also marked a set of programs designed to instantly update customers' personal accounts into whatever currency they wanted to invest in—which meant he had special-access permission to the account-balances database.

"There's our backdoor," Loren observed, scrolling through the list of permissions granted to Gsmith in the database security file. After a couple months of diligent work, he had managed to expand his original dispensation for the account-balance database to include access to the fund-transfer programs as well.

"Sneaky little pup, isn't he?" I said. "All bright eyes and wagging tail and what-can-I-do-for-you, then *stab!* Right in the back."

"Biting the hand that's alternately feeding and slapping him." Loren nodded judiciously.

"Excuse me, but are you waiting for Gideon?"

We both whirled around—Loren did it much more dramatically,

since he had a gimbaled chair—which caused the comfortable-looking woman who'd asked the question to step backward, bumping into the impressive paunch of the more senior security guard. Her expression shifted a shade, from casual interest to alarmed curiosity, especially when the security guys moved forward as if they intended to put her in a hammerlock for even mentioning Gsmith's name.

"Yes," I said, giving her a smile and waving off the nearest security goon. "Have you seen him today?"

"Sure. He asked me to tell you he'd be a minute," she said, waving a heavily ringed hand down the corridor. "He just came in, said he forgot his keys—"

Loren is fast for a guy who spends most of his time noodling on keyboards and slogging through code. We practically flew down the corridor, scattering programmers in our wake. Of course, we hit the elevator doors right as they closed. We bounced off them, and I charged for the door marked STAIRS.

Thank heavens for the medical establishment's never-ending crusade to convince Americans that they ought to get more active! The stairway doors were unlocked. Equally fortunately, the constant nagging wasn't actually very effective, so we didn't face a packed stairwell. We raced down the empty stairs, Loren taking them two— or more—at a time as I followed slightly more slowly but much more sensibly. Good thing I'd decided on jeans and sneakers instead of a skirt and dress shoes. The bank's hired guards galumphed loudly behind us, their heavy footsteps gradually receding into the vertical distance. Clearly they'd been hired for their bulk and intimidating demeanors, not for their fleetness of foot.

We burst out into the lobby, restartling a milling crowd of bank employees, and dove into the empty eddies our fleeing quarry had left in his wake. Another guard, this one doubling as a receptionist, shouted and gesticulated from behind the front-office bunker, either at Gsmith or at us—I didn't stop to find out which. Once again we reached the doors just after our quarry did, bursting out onto the concrete apron in front of the bank's huge oak portal. We looked wildly around, scanning the scene for anyone moving rapidly away.

Catching sight of a hefty, blond-topped figure diving into an expensive-looking silver car parked close to the building, I yipped "There he is!" and ran in that direction, Loren easily matching my pace. He wasn't as out of breath as I was, either—this tearing around stuff looks a lot easier in the vids.

I got a much better look at the car as Gsmith backed out with a squeal of tires and accelerated backward toward us. For a second I didn't believe he was actually trying to run us down—that kind of thing happened to field agents, not NIPC geeks. The wild look on the face peering over the back seat did a lot to convince me, but the unreality of the situation only contributed to my embarrassing inability to implement evasive maneuvers. I had never pictured myself in this particular situation, so I had no instant response prepared for a geekicidal programmer's attempt to inflict vehicular slaughter on me. I froze, my mind scattering through half-a-dozen bad adventure scenes, suggesting one amazingly acrobatic, impossible move after another. Half of my brain screamed *Run!* and the other half cried, *Which way?* while my feet just wanted somebody to give them coherent directions. Of all the times in my life to realize that my body was ruled by committee.

Loren solved the deadlock, grabbing me around the waist and lifting me away. The car kept coming, but Loren kept the momentum going, throwing us both over a set of ornamental bushes and onto the thin lawn fronting the bank building. We landed heavily, hearing another tire squeal as the would-be hit-and-run driver accomplished at least the second part of his goal and left the scene at high speed.

I disentangled myself from Loren—who smelled like soap and, disconcertingly, a hint of vanilla—and lurched to my knees, but I saw only the tail lights of the gray car as it swerved onto the road, causing even more screeching as another driver fishtailed wildly, trying to avoid it.

"He's gone." Loren caught my belt loop, preventing me from launching into futile foot pursuit of the rapidly disappearing suspect. (Sure. *Now* my reflexes decided to kick in.) "Unless you're up for a high-speed car chase?"

The look I gave him was answer enough; I didn't need to add, *In my car? At rush hour?* Actually, the idea intrigued me until I pictured myself behind the wheel of my beloved two-hamster-power vehicle, dodging in and out of heavy traffic. Eek. "Loren," I reluctantly admitted, "as much as I've always dreamed of having the grace and power of a balletic cheetah with NASCAR trophies on the mantle, I'm much more effective driving with datagloves, peering into a monitor."

"I didn't think so, but I had to ask." He shrugged. "Cheetahs are overrated anyway."

I half-smiled and slumped back down, patting his ribs where my shoulder had landed. He must have been taking advantage of our corporate gym membership for more than the showers, lifting me right off my feet like that. I felt a rush of embarrassingly warm gratitude. (Loren Tarzan. Me Jane. Blush!) "Thank you, by the way. Are you okay?"

"Fine," he said, wincing slightly as he rose to one elbow. "Good thing you're so dedicated about your aerobics."

The sappy affection caused by his heroic rescue dissolved into sisterly annoyance. (Maybe so I wouldn't have to acknowledge that flash of attraction.) "What, so I don't weigh as much?"

He looked genuinely surprised before pulling a sibling-rivalry sneer. (I'd like to think that he felt a bit of interest too, but I had to admit that was unlikely.) "Actually, I was thinking that it made you a lot faster going down those stairs, but the lighter weight is handy too."

I pulled myself to my feet, made a useless attempt at brushing leaves off my shirt — we'd kind of gone through the bushes rather than completely over them — and extended a hand to help Loren up. "Come on — now we call Stark."

"And the regular cops too," he said, accepting my hand but not putting any pressure on it as he rose to his feet. Show-off. "Since we've got a license plate for them to run down."

We managed to get loose of Mr. Gray and his cop mercenaries by firmly refusing any civilian help. "This is an FBI matter now, Mr. Gray," I said sternly. "We do not require the bank's assistance, except in collecting all the information you have about Mr. Smith and delivering it to us at NIPC. We do *not* want your security personnel showing up at Mr. Smith's apartment or attempting to investigate the matter for yourselves."

Mr. Gray backed down in the face of polite-but-firm federal stonewalling, but he certainly wasn't happy about it. He repeated his orders that we clear up the matter quickly, assuring us that he would be in touch with our superior officer later in the day. I felt a rush of petty satisfaction at his secretary's sudden appearance and urgent whisper of "Ms. Fiorello is on the line, sir, and she insists on talking to you." He'd have a lot more to do than call Dave today, trying to explain to the bank's wealthier investors just how their money ended up in a raft of peasants' accounts. Lucky man.

"Gsmith ever dares show his face around StarWest again, he's going to regret the day Mr. Gray was born," Loren observed, climbing into my car. "I wonder if they'd start skinning him at the fingers or the toes."

"Thugs like that probably wouldn't do anything quite so medieval," I objected, starting the car and flicking on the radio as usual. "They don't have the manual dexterity for it." However, I had to agree with Loren's graphically pessimistic assessment of Gsmith's chances if he ever dared show his face around StarWest again. Corporations like StarWest, with plenty of local law enforcement and politicians in their pockets, had very little patience with people who stole money from them, and they sometimes expressed their annoyance in unmistakably violent ways. At the very least they'd register their complaints with their local government flunky, I thought with a sigh, which meant I could expect another memo from Dave re emphasizing how important it was that we stop Gideon as soon as possible. Duh!

As I maneuvered us through the thinning flow of traffic, Loren called the highway patrol's dispatch office, identified himself as FBI and NIPC, and asked for a license trace. Lieutenant Gibson, the friendly-sounding officer who took the call, ran the license plate from the gray car . . . and came up with the address of a rental-car agency downtown. Dang! At least she wished us luck with the true empathy of a fellow professional, one who'd seen her share of unsuccessful pursuits.

The brush-cut, bolo-tied guy at the car-rental place had no such fellow feeling; in fact, he tried to give me the high-handed, customer-confidentiality brush-off when I approached the desk and asked to see the rental agreement for the car in question. I didn't totally blame him for his skepticism, watching him looking over Loren's casual denims and my tousled hair. Much to my satisfaction, however, the clerk's snotty attitude deflated immediately when I identified us as FBI agents — yes, a slight exaggeration, but justified in the situation — flashing my NIPC ID card just like Agent Cool on the crime vids. That perked up both his interest and his data-entry skills. (I quickly picked the last privet leaf out of my ponytail as he looked down at his monitor.) He found the rental agreement, which he printed and handed to us with a flourish, along with our quarry's name and address.

Loren gave him an authentic French-concierge look — equal parts disdain and boredom — and answered his eager questions about what we were looking for with a sub-zero "That's need-to-know, and you don't need to know."

On the way to Gsmith's den, I gently remonstrated with Loren over his giving the guy a hard time. "Come on, Sue," he replied. "He'd be disappointed if we didn't give him the enigmatic G-man act. Our public expects it of us."

The landlord certainly cooperated when Loren pulled the same arrogant civil-servant act on him, flourishing the electronic search permit Stark had flashed to us from headquarters. Stark and his Special Agents would arrive momentarily with the forensics team, but after I gently but firmly shut the door on the landlord's curious gaze, we had the place to ourselves.

From the look of things, Gideon liked to live up to stereotypical expectations as well. The address led us to the bottom flat in a short-lease apartment building, one of those half-basement routines with the front door conveniently obscured by an ancient, overgrown evergreen bush. Inside we found two empty rooms, a bathroom with only a few sample-sized toiletry items—toothpaste, toothbrush, comb, et cetera—and a brace of candy wrappers stuffed into the garbage along with yesterday's junk mail. The place didn't even smell lived in; if Mr. Smith had ever cooked anything in that tiny galley-style kitchen, it hadn't involved any meat, let alone spices, onions, or garlic, and the refrigerator was empty aside from the inevitable Chinese cartons and squeeze-packs of pureed salsa and soy sauce. The few pieces of furniture in the kitchen, small bedroom, and media nook had that unmistakable furnished-room flavor: aggressively neutral colors, slightly shabby edges, and styles that hadn't seen the inside of a showroom in ten years. The few clothes in the closet and dresser—another pair of suit pants, four pairs of socks, standard boxer underwear, two white-collar shirts, and a sweater—were slightly more recent in style, but no more distinctive in color or cut.

"If we were on the vids," I told Loren, "we'd probably have some cultural-studies class dissecting the rhythm of buildup and disappointment in the characters' lives as some kind of metaphor for the peaks and valleys of manic depression."

"Better than having them sit back, chow popcorn, and laugh about us being throwbacks to those ancient Keystone Kops flickers." Loren tossed a violently colored sweepstakes entry onto the pile of similar communiqués on the table, nearly all addressed to the nameless occupant of 164 Bluebird Avenue, Apartment 5. Most something-for-nothing junk mail had moved online decades ago, but some diehards still targeted the vast snail-mail audience. After all, not everybody had an ether-based avatar. Yet.

An elegant envelope from Aireon, personally addressed to Mr. Gideon Smith, gave eloquent evidence of their efforts to precipitate the eventual capitulation of the few nondigital holdouts. This letter assured Mr. Smith that Aireon's next release, version 11.4, would make his life easier in dozens of ways and that if he signed up now he would be able to take advantage of the unprecedented upgrade without lifting a finger. Obviously, as good as Aireon's name-gatherers were, they didn't realize they'd sent a newbie invitation to an overly accomplished and possibly murderous system cracker.

I poked aimlessly around the kitchen, trying not to rub out any personal evidence Gsmith had left. I was a lot better at tracking people through the virtual environment of computer systems than real-world settings. By this time, if I hadn't peripherally seen him and nearly gotten his rented tire marks engraved on my body — I'd have thought he was nothing but a virtual presence.

I sighed. "Well, he's gone, gone, gone, leaving nothing but his wrappers behind him. We won't get any more clues about Gideon until Stark and the forensics team get here with their fingerprint and DNA kits."

Loren came out of the bedroom. "We know three things about him. First, he's a pretty good programmer. Second, he's surprisingly quick for such a chunky monkey. Third, he's an arrogant hacker-thief with a sarcastic sense of humor. Look what he left on his night table, right in plain sight." He tossed the book he was carrying, and it thumped onto the wobbly table. HOLY BIBLE glowed in gilt letters from its cover, and PLACED BY THE GIDEONS adorned the flyleaf.

"That's four things," I said, letting the cover flop closed. "Computer criminal and Bible stealer." I didn't even bother to suggest he'd left it there because he'd been reading it every night.

"Make it five," Loren suggested. "This guy's not Gideon. Gideon hired him. Or Gideon is the *nom de guerre* for a whole bunch of discontented crackers trying to teach the world a lesson."

Something tickled at the back of my mind, Sekhmet scratching lightly at an idea as if it lurked behind the cracked floorboards of a mouse-infested barn. "Still, I'd like to talk to him."

As usual, I got my chance, but not really the way I wanted it. I had wanted Lieutenant Gibson and her highway-knight colleagues to run the silver rental car into a drainage ditch after a wild, tire-squealing chase, with plenty of random objects like extra wingtip shoes ejected from the fleeing suspect's vehicle, which the following media helicopters just love for some reason. The steely-eyed champions of municipal law would haul a dazed and staggering Gsmith out of his smashed getaway car and escort him to a nasty, gray tank in the city jail while Loren and I neatly summarized the unimpeachable evidence of his guilt and tied it all up for Dave with a lovely red cyber-bow.

Instead, I found two e-mails waiting for me when we finished warning Dave about Mr. Gray's impending call and endured another expected lecture on how important it was to bring Gideon in. The first message, from Lieutenant Gibson, told us that the police had found the silver car abandoned at the airport office of the rental agency. Gsmith hadn't even bothered to fill the tank, as required on the rental agreement—clearly a scofflaw of the deepest dye. Their sweep through the airport had turned up five heavyset blond guys, but none of them matched the security-badge ID picture from Star-West. None of the airlines' passenger lists included *Gideon Smith,* either.

"So either he's jumped the fastest flight out of there and is gone in any one of six directions, or he's got himself another car and disappeared into the wilds of Portland again," Loren said.

"Got himself another car?" I asked absently, opening the second electronic envelope.

"Sure—either used a different ID to rent it at another agency or found some poor idiot's unlocked car in long-term parking, one with no security system or GPS link. Take that one, switch license plates with another car out there, and he's gone, with nobody the wiser. Then, when the idiot comes back and calls in the theft, they're looking for the wrong license numbers."

"Sneaky," I said. "Sometimes it scares me how much you know about—" I stopped.

"I met a lot of juvenile delinquents in various foster homes. What?" Loren asked. I didn't have to answer; he read over my shoulder.

Dearest Sekhmet, the message began. *Bad kitty, chasing our loyal servant! Take up your true calling, seeking eternal truth rather than the pathetic blind justice so beloved of fallen, myopic Man! Seek and ye shall find, knock and it shall be opened unto you. I love them that love me; and those that seek me early shall find me. Your skills, under our enlightened influences, can contribute so much to the good of our beloved sheep. But our hand will not remain stretched out toward you forever. Be warned. She that diligently seeketh good procureth favor: but she that seeketh mischief, it shall come unto her. Those who are not with us are against us. Join the true believers, forsake your mistaken crusade!* Again, it was signed *Gideon* under a blank avatar.

"Well," Loren said, "that's one method of doing missionary work, alternating dumb compliments with insults and ending up with threats. Very persuasive." He punched me lightly on the shoulder. "Hey, you're already in one cult. What could it hurt to join another?"

"You're enjoying all this way too much," I growled. "Put that wit to good use instead of evil, and pull up the Bible for me, Jesuit-boy." He did, and after a few minutes of searching I clicked the REPLY button.

Gideon, I began, wasting no endearments on him, seek good, and not evil, that ye may live. I don't know whether you really believe you're on a holy crusade, but you're going about it all wrong. Remember that wickedness never was happiness. You're setting a very bad and dangerous example for the idealistic kids out there who don't know better yet. As Paul said, "But take heed lest by any means this liberty of yours become a stumblingblock to them that are weak." I'll go with Joshua: "And if it seem evil unto you to serve the Lord, choose you this day whom ye will serve; whether the raging ego that's got you in its grip, or the gods of anarchy: but as for me and my house, we will serve the Lord!"

"Nice," Loren said as I sent the message on its way. "Lots of venom. I think you're treading some heretical territory there at the end, though, wresting the scriptures."

I guffawed. "I think you'll find I'm within boundaries on the substitution there. Besides, I do have a household—I included you in that last bit. Sometimes you have to use strong tactics when you're dealing with a nut case. No matter how much you agree with him and enjoy his antics, this guy's not Batman—he's a sociopath."

Loren raised one eyebrow. "Is that an example of what you learned in the last mini-class at Home/Personal/Community/Social Propaganda Meeting—how to diagnose antisocial personality disorder over e-mail?"

His sharp sarcasm made me regret digging him about agreeing with Gideon. I'd told him about the monthly Relief Society Home, Family, and Personal Enrichment meetings the last time I'd let Jenni and the other femmes in the ward guilt me into showing up. As he was with everything church-oriented, he'd been half-interested, half-sarcastic about it.

"No, I learned how to debug the onboard navigation system

in my car." I gave him a sweet smile. "But this week we're going to find out how to use brainwashing techniques on skinny computer geeks, so I figure I really ought to go. Who knows, it may work on both Gideon and you!"

"You're assuming that G.D. Davis is the original Gideon," Loren said with a smile as he leaned back in his chair. "For all you know, Mr. Smith may represent the ideal cracker physique."

"Mr. Smith is a candy addict, and—bingo!" I leapt up in excitement.

"What?" Loren asked. "Tack on your chair, or another bout of divine inspiration?"

"You laugh, but I've just had an epiphany."

I opened the digital phonebook and pulled up the rental-car agencies at the airport. "Gsmith is a pretty decent programmer, but he's no secret agent—look at all the stuff he left in his apartment. Say Gideon did hire him to be a mole in StarWest's system. Okay, that gives him computer skills. But I don't think he'd know how to steal a car even if he did think about it. He'd do what I'd do in that situation—dump the one, skedaddle to the other side of the airport, and get himself another car from a different rental outfit. Then he makes his getaway, without any extra heroics."

"Not bad," Loren said. "For a civilian."

"Which is exactly what Gsmith is," I reminded him, dialing the first rental agency.

"Yes, this is Sue Jones, from the National Infrastructure Protection Center—yes, the FBI. Listen, we need to know everyone who's rented a car from you today, specifically walk-ins after noon."

It took only two calls to narrow down the search to two possible suspects, both of whom had used ID information that proved as shallow as Gsmith's résumé. One had used a corporate account to rent a minivan only an hour after Gsmith had tried to run us down in the parking lot. The other had sprung for a German convertible a few minutes later, using a credit card that belonged to a widow who'd died two months ago.

"Okay, which is our boy?" Loren asked.

"Convertible!" we chorused in unison. I sent the GPS code for the convertible over to Ed, our department recluse. Then we both charged around the cubicles to the other row and Ed's self-made cave.

"Ed?" I asked. "Wanna go sport fishing?"

He didn't turn around or acknowledge us personally at all, but a deep voice exclaimed "Neat!" through the surround-sound speakers. The map from the Global Positioning Satellite system expanded from one corner of Ed's monitor to fill the entire screen, grid lines flashing into existence and converging on a dot moving rapidly south. Ed locked in the coordinates and set his system to track the car's every move. This kind of satellite-assisted surveillance was one of his hobbies; he himself never traveled, but he was fascinated by people who did.

"Can you get into the onboard emergency-assistance module?" I asked.

"Child's play, Robin," blared from the speakers in a different voice.

Another playing-card-sized box opened, flickered, and then steadied. The thick, blond-topped face of Gsmith appeared, recorded by the tiny communication unit built into the car's system as an extra option for important customers.

I laughed. "Done in by his love of luxury. How perfectly appropriate. Should've gone with an economy model, Mr. Smith." I left Loren to argue with Ed's speakers about Gsmith's terrible taste in music, and I dashed over to Dave's office.

"Hey, Dave, you know all those motivational talks you've been giving us?" I asked.

He looked up from his monitor and indicating the phone handset he held, motioning for me to be quiet. Checking out the caller ID, I noted that it was Shawnie again and took special pleasure in saying, "Well, they worked. We've got Gsmith on vid right now—Ed's got his GPS box. How about you get *off* the phone and call Stark to go after him?"

I waited only long enough for Dave to hurriedly hang up on Shawnie, dial Stark's office number, and bark, "We've got Gsmith on GPS—get the specifics from Ed!" Then I tore off to the break room, bought a container of instant popcorn, and hauled my chair to Ed's cubicle to watch the show.

"The popcorn's a nice touch," Loren approved.

As I watched, I thought that Ed could have a promising career as a real-time video director, if only he could get over his people phobias. He alternated wide shots of the GPS tracking for the cars of both Gsmith and Stark with close-ups of their faces through the onboard AV, as Loren and I made soundtrack suggestions. It would've been more dramatic if Gsmith knew that Stark was rapidly closing the distance between them, but the cracker's oblivious calm added its own flavor to the proceedings. And it was gratifying to see his horrified expression when Stark's black, hopped-up FBI vehicle pulled up behind him and flashed its lights.

"Come on, run," Loren urged.

I thumped him.

Gsmith bit his lip, then obediently pulled over. Despite Loren's long-distance cheerleading—"Okay, Stark's out of the car. Gun it!"—he didn't give Stark any physical trouble. Instead he simply informed Stark that he wanted to speak to a lawyer and that he would cooperate "in any way I can to get this cleared up." We caught just a fragment of Stark's impolite answer before Gsmith turned off the car and we lost picture.

He kept up an impassive demeanor right through the drive back, despite Stark's patented bad-cop routine, and in the interrogation room at the field office as well. From behind the one-way mirror, Loren and I added our positive identifications to those of Mr. Gray and the coworker who'd pointed out Gsmith to us. The lawyer who came in answer to Gsmith's one phone call was Mr. Benjamin Yazzie, a professional cracker-defender we knew all too well. Under Yazzie's watchful eye, Gsmith—now revealed as Albert Anderson, a longtime freelance programmer with excellent skills but shaky ethics—said that he had never met Gideon either in person or on the V-Net. Gideon had contacted him, offered him a job at StarWest, and advanced him a respectable fee by depositing it in Anderson's private Aireon escrow account. Gsmith didn't know about Gideon's ideological goals and frankly didn't care; he'd simply accepted what he believed to be a well-paid contract assignment.

An assignment which, Yazzie hastened to add, his client had no reason to believe would result in any harm to either StarWest or his customers. As for the incident in the parking lot, his nearly backing into us at high speed was simply a panicked reaction that kept him from shifting into forward gear before he hit the gas. He implied that it was a totally understandable state of mind, given the reputation of StarWest's internal security. After all, Anderson had cooperated fully once he had time to calm down and assess the situation rationally.

"Oh, baloney," I sneered. "He would've hit us if he could've. Yazzie's good, though. A jury would believe him, once he trains Gsmith to keep a more pleasant expression on his face."

"So that's it," Loren said with disgust as we left the observation room. (We don't actually help interrogate anybody—that's the

Special Agents' job.) "He helps Gideon totally rearrange StarWest's customer accounts, tries to run us over, and what do we get? He admits only to bad judgment in using an unsigned driver in his program for StarWest, says another programmer paid him to test it out, and maintains that all he knows about Gideon is the guy was looking for superior programmers. And he gets probation or house arrest for it."

"Ah, I don't know," I said. "That Eichmann defense about just following orders may not cut a lot of ice with StarWest and Sunshine. Especially if we can prove he got a percentage skim on those funds he transferred."

We trailed back into our offices. In spite of my optimistic suggestion, the anticlimactic interrogation considerably dampened our elation at actually catching Gsmith.

"So," Loren said, flopping into his office chair, "we've caught a little fish and found out he knows less about Gideon than we do, if we believe the guppy. Do we?"

"Yeah, I think we do," I said. "Stark's going to give him the bare-bulb treatment for a while more, just to make sure, but I'm thinking Gsmith would give up Gideon in a flash if he thought it would get him off. Now that I think about it, Rang told me a while ago that he'd heard V-Net chatter about somebody hiring top programmers to help him prepare for Armageddon, which totally fits what we know about Gideon. I thought it was a doomsday cult or something, but it may be just a business deal—in which case, we may be able to bring Gideon down, if we catch a subordinate who knows anything real about him."

Loren nodded. "No loyalty among thieves. All right, another point for Gideon. I guess we'll find out if he's got other goons-for-hire and if he's been as careful to handle them with gloves. Now, where's the big fish, and what's he—or they—going to do next?"

Fortunately, I didn't have to think up an answer for that one because my console filled the pause with a sudden barrage of belling notification signals. Loren's promptly joined in, and the noise of e-mail boxes filling crowded in from all the powered-up terminals around us. I flicked open my in-box, only to be nearly buried in an avalanche of nonsense mail. The image of Sekhmet on my screen leapt for the treetops in slow motion, her usual lightning-fast movements painfully hesitant as the flood of messages sucked the work station's processing power.

A yellow-legal-paper plane flew shakily over the partition and bonked off Loren's shoulder. He opened it and tossed it to me. *Who ordered all the spam? I was in the middle of editing our movie for its V-Net premiere!*

"Don't know, Ed," Loren yelled back. He yanked the speaker cord on his own console to stop the frantic signaling. It made hardly a dent in the cacophony filling the room. "I told Dave we didn't need to turn on notification for everybody and their dog. For crying out loud, we're big people — we can be relied on to check our own mailboxes occasionally!"

Real voices had joined the electronic chorus of beeps, bells, chimes, monkey screams, dripping water, and Aireon's default "You have a message." As I rapidly discovered, no one could do anything under the blizzard — we were all locked out of our mailboxes, V-Net connections, and even local files as the computers tried valiantly to deal with the flash flood of messages. Leaving Loren to try to find a way to preempt the message processing, I ran through the offices, finding the same situation wherever I went.

"Where's Jacques?" I yelled over the electronic pandemonium. Someone pointed downstairs, so I changed course and charged into the basement.

"Jacques!" I found our system administrator hunched over our primary V-Net computer, grimly glaring at the screen as his fingers flew inside the datagloves. "Everybody upstairs is snowed under with e-mail. What's going on?"

"Denial-of-service attack," Jacques growled. "Mother-loving phone phreaks — I know, I know, they've downed our V-Net site. I'm working on getting it back up, already!"

"Downed the V-Net site?" I asked.

"Snowed under with e-mail?" he asked at the same time.

It took only a few seconds to get our stories straight, once I had his full attention. Then I wisely left him to exercise his considerable troubleshooting expertise. Jacques was an extremely competent network administrator and an unruffleable Canuck as well, but I certainly didn't envy the guy his job. As if battling outside jokesters, irritated criminal types, and budget-cutting bureaucrats wasn't enough, he had the daunting task of maintaining our system in a department full of hackers who thought it was amusing to telecommute by hijacking connections rather than signing in the normal way.

"The entire office is snowed under with connection requests and electronic messages. The filters are totally blown," I told Loren, flopping into my chair once more. The noise level had gone down dramatically; apparently Loren had enlisted Ed's help in turning off all the speakers around the room. For a guy who rarely worked without his headphones pouring music into his ears, Loren was certainly sensitive to sounds. "Plus, Dave called Jacques all in a flutter because the NIPC site wasn't responding. Jacques checked the computer, and we've got an old-fashioned denial-of-service attack going on."

"Aren't there safeguards to prevent that kind of thing?" Loren asked, surprised.

"According to Jacques, the crackers've managed to slide by them. We're deaf, dumb, and blind on the V-Net. Nothing's getting in but spam, and we can't get out." I poked at my datagloves, watching the counter on my in-box spin. Abruptly the monitor filled with an admin-error message: *The network is offline. Please wait.*

"Looks like he's taken down the computers," Loren said needlessly. "So, you want to sit here staring at Jacques's version of a customer-service announcement or take a long, late lunch?"

"Like you have to ask!" I grabbed my purse and jacket.

"I figure if we talk about work, we can charge this whole thing as a business expense," Loren told the waitress as she reclaimed our menus. "Does that sound fair?"

"Oh, sure," she said, leaning against the bench beside me and giving him the full benefit of her attention. "What business are you in?"

"Decentralized distributing," Loren said earnestly, checking her name tag. "It's really not a pyramid scheme. Whitney, how much do you know about the ease and convenience of pharmaceutical-of-the-month club subscriptions, and would you like to know more?"

"Um," she said. "I'll have your order right out."

I watched her hustle away and poked Loren's leg with my foot under the table. "All right, enough playing with the natives' minds. Why do you do that? Give her an opening for flirting, then chase her away?"

He shrugged, straightening the condiment tray. "Like Demosthenes on his quest for an honest man, I am constantly searching for a wise and witty woman. 'What business are you in' doesn't qualify. Neither does getting nervous so quickly. Besides"—here he flashed me a blue-eyed Valentino look—"she should've noticed I already had a date."

I wrinkled my nose at him. "All right, Romeo, let's talk business. We've got to figure out who Gideon is, what he's going to do next, and why he's downed our system—if it's him."

"That last is pretty easy. Of course it's him—he's punishing us, and you in particular, for seeking mischief, as he put it. It's meant to show us that he can get to us if he wants to." Loren leaned back to let Whitney put a pair of condensation-speckled glasses on the table, then he gently touched her cold hand, preventing her quick retreat. "Thank you, Whitney."

We watched her bustle away, pleased that her charms were working after all. Loren met my eyes and raised his eyebrows. "There. Amends made for playing with her mind. I'll even leave a nice tip. Satisfied?"

"Well, I don't know. What happened to you already having a date?" I dumped a packet of sweetener into my lemonade and waved the torn envelope at him. "Anyway, chalk this one up to Gideon saying 'I know where you live.' No big surprise there. On to the next question. What's he going to do now? And does he know we've caught Gsmith?"

"We'll reserve judgment on that for now—no media coverage yet, so he might not know. As for where he'll strike next, that's elementary, my dear Watson. He'll hit the Sri Lankan Import Company." Loren raised one hand against my incredulity and perhaps as a shield against a possible lemonade geyser. "First Sunshine, then StarWest—he's got to go to the Sri Lankan Import Company to keep up with the reverse alphabetical theme."

I managed to swallow my mouthful of lemonade instead of spraying it. "All right, you're inspired. Is it the tacky seventies decor, or what? We're on a roll here. Okay, last question. Who is Gideon?"

Neither of us answered immediately, falling discreetly silent as Whitney reappeared with the rest of our lunch order. This time she didn't get any special treatment, just the usual half-absent recital of "thank you" as she set down our plates. The moment she was out of earshot, Loren said, "I think we'd better ask who *are* Gideon?"

"Right," I agreed, snagging a fry from his plate as he took a forkful of coleslaw from mine. "The two guys we've seen so far don't look anything like each other, but both of them are calling themselves Gideon something—which has got to be intentional, part of the deal in Gsmith's case. It'd be way too much of a coincidence for them to just happen to have the same name, right?"

"Right," Loren mimicked me. "But the way I see it, we're looking for at least three guys."

"Why three?" I asked. "We've got G.D. Davis and Gsmith already. We know Gsmith isn't Gideon, but G.D. Davis may be. College students are notorious for having these huge ideals and nearly no sense to go along with them."

"That may be, but the code's the clue," he said. "The transfer virus we glimpsed at StarWest before I blew it up looked like the same kind of really tight coding we saw in Gideon's additions to Sunshine's drone-fleet system. It's way more elegant than the code Stu said G.D. put in. And the currency-translation routines Gsmith wrote didn't look anything like that. Sure, it's nice enough, very workmanlike, but it lacks the elegance of Gideon's other pieces."

"Maybe Gsmith really is Gideon, lying to get out of it, and he wasn't very interested in the actual bank job," I suggested. "He didn't bother to do his best work, because it was just a cover anyway. Or he's really G.D. Davis, doing a terrible job to throw us off the track."

"No." Loren shook his head and gestured with a fry. "I can't go for that. Good programmers, and especially binary artists like Gideon, don't just get sloppy like that. It'd be like a pastry chef at a five-star restaurant suddenly deciding he didn't need to throw sprigs of mint into everything."

"All right," I conceded. "So we really do have three different sets of fingerprints here. Gsmith, workmanlike but uninspired. G.D. Davis, whose extremely sloppy programming was actually his, not merely camouflage for what he was really doing. And finally the real Gideon, the one who writes half-baked scriptural messages to me and codes like a base-two angel."

"That's how it looks from here," Loren said. We fell silent, looking at it from there as we finished lunch.

Ed's origami memo awaited us when we returned, a physical companion to the message lights blinking on our phone sets. Jacques had managed to stop the crippling flow of nonsense into our mailboxes, but he needed help digging the computer out of the drifts of unwanted — and supposedly impossible — messages. *You're elected for stable duty, suckers. Shoulda got out when you could.* Ed even managed to scribble a snigger.

I climbed up to kneel on my desk ledge and looked over the partition into Ed's lair. "I don't believe this — even Ed's pulled a bunk!" I flopped down again. "We should've let lunch stretch right into dinner and come in tomorrow, say we thought the workday was over. Like everybody else is going to do."

Loren tossed Ed's unfolded crane back into the depths of its creator's cubicle and raised an eyebrow at me. "Oh, come on—you know that Mormon conscience of yours wouldn't let you relax in front of the vid when there's a service project available. Anyway, you wouldn't be able to sleep, wondering how they got past our filters."

"I'll give you that last part," I told him. "But one of these days I'm going to drag you along when the ward goes planting trees down in the park. It'd do you some good to get some sun, fresh air, and exercise."

By the time we got to the bottom of the virtual avalanche, my shoulders and neck felt like I had been shoveling manure for hours. I pushed away from the console, bone-tired and worried. Loren turned to look at me, his expression as solemn as mine. Sekhmet's ID had appeared on the SENDER line of each one of the auto-generated messages, neatly letting it through the filters because I appeared on all the computers' access lists as a registered user. Even worse, the bogus connection requests that downed our V-Net site also used Sekhmet's basic identity string as a key.

The worst bit was the message from none other than Gideon that I unburied from the muck. *Our servant, Albert Anderson, was unworthy of his hire. From him shall be taken even what he had, as is just. You were an agent of divine justice in that. But beware, Sekhmet, the fate of those who despoiled the Master's vineyard.*

"I guess this is Gideon's way of letting us know he found out about Gsmith, and it didn't cripple his operations," I said, trying for a light tone but knowing I'd missed it completely. I took a deep breath, fighting down the irrational fury rising in my chest. "Remember the basics, keep it professional, don't let it get personal. He doesn't know who I am—I'm just the cop on his trail."

"He's got good reason to want you off his case." Giving me a reassuring look, Loren toed my chair. "You've blown his access at Sunshine, and he won't be able to pull anything at StarWest again either. If you weren't doing a good job, Gideon wouldn't bother with all the personal stuff."

"So why are you looking a wee bit concerned?" I asked, flattered by his confidence.

He shrugged, hitting nonchalance much more expertly than I had. "Nothing really—just thinking that getting personal isn't cool, but being cautious never hurts. Since we're in Jesuit mode anyway, might as well remember another scripture: 'Be sober, be vigilant; because your adversary the devil, as a roaring lion, walketh about, seeking whom he may devour.'"

Having the extra-light complexion that goes with red hair is inconvenient sometimes; I must've changed color pretty dramatically, because he quickly leaned forward and caught my shoulders. "Hey, it's not that bad. Wrong reference. This is just some crazy cracker who thinks he's Robin Hood and the Pale Rider all mixed up in one computer-headed package. He couldn't even really damage this system, and he can't get to the real you—he picked up Sekhmet's ID, sure, but anybody with a packet-sniffer can do that. It's not confidential. All your real info is safe behind sixteen different locks in Aireon's databases."

I firmly squelched both the shiver of fear at the thought of Gideon targeting me personally and the impulse to snuggle into Loren's arms. *Keep it professional, Jones.* "And you know this from personal experience trying to crack Stanton's safe, right?" I asked, managing a smirk.

Loren sat back, satisfied that I had recovered if I could tease him about his personal crusade against Stanton's empire. "Yeah, and if I can't get in, you can bet that nobody else can either. Come on, I'll show you that all your personal info is locked up tighter than a spinster's—" He stopped himself. "Well, tighter than Gideon can get into, anyway."

"Good save," I jibed, punching his shoulder. "Almost."

Loren slipped his fingers into his datagloves, switched on his terminal, and opened the portal to Aireon's V-Net site. I swirled back my chair and piggybacked my console onto his connection. An immaculately groomed landscape spread its pixels around Sekhmet and Secret Agent Man, Loren wisely having decided to use his registered avatar to visit the headquarters of the supreme registrar of the wired world. The thin, twisting stream of virtual smoke from Sam's cigarette utterly failed to dim the glory of the chaos-generated clouds in the sapphire sky. (I'd tried to get him to put Sam on a strict no-nicotine diet, but he insisted the cigarettes were necessary for authenticity.)

The digital smoke also failed to affect the smile on the sylph-like maiden who rose gracefully from a bench in the rose arbor beside us. "Welcome to Aireon," she said sweetly. "May I act as your guide, or would you like to explore on your own?"

"We're solo this trip, doll," Sam graveled in a voice that reeked of a sad-looking office with secondhand furniture and a depleted fifth of whiskey indiscreetly stashed in a drawer.

The maiden obediently subsided back to her bower perch as Sekhmet and Sam brushed past. Signposts beneath a statue of Paul Stanton and his design team—arranged like Revolutionary War heroes or Catholic saints in simulated granite—marked the paths that branched in all directions through the park: CUSTOMER SERVICE CENTER, GAMES AND AMUSEMENTS, ENHANCEMENTS, PERSONAL INTERESTS, SPONSORS, and so on and on and endlessly on. The paths were relatively empty; most people who visited Aireon's virtual playground knew exactly where they were going and arrived through more specific portals.

A gaggle of tourists wandered past in the distance, potential customers wearing standard-issue avatars as they listened to the practiced spiel of one of Stanton's professional guides, trying on Aireon's world-leading software for size before they actually subscribed. Probably European or African businesspeople—Aireon's spectacular recent rise had come primarily from North American and Asian markets, but it was expanding its domination across oceans at the speed of light through fiber-optic cables.

Nearer by, a group of teenagers lounged around a small group of benches. They were probably waiting for the latest death-match arena to come free, spending their downtime gazing at the wonders of the online world and their fellow V-Netizens through jaded eyes and carrying on desultory, slang-filled conversations in customized thought balloons.

"Were we ever that young?" I asked Sam, pointing them out.

"Young?" he asked before he got a good look. He spotted them for teenagers too—their zombie-vampire avatars' black rags, gaping death wounds, and bloody mouths hewed too tightly to the fashion of the clique for them to be anything other than fiercely independent sheep adolescents. "Oh. No, we weren't. You were never a teenager, and I didn't like them when I was one."

They'd picked a spot mostly free of adult supervision for their angst-fest; maybe they'd gotten thrown out of the online malls. No security guards strolled the grounds here. Birds twittered through the skies, however, keeping their sharp, sparkling eyes on us and the other visitors. The spy-sensor on my belt hummed steadily, tracking the presence of monitor features hidden behind the idyllic setting. So far Aireon's security arrangements impressed and reassured me.

Sam struck out on the graveled walkway leading to the Kid-Zone as I prowled along in his wake, my hind claws tapping softly on the paved surface. We passed the entry portal and made our way into the virtual summer, leaving the imposing glass domes of the Customer Service Center rapidly behind us. The brightly colored tents of the under-sixteen playground came into view over the short rise.

"Yah! Hands up or you're toast!" A grenade-hung, hugely muscled Marine Corps caricature erupted out of the trees beside the path, brandishing a huge rail gun as he roared his challenge.

His comrade, an outrageously proportioned Amazon holding an imaginatively constructed crossbow, jumped out of the branches to land behind us. Her attire confirmed the suspicion that the Marine's words sparked—the uniform she wore hugged her superhero curves like paint, but no actual flesh tones peeked from the camouflage cloth. We were dealing with a couple of kids. Public outcry about the influence of the V-Net on juveniles had long since resulted in a set of regulations about exactly what a child could do, see, and be in virtual reality. As a result, our new acquaintances' overbuilt avatars could carry somewhat dumbed-down virtual weapons but could not incorporate any suggestive characteristics, such as skin. I had no problem with that rule—in fact, I personally favored a general ban on all sexually oriented avatars. I just wished they'd put more brakes on the little idiots' access to firepower as well.

The blast that the Amazon unleashed at me didn't cause any damage or even briefly fuzz my connection, since I hadn't turned on Sekhmet's gaming interface, but it did annoy me. Before I lost my temper enough to toss a logic bomb in her direction and disable her avatar for several minutes, however, she froze, her entire body as stiff as the permanent comic-book sneer on her face. Sergeant Slaughter managed to turn away before the same spontaneous stasis locked him into place. "Aw, crap," he muttered.

A column of flashing lights bloomed on the path, coalescing into a neatly uniformed, blandly handsome male Aireon C.O.P. (Customer Operations Person—cute, huh? They're actually elves, online robots who monitor the system and refer problems to a real employee only if necessary.) "Aireon Unlimited prohibits gaming outside designated zones," he intoned. "Game sessions require the consent of all parties who wish to participate. Violation of V-Net site rules results in sanctions. Gungirl32 and Meat Grinder, you will accompany me to discuss your netiquette infractions. Control of your avatars will not be returned until you comply." He turned to us, his stern expression changing immediately to a sunny smile. "Please accept our apologies for the interruption. If your avatar or your system have suffered any damages, please inform the Customer Service Department. We hope you enjoy your visit to Aireon."

The C.O.P. marched the two renegade juveniles off toward the circus tents, to the delight of several equally improbable creatures watching from a distance. "They got Grinder!" one of them happily reported to its buddies.

"Kids," I hissed.

Sam shrugged. "Mark Twain's old raising-kids-in-a barrel idea has some merit, but the little brats came in handy this time, distracting the C.O.P. Hold on a second."

I obediently waited until the gang disappeared after their apprehended members, and then I dove off the path in Sam's wake. He fished in the deep pocket of his trench coat and pulled out a filmy length of cloth, which he threw over both of us. We instantly paled and faded as the cloak of invisibility turned us into shadows of our former selves. (This was a Loren custom job, one of the many things that made me glad he was on our side now.) He then tossed a key at the trunk of a huge, spreading oak complete with currently unoccupied tire swing.

The bark sparkled, glowed, and swept apart like a velvet curtain, sucking us both into an oriental-carpeted hallway that seemed to extend forever in both directions. Windows showing scenes from a thousand imaginary worlds punctuated the bland walls at regular intervals. Dinosaurs, their muscles rippling under multicolored crocodile hides, roared and slashed at each other in a jungle of emerald ferns. Two suns cast dual shadows through rock arches and cliffs carved into whipped-cream peaks by howling sandstorm winds. A bustling city's lights glowed through the darkness of a future night, simulated citizens striding or slinking along on their errands through the mists wrapping the shop fronts and light poles. Codes scrolled beneath each window, initials and numbers creating an unintelligible closed captioning for the action within the frames.

"What are these?" I asked, intrigued.

"Production area," Sam informed me as he tucked the cloak of invisibility back into a trench-coat pocket. "These are all the scene-theme projects Aireon's drones are working on at the moment." He pointed at the ever-changing litany of statistics accompanying the playback of an idyllic underwater tea party. "Those show bug reports and fixes, status reports, progress made toward the day's goals — probably the keystroke counts for every programmer working on the thing. You know a theme's getting closer to done when the cascade slows down. This one's still got a long way to go."

For this one, at least, it was pretty easy to tell the scene-theme wasn't done. The fish at the tea party tended to ripple and disappear, and the octopus serving plates of cookies had sunk into the fabric of its chair. I had to pull my attention away from the moving wallpaper and hustle to catch up with Sam, who managed to look black and white amid the (properly subdued) jewel-tone splendor as he marched up the corridor.

"Sure does — right now, even Alice would feel out of her element there. So, how did you manage to get that key?" I asked. "I'm sure they don't give those out at Aireon developer conferences."

"Nope." Sam's expression didn't change, but he radiated satisfied smugness. "I had our sweet little Copycat get snuggly with one of the C.O.P.s and then did a bit of vivisection on the clone. Turns out they have a multipurpose key built in, to make it easier for them to appear wherever they're needed. It doesn't have full privileges, of course, but it's pretty much a free pass into any unencrypted area."

"Sneaky," I said. "No wonder you like cats so much. It really is going to be a pity when NetSys 11.4 comes out and kitty doesn't work anymore."

"I'll miss her," Sam admitted. "But them's the breaks. It's a tough town."

After passing the fourteenth animated scene, we took another sudden detour through one of the windows into a lovely Victorian-era living room. The bug-counter on the frame ticked over very slowly indeed, and the environment inside the simulation wrapped us in gorgeous detail. Tall, narrow windows shone behind velvet curtains that spread in precise, wasteful pleats across the floors. Neoclassical brass andirons guarded a crackling fire. Knickknacks, tchotchkes, and bric-a-brac cluttered every mirror-polished surface, echoing on the complicated patterns in the piles of antimacassars draping the backs and arms of the chairs. The piano even wore a skirt! I could almost smell the attar of roses scenting the gaudy china bowls of potpourri.

"What a lovely little place you have here." I settled onto the camelback sofa, its elegant lines completely buried in a mound of hand-woven lace, and I flicked my tail languidly. "What shall we do? Have a spot of tea or write a couple of eccentrically spelled letters?"

My feline version of a Victorian seductress lasted only until I caught a glimpse of us in the intricately framed mirror across the room. "We look like refugees from a different genre," I said, laughing.

Sam looked around the great-aunt habitat and blew a derisive smoke ring. "Yeah, what this joint needs is a stiff on the floor next to a bent poker. Give it some character. Don't get comfy—we're not staying."

The warped effect deepened as he popped open a china hutch and stepped through the Wedgwood dinner set. I stared, amazed, until his hand and coat cuff reappeared, beckoning curtly. Fighting a shudder that rose out of a childhood memory of a ghost story involving an antique chest and phantom hand, I paced cautiously across the floor. The china cabinet looked as real as the rest of the decor, as tangible as Aireon's reality could make it. None of the usual subtle cues—seams around the cabinet, slight color differences, a certain vapor quality—that usually indicated a hidden portal marked either the dishes or their shelves. I extended a claw to tap the huge silver soup tureen.

And let out a yowl as I was abruptly jerked through the back of the cabinet. I made a three-point landing, all claws extended, my free hand brandishing a tangler to entrap an opportunistic assailant. (Just because I don't choose to play point-and-shoot games for fun doesn't mean I don't know how to go about it.) In the gloom I caught a glimpse of familiar faded-gray trench coat out of the corner of my eye, but the flash of movement in front of me grabbed my attention. A Fenris leapt for my throat, its three heads snarling and darting in perfect synchronicity. The tangler spat and crackled, wrapping the canine guardian exie in an endless loop of instructions. It crashed to the rough-hewn floor, its snarl wavering into an unintelligible aural drawl. I backed up a step—it's always best to get out of your enemy's reach before turning your back, in both real and virtual fights—and spun three hundred and sixty degrees, checking for more threats.

Another Fenris writhed in slow motion, pinned to the rocky cave wall in a web of shining threads. Sam stood coolly regarding the hot-crimson blood running from a nasty gash on his arm into a widening pool on the ground.

"Are you all right?" I whispered, my usual purr dropped down a register.

"Minor corruption and a touch of data leak," he said flatly but also quietly, stroking the wound with his other hand. The rip instantly vanished, flesh, skin, and coat rejoining seamlessly. Another casual flick vanished the blood, wiping all evidence away from the surfaces around him. "No problem."

Apparently he'd spent Sam's allotted avatar-ability points on resilience and deep pockets for carrying gadgets like the cloak of invisibility. Occasionally, Aireon's game-world origins showed through their multipurpose present; avatars were essentially independently running programs that moved themselves from one computer to another over the V-Net, used the computer's processing power, and interacted with the other programs running on the computer. If an avatar sustained too much damage, which the Aireon interface visually interpreted as blood and broken bones, it essentially died until its owner restored it from the original version on its home system. Because an avatar could incorporate only a few features in its data package, you had to choose what kinds of capabilities you wanted it to have—which meant that problem-solving talents, heavy weaponry, turbo speed, tough armor, and other flashy abilities took their toll by making it harder for the avatar to recover from attacks. Carrying backup routines meant less space to devote to other skills—Sam was rather plain on the outside, not particularly strong, and not armored—but in some cases it was worth it. Like this one.

I knew the blood wasn't real—even though it was so vivid that I could almost smell it in my imagination—but seeing Sam (and by extension Loren) hurt chilled and upset me. So, naturally, I expressed my distress and concern by swatting his trench-coated shoulder. "You could've told me that here lie monsters!"

He absorbed the few damage points easily—it was nothing compared to the wound he'd already healed—and shrugged. "I didn't know they'd be here. They weren't last time, which means somebody's found this crack. Come on—we don't have a lot of time."

We detoured in a wide circle around the stymied watchdogs and sprinted down the twisting turns of the cavelike labyrinth. "What's this for?" I gasped.

"Training ground," Sam replied without slackening his speed. "They create learning programs—like the ones that do stock market analysis or combinations of behaviors for automated planetary probes—then set them loose in this area to evolve with and against each other. The team leader, Ozuri Katzumi, has this sense of humor—things evolve in caves."

"We're not going to run into a ravenous stock-picker, are we?" I asked, scanning the dark mouths as we ran through a three-dimensional cartwheel of tunnels diverging in a circle off the main path, passages leading left, right, forward, back, up and down.

"No," he said. "They're between cycles, won't start another till tomorrow. The only thing that might happen is—"

"A system-flush to wipe the DNA of the last generation before beginning the new round?" I suggested, as a warning rumble thrummed behind us. With impeccable timing and a sound like a rapidly approaching waterfall, a sparkling flood poured from every opening, its overwhelming tide surging toward us. It roared around every curve, wiping away any program in its path.

"Like I said," Sam said calmly, catching my hand once again and propelling us toward the blank rock face of a box tunnel, "not a lot of time."

I fuzzed slightly as the first lap of the flood caught my heel, and then we were through the door that I guessed Ozuri must use to dump his sub-evolved programs through. We fell, twisting through a black, neon-shot tunnel before it spat us out into a slick silver funnel, where we substituted sliding for tumbling. I dug my claws into the mirror-bright surface. The shriek filled my ears, vibrating my brain, but it worked—our wild descent gradually slowed. I whipped my tail around Sam's arm; his fingers locked around it instantly. We hung there, two small specks on an endless, brilliant slope.

"Um, now what?" I asked. "Hope you have a key. My hind foot's zonked, and I think it's slipping."

"Yup." He reached up and patted the leg attached to the foot in question, then touched the smooth cliff under us. It shimmered, twitched, and dumped us into another alternate reality. This time, however, the scene change left us in much more familiar territory. Gray walls rose around us, with hieroglyphics against the blank background. V-Net portals hummed and whispered behind firewall shields as packets flowed in and out of Aireon's database network.

"This is it?" I asked softly, shaking the life back into my hind leg. "The world-famous Aireon database?"

"Yup," Sam returned, glancing around cautiously.

"And you found a way in. I would have thought you'd find a back door in one of those World War Three battles or vampire gothic haunted houses they had out in the corridor. Seems weird to break into their goldmine through a Victorian parlor."

Sam gave me a long look. "Hit it with everything you've got, hacker-cat. Let's see if you can get in."

I laughed, touching an access terminal with two clawed fingers and tossing out a display request to the system. "All right, point taken—most crackers are guys, and no guy in his right mind would try to break into the ultimate girly vision of a Victorian parlor. Let's see what safeguards they've got."

Aireon permitted no unguarded display windows here, I quickly found, and the company had made sure to leave no passwords or user accounts still valid on this system. The databases steadfastly resisted my seasoned arsenal of blandishments, as I tried a fast succession of techniques from subtle requests to outright force. I thought nonsensically about resorting to bribery when nothing in my usually excellent tool belt made any headway through the walls to the data mine inside. I launched an electronic carrier pigeon at the nearest V-Net link, an elegant little exie designed to fly back to my console and create a permanent connection between it and the database computer. But the virtual bird barbecued in a puff of charcoaled feathers when it hit the firewall. Suddenly the world filled with invisible molasses. I could move, but just barely; even the curl of smoke from Sam's cigarette writhed ceilingward in extreme slow motion. The freeze-frame didn't make his smug grin any more palatable.

"Your connection has been seized. Cease all activity to avoid damage to your system." The words bellowed at us through the speakers and from the red-and-white face of the sign that spilled over the display like a very final curtain. "Submit your avatar id and registration now."

"All right, you sorry-butt hackers," a live voice said in much less impressive tones. "You know the drill. Assume the position."

"Busted," I said aloud, shaken out of virtual immersion only to find that my console was as sluggish as Sekhmet. "That didn't take long at all. Did he really call us what I think he did? And more important, can you get loose?"

"Yup and nope," Loren told me. "Their watchdog's grabbed my connection and got control of my console, and it's wormed through to yours too. Very nice boomerang exie they've got. I'm going to have to find a way to steal it."

"Or maybe we can tell them we're FBI, and they'll give it to us," I suggested, obediently keying in the code that let Aireon's probe X-ray Sekhmet's digital innards for their maker's mark.

I knew that Loren had done the same when the automated voice intoned "IDENTIFICATION ACCEPTED. VERIFYING."

"So, what can we do for the Feds tonight?" the tech asked, still with that irritating superiority in his tone. "If you need user information, all you've got to do is ask for it—after you get the search warrants and all. Or are you in a hurry?"

"Actually, we're just making sure you guys are on your toes," Loren assured him. "You can release the boomerang now, by the way."

"How about you explain what's going on first, and then I'll uncuff you?" It clearly took a lot more than flashing a cyber badge to impress this technician. He did, however, relinquish total control so that we could reanimate our avatars.

Loren recalled his avatar instead of simply reanimating him; Sam pulled his Bogart half-smile and disappeared.

"We're looking for a cracker calling himself Gideon," I said through Sekhmet.

"The one who's been in the news," the tech finished for me. He hadn't bothered with the polite gesture of inserting his own avatar into the scene, so I pulled out Sekhmet as well.

"Yes, that one." I simply typed my responses through the datagloves, wondering how my "voice" sounded on his speakers or if he had turned on a voder at all. The midnight shift guarding Aireon's databases probably didn't attract the kind of person who liked a lot of bells and whistles. In my mind this guy looked like Ed, only more hygienically challenged.

"We told you we didn't have him registered," the tech informed me peevishly after apparently checking a file.

"We know that," I shot back. "We simply wanted to be sure he hasn't managed to compromise the security of Aireon's databases."

"And you figured you could find out by trying to hack it yourselves?" The tech laughed. "Listen, you're worrying for no reason. Nobody, but nobody, can bust into Aireon's records. That's what makes us the very top V-Net service in the world. You guys keep chasing runaway grocery trucks—we can take care of ourselves. And if you need any help, just ask next time." The connection light on Loren's console blinked from green to gray.

Hunched over his freed console, Loren muttered, "Talk about pride."

"And no manners, either. Still, it does look like those databases are secure, at least from outside attack. And they'll be combing through them extra carefully tonight, just to make sure they are."

A thin shudder wrapped itself along my spine. It would be a megadisaster if somebody did manage to hack them, with eighty percent of the V-Net users in the United States and fully sixty percent worldwide happily storing their information in Aireon's databases — financial, personal, business, physical, everything. Sure, it made the world an easier place, not having to pay cash, never having to deal with junk mail you didn't explicitly order, all your numbers kept private — but it all came down to a very basic equation: As Aireon went, so went the world.

"They'd better," Loren informed me. "They're not perfect yet. *Voila!*" He smiled sharply at me. "Left their boomerang on my system for just a nanosecond too long. Copycat got it."

"Silly creatures," I said disdainfully. "Before they know it, you'll have their megacomputers eating out of your hands. So, my dear Watson, how did you know so much about that learning-program arena?"

"Know the enemy. Basic strategy." He gestured to the pile of industry magazines and computer-science journals filling a printer-paper box under his desk. "Ozuri and his team published their findings, including the methods they used — throwing their candidates into a hyped-up MUD and letting them run. I figured they'd used a section of Aireon's existing site, and I went looking for it. Finding the right project was the tough part, but once I narrowed it down to that Victorian parlor, getting in wasn't too hard. It's keeping the door open that's tough — those Fenrises prove they knew somebody'd poked around in there, even if they didn't know who. That door's closed tight now." He sighed philosophically. "But one of these days they'll screw up, and I'll get past their wall. Then they're mine! Bwaa-haa-haa!" He had a great mad-scientist laugh.

"Loren, Aireon is not your enemy," I said slowly, enunciating each word. "You are one of the good guys now."

He tossed a wadded-up printout at me, and I laughed and ducked.

"All right, Counselor Jones, get off it," he pretend-growled. "I know my FBI boundaries. But I also know they're up to something in there. One flick of the switch, and they could take down V-Net access for just about everybody in the world — or take over their computers. They could completely rearrange half the world if they wanted to — ownership titles, financial records, data files, whatever. It's all wide open to them."

Our staring contest, bright blue against hazel green, lasted several moments. Finally he admitted, "Not that I've got any proof that they're going to. It just bugs me that they could."

"Seriously, though," I said, "it's more than a good thing they're so careful." I tossed back the printout, making a neat basket into his trash can. "I know it's fun to poke around in there, but for right now we better save our energy for grabbing Gideon. Whoever they are."

Loren cast a longing glance at the boomerang exie caught in his Copycat's claws, and then we both turned back to the heaping piles of spam Gideon had used to choke our computers. Handily, every e-mail message had to contain a destination and source address. Unfortunately, the source address could change. It was like mailing a letter to New York and having each post office along the way overwrite your return address with its own—and some post offices guaranteed anonymous service and didn't put anything in the return address at all. Various governments had tried to slap regulations on anonymous-messaging computers, but even in the few cases where the laws actually passed, the problem came down to enforcement. How do you stop someone from hooking his console to the V-Net and offering his or her services? You can't—which is where we come in. Even with all the overwriting on the outside of the envelope, traces of the message's origin still lurk inside.

"He's using two different anonymous-message computers to launch his spam," I told Loren, after dissecting the fingerprints on a handful of messages.

"He's also hijacked at least three relay computers, to bury us in repeats of the stuff," Loren said. He had concentrated his search on the paths the messages took rather than on their origins. "No, make that four. And there they are." A quartet of bright dots appeared on the V-Net map glowing from his monitor. Information scrolled beside each one, detailing ownership, activation, transaction records— all the data our search programs could pull from their computers. Gideon had sent his junk e-mail to these computers along with a zombie routine that instructed them to send millions of copies to the NIPC mail computer. And the poor stupid-but-obedient things had done just that, using their owners' identities and connection time to bring our system to a crashing halt.

"All unguarded terminals in small businesses," I noted. "Probably don't even realize Gideon used them. Why do people leave their systems wide open like that?"

"Because they don't have anything interesting enough to steal, and they're not high-profile enough to attract vandals. So because nobody's ever done anything to them, they don't think about security. Like they say, a conservative's just a liberal who's been mugged."

"Well, these guys are going to get conservative real fast," I said. "Wait a minute—where's that line going?" We watched it take a sudden upturn, launching itself off the two-dimensional grid to hit a satellite relay before diving down toward earth again. To my disappointment, it didn't burn up on reentry. "Overseas. Dang!"

"Looks like you get to talk to Shawnie again," Loren said.

"Oh, wipe that grin off your face," I told him, but I didn't suggest that he talk to Shawnie—I knew better, from past sarcasm explosions. Having to tell her that we were the victims in this case made it even worse. I'd just as soon let her keep her "How's it going way out there?" comments to herself, but in this case I didn't have a choice. The E.U. had finally set up a pretty good computer-security organization, but they got extremely prickly about investigators from either China or the United States digging through their phone and V-Net connection records. They'd rather handle it through their own intelligence agencies. Thus, we had to contact Shawnie in D.C. whenever one of our hunts "jumped the pond"—as she said—so she could contact the Foreign Liaison Office, who could ask the guys at Interpol to track it for us.

Inaccurate but funny visions of James Bond as a computer geek—less well dressed, more squirrelly, with a tendency to drool over processor ads—wandered through my head as I listened to Shawnie's phone ring. Much to my surprise and delight, the voice saying "You have reached Special Agent Shawndell Lincoln at the National Infrastructure Protection Center of the Federal Bureau of Investigation" was recorded rather than live.

"Hi, Shawnie, Sue Jones from the northwest division here. Sorry I caught you out. We're tracking a denial-of-service and spam attack that used an overseas satellite connection." As I spoke to her electronic secretary, I dumped all our data into a neat package and addressed it to her mailbox. "I'm sending you the info now. Looks like Gideon feels we're getting too close to his heels, what with us catching Albert Anderson and all, so he's throwing out tacks. Let us know as soon as you pass along the message to the Euros. Bye."

"Nice face-saving maneuver," Loren said approvingly.

I grimaced. "I know, that was weak. Should've stuck by

Sensei Rick's rule, 'No excuses, no explanations.' I just couldn't help it. She's such a toastie sometimes."

"Rick's got a macho stick up his—shirt. Toastie?" Loren asked. He's pretty good at the old face-saving maneuvers himself.

"You know—the old cereal slogan, 'Just a little bit better.' Makes me crazy. At least I didn't have to talk to her in person."

"No, you just left a sweet college-girl voice-mail message," Loren teased. "Haven't you watched enough cop vids? We don't say hi and bye, we don't ask nicely, and we surely don't apologize for calling when somebody's out. You should've said something snarky like 'Gone home already, Agent Lincoln?' and made her feel like an idiot for not living in her office chair."

"Oh, yes, that'd make her tons easier to work with and motivate her to get right back to us the minute she finds anything out."

"Like she would anyway," he shot back. "Loving your neighbor doesn't always work."

"This kind only understands the language of power, eh? I'll atone for the time my blunder has cost us by studying *The Prince* a bit harder."

"Ah, go straight for Nietzsche," he suggested. "Christianity is a religion of slaves. God is dead."

"So is Nietzsche," I said, laughing at his exaggerated German accent. "But God in heaven reigneth, loving forever, with his Son at his side and his children before him."

"Who's that from?" he asked curiously.

"Me," I said. "With a little help from Handel and Isaiah."

"See if they'll help you figure out where Gideon is before Shawnie's MI-5 and Mossad buddies do," he suggested, turning back to his own console. He waited until I'd done the same before adding, "Good come back, though."

The compliment buoyed me through the next few minutes, but the tingle of pleasure quickly dissipated as I stared blearily at the endless lines of garbage characters I had reconstructed from the layers of spam in the computer. *Halogen* swam into my view and then *Hot*, repeated down the columns of code again and again. *Hot Halogen. Halogen Hot. Halogen.* "Loren, have you ever heard of something called halogen? Something Gideon might consider hot? Other than the lamps. I don't think he's trying to include a public-service message about the dangers of halogen lights here."

"Hot halogen, huh?" he said, turning around in his chair. "Actually, I have. Halogen. It's an online club, independently sponsored, not one of Aireon's or a community party. But you wouldn't like it."

"Well, it keeps coming up, so somebody's got to go check it out." I fluttered my eyes at Loren. "Since you already know where it is . . ."

"Oh, no. I couldn't dream of depriving you of a real growth experience. Besides, I'm pretty much *persona non grata* around there. Beat up their bouncer when he tried to toss me out for apprehending the Mad Multiplexer."

"You and your Dirty Harry ways," I tsk-tsked. "Leaving me to plunge into the wilds of some virtual red-light district all by myself." I drew back my shoulders and lifted my chin bravely. "Sometimes you just have to do things that aren't fun in order to build character."

"Character—right," Loren said, laughing as he sent the V-Net site address to my console. "You're definitely going to learn something. By the way, Trixie was a real hit in that joint. Be sure you turn on PrudePro before you go in."

He wasn't kidding. I caught a mere glimpse of the elaborately feminine door attendant before a shiny silver jumpsuit washed over her gravity-defying triple cleavage, and that glimpse was more than enough. PrudePro was one of Loren's copyrighted programs, the ones that made him his legal connection money before we caught him. He published it over the V-Net as an avatar enhancement, allowing anyone to download it for a nominal fee and add it to their online personas. It actually earned him several hundred dollars a year from people like me who preferred not see the details of others' exhibitionist and anatomically imaginative avatars. While tightly written private and legal rules surrounded the appearance and capabilities of juveniles' online identities, adults' pixilated manikins were limited only by their owners' imaginations and the ever-receding technical boundaries of Aireon's interface.

The imagination of Halogen's owners and patrons definitely went in directions I didn't want to follow. Even with PrudePro metaphorically hiding my eyes, I avoided glancing directly at the virtual club's central stage as I slunk into the strobing darkness, tail twitching. PrudePro neatly black-markered the closed-captioned conversations swirling around and at me, while using my specified substitution list for the audio file. Thus, whatever the fig-leafed, muscle-bound robo dude in the horned helmet actually said when he grabbed my arm, it came out, "Hey, kitty, nice tail—wanna go to a private room and let me use it to swing from the rafters?"

"*No!*" I snarled at him, showing my fangs and claws. Places like this raised my hackles even more than real-world boho strip bars—pathetic and creepy as trolling for casual sex was in real life, it got even slimier in a world where you could add deep-gouge blood and guts to the usual Babylonian perversions. The argument that it wasn't real and therefore didn't matter simply cut no ice with me. Where your thoughts are, there your heart is also, to paraphrase the dead-on scriptural warning.

The robo dude backed off, muttering a stream of blacked-out words that sounded as, "Touchy lady."

After the third vigorously censored and equally sharply refused proposition, I leapt for the hall's exposed rafters. I slunk along the catwalk over the heads of the crowd, scanning conversations with Sekhmet's enhanced hearing. Between the terrible spelling and the swatches of black ink, nothing drew my attention for several long minutes, during which the pounding grind-hop soundtrack changed songs twice but didn't change beats even once.

As I scanned the bobbing, shifting mob, a sudden whirlpool of activity in the hall's far quadrant caught my attention. The bouncers—huge virtual eunuchs and butch-cut, single-breasted Amazons—promptly plowed wakes through the dance floor, quelling the disturbance and summarily ejecting a flailing, bleeding cowboy for pulling his pistol on a special guest of the owners. The crowd milled, realigning according to the new power structure. Apparently Black Bart used to be somebody, but there was a new sheriff in town. I sprang from beam to beam, neatly landing on the thin support above the center of the new constellation.

"Let's just say that I know plenty about Gideon," a familiar voice boomed into my ears. Sure enough, a crested helmet bobbed beneath me, overshadowing narrow, plaid-covered shoulders. A soul string trailed up past me, connecting the avatar we all saw to the real person—G.D. Davis—manipulating the datagloves at a remote console. The cluster of creatures around him had only soul strings and excessive mammary development in common.

"Shh—you shouldn't talk so loud," breathed a bombshell redhead clad almost entirely in PrudePro's default silver paint.

"Don't worry, baby." He did something that made the redhead squeak. "Those Nipsies have their hands full tonight. They know what happens when they mess around with us."

Well, that answered one question — G.D. Davis was *not* Gideon. I landed right in front of him, giving him and his entourage the full benefit of my gleaming, feline grin. "You get caught?"

I blasted the entire area with a set of data packets identifying me as FBI and informing everyone of his or her or its constitutional rights, and then I straight-armed the redhead and lunge-kicked the blonde behind her, who'd started to morph into something reptilian but still with the cleavage.

"Loren!" I yelled aloud. "I've got him — G.D. Davis! He's at Halogen!"

G.D. was yelling too, a frantic gush of clichés — "You'll never take me!" — bad spelling due to his voice-recognizer malfunctioning under pressure, and blacked-out swear words. He pulled a pen out of his pocket and turned it on me as the glowing thread of a tangler shot out. I flipped and hit the floor, avoiding it; the threads wrapped one of the bystanders, which pushed the crowd a cautious pace back. No one else showed any desire to interfere, but they didn't leave, either; since nobody was throwing logic bombs, they felt safe to observe. The bouncers hovered, held back by the might of NIPC and the FBI — or maybe just their own curiosity about how this match would come out.

Rolling to avoid the next volley of tangles, I tossed a homing pigeon at G.D. It fluttered unerringly at him, flashing into the soul string in a puff of white feathers.

"Trace on!" I told Loren as the avian exie locked G.D.'s connection and flew toward his console through the V-Net, leaving a vivid trail.

"Got it," he said. "Trace coming in."

G.D. knew it too. His avatar threw away the pen and pulled a cell phone out of his overloaded pocket protector. "Shibboleth!" he shouted into it. "Shibboleth!"

The wall shimmered and faded, the rushing of an open V-Net connection growing into crystal clarity. *Nice add-on,* I thought; I'd never seen an avatar that could spontaneously establish a V-Net connection. I pulled Copycat out of my bag, set her on the floor, and activated her. She scampered toward G.D. Davis as he ran for the portal. Just as he reached it, however, the portal hazed over with mother-of-pearl.

"Unworthy," a baritone voice intoned, soft but filling our ears. "An unfaithful servant has no place in his master's house." With that, a flash of lightning lanced out, neatly slicing G.D. Davis's soul string, before the portal closed with a thunderclap. The avatar froze, the program cut off from its master's control but still completely intact. I slipped a code-lock over the unresisting figure and then cast a sharp-toothed smile at the Halogen denizens. "As the man said, remember what happens when you mess with us NIPCs." Copycat leapt to my shoulder as I bowed and vanished out of the scene.

"Gideon," I semi-swore, slipping my hands out of the data-gloves and rubbing my temples tiredly. "Loren, he had a soul-snipper. We've got G.D. Davis's avatar, but the connection's gone. I figure G.D. set the spam attack himself. Not only did Gideon seem really ticked off at him, but Gideon's last message about Gsmith came during the storm. He wouldn't have sent it then if he'd known it couldn't get through."

"Sounds like Gideon did us a favor, then. G.D. Davis's avatar is all we need," Loren said smugly, scooting his chair over to me. "We've got a trace to his console—Vancouver. I already snapped a line to Shawnie to get our Canuck friends on his back. Mounties always get their man." He gently moved my hands and used his long fingers to rub the tightness out of my temples, and then he squeezed my shoulders lightly. "Just like us."

The bell on my in-box interrupted whatever foolish thing I was about to say. We both tensed, dreading a barrage of ringing, but it fell silent after a single tone. *Apologies*, it read, Gideon's blank-faced icon somehow managing to convey a sense of noble pique. *Our crusade is no place for light-mindedness and loud laughter. The liberation of the flock from the heel of the oppressor is a holy crusade. We have put the goat out from among us, an unworthy sacrifice.*

"Great—Gideon's thrown us G.D. Davis." I sighed.

"And a really nice soul-snipper program," Loren added, settling back into his chair and rubbing his hands gleefully. "And a free-floating link opener, and a boomerang. We've made out like bandits! Next time, we'll have them all backward engineered, and we'll take over Gideon's console with him sitting at it."

"Great." I yawned hugely. "You do that. I'm going to go home and sleep while the Mounties run down Nerd Boy Davis."

After a few more minutes, during which we carefully checked our consoles for leftover programs—I didn't find any, but you can never be too careful; who knows what kinds of viruses you can pick up at a place like Halogen—I grabbed a pizza slice for the road and finally made my escape. But first I paused for a second, watching Loren chortle over his latest acquisition from the unwitting—or at least arrogantly careless—Aireon tech as he spread G.D. Davis's avatar across his console for an autopsy.

I leaned over and brushed my cheek against his for a fleeting second as I said, "Remember to wash your hands after you're done, Dr. Macabre."

I got out of there, feeling my face burning with a blush as well as the feel of Loren's ten o'clock shadow. That'd get him back for the shoulder rub.

The parking lot lights gleamed prettily from the water-beaded surface of my car—the only one left in the lot. As I dug out my keys, I finished off the pizza crust I'd been nibbling—the last bit of the dinner Dave had ordered for everyone who stayed to help Jacques clean up the e-mail problem—in other words, me and Loren, Ed having escaped this time. Yes, it showed Dave's generosity and compassion for his team to buy us two free dinners so early in the week. But I decided I would still bug him about that old prejudice-against-singles attitude—all the married people have families, so of course *they* get to go home instead of staying until midnight for the second day in a row). He would squirm before he realized I was teasing and told me not to give him a hard time.

I stretched hard and then settled into the car, flipping on the radio as usual, but the song it played didn't make any headway against the tune dancing around in my brain. It was one of my mom's favorite songs from way back when, the one the girl sings about kissing her teacher in the middle of geometry class—except that my mental video version starred Loren, not a blushing young math professor. I sighed. Clearly, it was time for The Talk again.

"Jones," I sternly told my reflection in the rearview mirror, "you are not going to do this. First off, you're overtired. Second, you're attaching more significance than necessary to a totally natural, casual touch. So he rubbed your shoulders for a second or two—you'd just tracked down G.D. Davis! Loren was just sharing the general excitement of the moment. The mere fact that he invaded your wider-than-usual sphere of personal space doesn't mean you need to go having emotional reactions or acting out like that. You practically kissed him goodnight, you goose. No, no. You know he doesn't mean those flirty things he says—he flirts with everybody except Stark, for crying out loud. He can't help playing with people's minds. It's like an addiction with him. Just a sec."

I turned the radio to avoid another stupid jewelry commercial. February! Yuck! "Third, I know you're lonely—we're lonely, I'm lonely, whatever—and he *is* cute, in his own infuriating way. Yeah, having somebody to massage your aching back and cuddle you would be great, but the point is, Loren's not the one. He's a friend and a colleague and the only guy you really associate with, but all that means is you're overreacting to a completely unconscious, platonic gesture. Get a grip on those maiden-lady hormones, girl. And fourth, this particular guy is not in the running, because for all his sense of humor and wit and competence, he's a hostile agnostic with severe abandonment and family issues, and you don't need that kind of complication in your life. Friend, great—boyfriend, trouble. You're looking for a nice Mormon guy with a testimony and a mission pin and all the other stuff your mom told you. Got it?"

Talking to yourself, according to my unpublished and original *Single Mormon Chick Handbook*, was a perfectly natural and acceptable thing to do when you lived alone—as long as you didn't answer back. So I had to swallow the irrational arguments that Loren wasn't exactly Mr. Touchy-Feely himself or that there were moments—like just after he literally swept me off my feet to get me out of the path of Gsmith's car—that he seemed to notice me as much as I noticed him. Or that the supply of nice Mormon guys with testimonies dropped down to virtually none, once you eliminated the ones who were already married and the rest who promptly got interested in someone else once they'd heard "thirty," "master's degree in computer science," and "FBI."

I took a cue from the last guy my visiting teachers had set me up with and promptly got myself interested in something else too, changing the radio station and singing along to the howling angst blasting out of my speakers. Well, as much as I could, anyway—the vocalist femme wasn't exactly singing as much as wailing her woes to the world, and I'm definitely not a soprano or a screamer. I do much better accompanying bands whose lead singers are mid-range tenors who don't go in for a lot of flourishes, so that's what I usually sing while I play my guitar. I'm not professional-musician caliber, but I do enjoy musical messing around. (The guitar is a big hit in Sunbeams, too.) However, I do enjoy hair-flinging dramatics—especially when I'm tense.

I had gotten halfway home and just about had the growling harmony on the fist-shaking chorus nailed when the song ended and the DJ came on, unusually sober as he informed all us night owls and insomniacs that Gideon had done it again, but this time it was even worse. I groaned, knowing what that meant even as the dash phone rang. Of course, the readout displayed Loren's number.

I poked the channel selector and picked up the receiver with the same motion. "I heard," I told Loren. "I've got it on 92.8 now." Tucking the receiver against my shoulder, I flipped a U-turn.

"Those, like General Alliance Motors, who value filthy lucre above human life, who sell the righteous for silver and the poor for a pair of shoes, shall be repaid according to their deeds. The Lord's enemies shall receive the just recompense of his fury, despite all their attempts at creating secure havens for themselves. The righteous servant, as Moses, will smite the Egyptian, defending those of my children who are oppressed and suffer wrong. Remember the warnings you have received: I will punish the world for its evil and the wicked for their iniquity; and I will cause the arrogance of the proud to cease and will lay low the haughtiness of the terrible.

"That was the statement KWAT received just thirty minutes ago from the cyberterrorist known as Gideon," continued Ayesha, the newsreader for FM 92.8, her husky voice solemn. "During the last hour, a source calling itself Gideon claimed responsibility for another attack on a major U.S. corporation in northwestern Oregon, this one against the automated GenM factory outside Portland. Reports at this time indicate that the factory may have been bombed in addition to the damage done to the computer system. The attack has caused millions of dollars in damages and left one man dead. According to material sent with the statement, Gideon accuses GenM of putting public safety in jeopardy by ignoring known defects in the design of its vehicles. Elian Cortez, a night security guard at GenM, was on duty when Gideon's attack occurred, causing the robots on the line to malfunction. Cortez was killed by the machinery, but the exact cause of his death has not been released."

I turned off the radio and ran back into the building. Loren intercepted me at the door with all the unreleased information saved on his portable console. "Give a guy a lift, lady?"

"Sure. We're going in person?" I asked, surprised. "Shouldn't we do some V-Net recon first? It's going to be a total media circus out there."

Loren caught my hand and spun me around—that ballroom-dance class came in handy at the strangest times, as I managed to follow the move and turn gracefully, back toward my car again. "Yes, we're going in person," he said. "GenM's factory bots aren't connected to a V-Net portal—I can't even see them from here. Another patented Gideon inside job, and I want to get there before some thumb-fingered civilian manages to erase whatever traces he left in their system."

"And Dave's okay with us going?" I let him into the passenger side and slid into my own seat without having to unlock the driver's door, as he'd leaned across and popped the door for me.

"He's great with it," Loren assured me, flipping his portable console open and jacking it into my car as usual. "He's got his hands full, negotiating with the Mounties about extraditing your little buddy G.D. Davis back here to face the wrath of Sunshine."

I smiled nastily, pulling out of the lot for the second time in an hour. "Three cheers for the intrepid denizens of the Great White North!"

"Too bad he doesn't have antlers. They could stuff his geeky head for your mantle."

Loren's playful expression suddenly sobered in the soft glow from his screen.

"What?" I asked, flipping on the GPS unit and specifying the GenM factory as the destination.

"You've got mail," Loren said.

The GPS grid wavered and then steadied, a bright green line snaking along the phantom roads. As I pulled out of the parking lot, the dot representing us glowed into amber life as it moved along the path. Ah, how I loved Gypsy, my ever-faithful navigator.

"I think that's supposed to sound perkier," I said lightly. But then a shiver of dread fluttered over my shoulders. "It's Gideon again, isn't it?"

"Yup. Addressed to Sekhmet, as usual. Get this—'*Do not rush to judgment. Remember, he that findeth his life shall lose it, and he that loseth his life for my sake shall find it. Elian Cortez, though his efforts to thwart his employer's just punishment were wrong, has gone to a better place. His blood will cry from the ground against General Alliance Motors, yet another victim of their lust for gain. They shall be as a fiery oven in the face of our anger, they shall be swallowed in wrath, and the fire shall devour them. It is regrettable that innocents should fall in the battle against evil, but it is better that one man should perish than a nation fall victim to wolves.*' So it's not Gideon's fault—big, nasty GenM made him kill somebody, and they're the ones who are going to have to pay for it."

"'Than a nation should dwindle and perish in unbelief,'" I said, correcting the misquotation as the shiver became an icy jolt down my back and arms.

"What?" Loren looked across at me, raising his eyebrow.

I stared out the windshield. "He used it wrong—the quote. It's first Nephi four-thirteen."

"From your Book of Mormon."

"From the Book of Mormon, yes." My mind spun through the possibilities: he knew who I was, knew I was Mormon, had finally managed to crack the encryption and careful habits that kept Sue Anne Jones separate from Sekhmet. Eep!

"Pretty good—the boy's broadening his horizons. Wonder if he'll pull something out of the Koran or the Bhagavad-Gita next." Loren reached over and shook my shoulder. "Hey, it's all right. It's also in the New Testament—that's what the Jewish leaders said to justify throwing Jesus to the Romans."

"I don't think Gideon sees himself in that light," I objected.

Loren shrugged. "Maybe not. But even if he is quoting the Book of Mormon, it doesn't mean he knows who you are. If he did, he would've sent it right to your personal account. Looking at it one way, it's an even bet—a lot of FBI types are Mormons, due to your never-ending patriotism, clean-cut lifestyle, and android work ethic. Looking at it another way, that's a heck of a quote to use to justify civilian casualties. What's the story with that, anyway?"

"It comes from Nephi, the prophet who wrote the account that starts the Book of Mormon." My heart rate was gradually slowing. He was right—plenty of wackos used that scripture; the church's exponential worldwide expansion had its drawbacks.

I filled Loren in on the story of Nephi and his brothers' quest to get their family records and scriptures from a despotic Jerusalem official named Laban, whom Nephi was commanded by God to execute. "It's better that Nephi kill Laban than Laban stay alive and Nephi's family leave for parts unknown without the scriptures—that's the 'dwindling in unbelief' part."

"And because Laban was a lowdown thief anyway, it's no big loss, right?" Loren asked sharply. "A license to kill. Handy. Why don't you guys invoke that escape clause more often? Make it a lot easier to deal with those nuts who go after your missionaries every once in awhile, if you declared open season on enemies of the church and issued pistols along with pamphlets."

"Excuse me, Mr. Vigilante," I said. I'd pulled the same argument on my mom when I was fourteen and had prayed about it since, so I knew the answer to this one. "But the situation's entirely different. Nephi acted on a direct order from God himself, in what you could consider defense of his entire family's spiritual lives. And remember that he didn't jump at the chance — it took a personal revelation, and even then God had to tell him twice."

"Or the voices in his head had to tell him twice," Loren suggested.

I shook my head. "Uh, uh — can't go there. If he's a fictional character, he can't have schizophrenia. If he's real, he had to have real revelations, or God wouldn't have included his experiences in divinely preserved scripture."

"So God ordered a hit on Laban — that's extreme," Loren argued. "Why not just take the guy's clothes? He's already passed-out drunk."

"All right, I'll give you my take on this, but I'll warn you, it's not scripture."

Loren nodded.

"I just think that God sees death differently than we do. For him, it's just leaving one state for another. From everything I've seen, he cares less about how you die than what state your soul's in when you do. He wasn't telling Nephi to completely annihilate Laban, just to get him out of the way of a vital operation that he'd already refused to cooperate with."

I glanced at Loren's still profile and then continued. "I know it sounds weird, but in a cosmic sense it works. I'm willing to trust that God knows what he's doing, and that he loved Laban as well as Nephi, and that Laban got all the chances he let himself have. It all comes down to him loving us and us trusting him."

Please believe that, I added silently. *If you possibly can — it'll make your life so much less of a struggle.*

"So, anyway," I went on, "we'll go with what Jesus told us in everyday life and not make ourselves exceptions to the rules. The standard operating procedure is turn the other cheek — we don't kill anybody. And we surely don't appreciate wildebeests like Gideon trampling the scriptures to justify themselves."

I looked over at him again, trying to judge whether he got it — and even more importantly, whether he accepted it.

"Hey, I'm not arguing that your God's always compassionate," Loren said. "There are plenty of precedents for divinely ordered vicious behavior — the Israelites wiping out the indigenous inhabitants of Palestine, for instance." He met my eyes and smiled. "Okay, you win. Lying, cheating, killing, stealing, abandonment, adultery, ordering hits on people — the Bible's full of situational morality, and it looks like the Book of Mormon is too."

"So it must be inspired," I suggested brightly. His hostility toward a Heavenly Father he refused to admit he believed in wasn't something I really knew how to address, so I settled for the next best thing. "You ought to read it for yourself, so we can have all kinds of passionate arguments before you finally admit it's both true and okay."

"Mm-hmm." He turned back to his screen. "Tell you what, let's read this instead. Gideon's hit the automated GenM factory out here—specifically, the one that's been turning out cars with known safety problems. Seems the doors on their vehicles have a tendency to lock up at unfortunate times—specifically when there's a crash and the car's under water or on fire."

I blinked. "And they can keep selling these things? What about the safety regulations?"

"Doesn't happen enough to qualify for recalls or sanctions, and GenM's been very slick about keeping most of the information under wraps and using their influence to keep the powers that be from officially noticing. It's one of those situations when the company board asked, 'How many people will be badly hurt in accidents, and how much will they sue us for?' and weighed it against 'How much money will we have to spend retooling our plant and redesigning our cars?' Turns out they decided it was worth their while to pay the settlement money. So far, they've paid out settlements for three fatal crashes and twenty-seven maimings—without even putting up much of a kick with the insurance companies. How considerate of them."

"Very," I agreed. Once again I found that I had a hard time faulting Gideon for his choice of targets—but this time the real victim and his family got all my sympathy. Gideon hadn't just financially hurt companies or stockholders this time. "What about Mr. Cortez?"

"As usual, the media got it wrong out of the gate. Cortez isn't a night guard—he's an engineer supervisor, there to oversee the plant's operation after an upgrade to the robots' program. GenM's official information on him is pretty sketchy, as usual— Elian Cordova-Cortez, thirty-one, married to Reiko Mara Cortez, two kids, lived in Portland, worked for GenM for two years, one letter of commendation for suggesting design improvements."

After reading the vital statistics off the monitor, Loren turned it to show me the security-badge photo included with the personnel file. I glanced at it, catching an impression of dark-brown eyes and a wry smile before the traffic light turned green. "Gideon didn't send in a hit squad and shoot him, I hope."

"No, nothing so direct," Loren replied. "The update to the robots' operating system apparently included one of Gideon's patented additions. It turned the robot assemblers against each other and the line, so they started to disassemble and destroy each other, starting at one end of the plant and going right down to the other. Cortez called in an emergency and left the control booth, probably trying to get to the power breakers. He got partway there, but one of the swinging robot arms smashed into him. The troubleshooting team got there and managed to pull him out, but by the time the police and ambulance got there, he didn't need them."

"Interesting way to put it. What about Gideon's agent this time?"

"I found a Gideon Johnson in the employee database—again, hired in the last three months, a pretty good programmer doing clean-up work on the latest operating system upgrade for the robots. Stark's on his way to ask him some questions right now."

"Did he look like anybody we know?" I thought about G.D. Davis and his skinny-nerd avatar and about Gsmith's round, bland face.

"No, not from his temporary ID photo. That photo is all the identification we've got, too, if the address and contact info he provided turns out as fake as the others have been—which it probably will." Loren added philosophically, "These guys are slick, gotta give them that."

"G.D. Davis wasn't so slick," I reminded him, still feeling nastily satisfied at the nerd boy's public repudiation. That'd show him to brag in a low-down pickup joint about beating NIPC.

Just then, the factory's sign loomed above us: GENERAL ALLIANCE MOTORS—TRANSPORTATION FOR THE NEXT MILLENNIUM.

"And Gideon promptly tossed him out of the club for it," Loren reminded me right back. "They've got a tight no-slipups policy, which is good for them but bad for us." He leaned forward, looking toward the cluster of flashing lights down the dark road. "All right, there they are, the media pack in full cry. Turn down over here—there should be a back way in. We can avoid the prying eyes of the public's right to know."

There *was* a back way, and the sheriff's deputy guarding the narrow gate waved us through when I showed him my FBI credentials. We pulled into the lot behind the huge, boxy line of factory buildings to find another deputy nervously guarding the door. Viewing Loren's laptop with deep suspicion as he inspected our IDs, he gave me a short answer when I asked where the control booth was located. "Down to the left. You'll see it."

We slipped through the service door — marked Authorized Personnel Only, which I figured included us under the circumstances — and into a cavernous space so huge that it felt like it should have its own clouds. At the far end, bright spotlights and noise filtered through the factory's open main doors, but back here the silence reigned supreme, broken only by the sluggish drip of lubricating fluids. The assembly line occupied the center of the room, large bins and racks of entire car sections and other miscellaneous parts lined up along the walls.

That summed up the organized aspects of the scene. The contents of the bins lay strewn across the line and the floor, random parts and auto carcasses thrown hither and yon in wild abandon. The gigantic mechanical arms of the assembly robots jutted at bizarre angles, some broken off at the bases or joints, others frozen in full extension as they reached for each other. The running track itself was in ragged pieces, entire sections ripped from the floor and warped into a nightmare roller coaster. An occasional burst of sparks erupted from a dying battery or as the last discharge from a ripped cable. Orange and yellow emergency lights glinted off the bright edges of torn metal and cast chaotic shadows.

"It's like a *Motor Trend* cover designed by Hieronymus Bosch," Loren said, poking the stripped gears of one machine with his toe.

"Or a dedicated Luddite's vision of *Paradise Regained*," I added. "We're way beyond throwing wooden shoes in the works here. Maybe this wasn't Gideon at all — it could've been the unions. They're not big on the whole idea of unmanned factories, worker shortage or no."

"And they just imitated his psycho-prophet writing style?" Loren gave me an impatient-patient look. "And just happened to send you an e-mail about it? Nah. This is Gideon, all right. You want to hope for something, hope that nobody out there turns the power back on. This wouldn't be a comfortable place to stand if these big buggers start moving again."

I rolled my eyes at that, but my imagination gladly conjured a vivid scenario: the huge, metallic arm hanging over us, the one with the four claw-looking things on it, finishing its grab and lifting me to the ceiling before squishing me into Sueberry jam. I shook my head to wipe out that preposterous vision and stepped gingerly over a skeletal armature, broken cables trailing from its metal bones. I had just gotten one foot over the thing when it whirred and shifted.

"Yow!" I leapt backward, slamming into Loren.

He held onto me, putting both arms around me and turning us around to look at the offending bit of wreckage. "Hey, hey, it's all right—it just shifted when we stepped on the plate it was resting on. See? It slid a little bit, and now it's stopped. No worries."

So much for my stern soliloquy in the car; why did he have to smell like that? I bonked my head on his shoulder and wiggled away, fixing him with a reproving stare as he struggled to hide a smile. "Did you do that on purpose?"

"Do what on purpose?" He lost the struggle. A wicked grin spread across his face.

"Give me the big imagination boost, then make that thing wiggle when I stepped over it." I knew it sounded silly and vain even as I said it. Great—embarrassing myself twice in under a minute. This had to be a personal record. To quote one of my favorite realist philosophers, my life needs a rewind/erase button!

"Well, if I'd known you were going to leap into my arms and climb me like a tree—" He paused, then finished thoughtfully, "I probably would've done it on purpose."

Maybe I didn't need that button after all. I looked away, irrationally warm from the implied compliment. Then I pointed through the frozen melee. "Looks like that's the control booth."

We picked our way through the metallic mayhem, avoiding twisted wrecks, crunching over tiny cubes of shattered glass, and skirting pools of oil and transmission fluid, without any more false alarms. Loren reached down to pull me up onto the massive grappling arm of a toppled crane, and then he neatly slithered down the other side. I balanced on the upturned platform, surveying the devastation. It amazed me that all this twisted metal sprang from a few lines of saboteur code. I knew that computer malfunctions could and did lead to real-life consequences, but in my experience they'd always involved more abstract elements, like bank-account totals or identity theft or erased data.

"Come on, Sue." Loren held up his hands. "Computer first, gawking later."

I slid off the metal, catching his hands as he jumped me down. "It's unbelievable. All this wreckage just from a program."

"Believe it," he said, pulling me along. "You're probably going to see more of the same, with all the companies turning to automation to save themselves payroll money. Even if it's not crackers infecting the system, accidents happen."

"I hope no more like this," I said as we came to a halt beside a gruesomely dark-red stain marking the wall and spreading across the floor under a broken crane arm. Cortez had been only ten feet from the breaker circuits when the flailing robot caught him.

"Me too." For once, Loren didn't add a flip comment.

"How'd they turn it off?" I asked softly.

"Support team cut the power from outside. The line wasn't hooked to the UPS." Loren's voice was lower and more sober than usual.

The computer system in the control booth still hummed faintly, however, drawing its energy from the uninterruptible power supply lurking in the utility closet. I pulled my hand into my jacket sleeve and brushed broken glass off the desk and seats. Loren hefted the tireless axle that had flown through the windows and landed on the other side of the desk. Then we checked the four monitors that beamed security-camera pictures from various sectors of the line. Three reflected the robotic wasteland we had just passed through; one displayed the crowd filling the loading area in front of the factory, sheriffs keeping reporters, gawkers, and possible looters far outside the doors.

"Gideon sent word to every major media outlet in the region about fifteen minutes before the altered program drove the machines wild," Loren told me. "They got here only a few minutes after GenM's support team did."

"Too bad he didn't see fit to warn Cortez," I growled.

"Didn't want to give away his game, especially not to a competent programmer. If Cortez knew what was happening, he probably could've stopped it—or at least turned off the system before it took effect." Loren keyed into the system, settling into the chair Cortez had abandoned. A few moments of exploration and muttering crescendoed into an expletive that he had to abruptly strangle. He hit the desk with his fist.

"Rats!" I supplied helpfully. Actually, I put more than a little fire into it myself. On the screen I'd co-opted, the innards of the computer system resembled neatly structured programs as much as the scene on the factory floor recalled the orderly precision of a Swiss clockmaker's shop. Gideon had finished off his latest magnum opus with a final line that completely destroyed the system's memory. Yes, we could probably reconstruct the programs out of the digital spaghetti and meatballs, but it would take tons of effort—and time that I didn't think we had.

"He's done a real job here," I said. "Being up on criminal mischief and theft charges is nothing at all compared to a murder rap. He knows it, too—wiping out the system to cover his tracks and trying to justify killing somebody by quoting scriptures out of context."

"Aren't we supposed to liken scriptures unto ourselves?" Loren asked.

"*Et tu*, Brute?" I snapped. "You've been digging into the Mormon quote file too? You're supposed to read the whole thing, not just pull out the bits that suit your current purpose and shrug off the real meaning."

"That, however, is exactly what our killer excels at doing," said a voice behind us.

Loren and I skewed around in our chairs to see a rumpled Dave standing in the doorway with the much slicker-looking stranger who had broken into our conversation. The new guy actually wore a hat, one of those snap-brim affairs, and a vivid stripe of starched white shirt showed under his black-cloth coat. He looked like something out of a black-and-white film, only somehow less warm and alive.

"Sue Jones, Loren Hunter, this is Charles Von Towe, a psychological specialist from bureau headquarters. Special Agent Shawndell Lincoln recommended him for the assignment after reviewing the preliminary statement G.D. Davis gave the Canadian authorities." Dave made the introductions with the completely neutral expression of a supervisor who knows he's about to get trapped between his boss and his subordinates.

"A psychological specialist, huh?" Loren asked disgustedly. "You mean *profiler*, right? Our Gideon's coming up in the world. Obviously the bureau's decided he's not just a slippery cracker— he's a career murderer and possible serial killer, so they send Dr. Van Helsing here to solve this whole case for us."

"Well, you know, Loren," I broke in, "it's totally appropriate. In fact, it hearkens right back to Gideon's first job at Sunshine Foods— the guy's a cereal killer." I couldn't keep a straight face any more as I added, "Well, at least a cereal kidnapper."

At least Loren cracked a smile at that. Dave's stress level, however, had obviously trumped his sense of humor. He didn't even blink, let alone smile.

Von Towe's cold expression failed to thaw even half a degree. "The individual to whom you refer as *Gideon* is a megalomaniac narcissist with antisocial personality disorder. He seeks to reaffirm his internal self-portrait by creating powerful reflections in the stream of others' social interactions. With each successful foray, his hunger for external reinforcement increases."

"Oh! Doc! I know this one!" Loren couldn't restrain himself even in the face of Dave's warning look—or maybe because of it. "So Gideon will keep pulling these hacks, getting bigger and wilder with each one, until we either catch him or he takes over the entire world!"

"Or until he undergoes a complete psychotic break," Von Towe intoned, "which will make him even more dangerous than he is now." He cast his Olympian gaze in Dave's general direction. "I shall inspect the scene of the crime."

"Do tell us what your visions reveal," Loren called after him as he stalked into the chaotic mess of the factory floor, Dave following after a very indiscreet eye roll at us.

I leaned back in the operator's chair, crossing my ankles on the console desk. "My, aren't we lucky we've got an expert psychologist here to fill us in on such unusual conclusions? Thank you, Shawnie. I wonder what G.D. Davis told the Mounties."

Loren leaned out the broken window, watching Von Towe's progress. "I wonder if his extraordinary powers of perception will tell him that the actual scene of the crime is right here." He stood up again, tapping the monitor absently. "He's putting on the big black-cape show, pretending he's something out of a detective movie. Thinks he's tracking a thrill killer. Guy doesn't even realize that Gideon isn't one person—it's a bunch of hackers making a backward attempt to put a little justice into the world."

"Justice?" I yipped. "Justice by stealing? Justice by destroying property? Justice by killing somebody who was only doing his job?"

"That wasn't part of the plan," Loren said tightly. "Cortez was just in the wrong place at the wrong time."

"Oh, like Gideon really cares who he hurts, as long as he gets his big media circus!" I pulled the forensic program out of the half-wiped computer and tossed it toward Loren. I didn't notice that he looked a lot paler than usual until he leaned into the monitor light to catch it.

"They're doing what they think they must to overthrow the

vicious corporate system that this factory represents," Loren said, snatching the disk out of the air. He scowled at me. "Oh, yeah—you can't understand that, can you? You and your nice sheltered life. You're as bad as that charlatan Van Helsing. Worse—at least he realizes he's a fraud."

He stomped out, muttering about trying to track down somebody who probably saved dozens of lives by destroying this particular factory.

I tried to catch his arm, but he shrugged me off without even looking. I watched him brush past Dave and the bureau's profiler, stalking into the mangled darkness. The shadows blended into his black hair, swallowed his dark jacket.

The horrible suspicion growing in my mind got brighter as his silhouette faded. Gideon knew so much about me, quoted Book of Mormon passages at me, sent me personal e-mails trying to convince me he was right; Loren was extremely socially conscious, he hadn't been very intense about finding Gideon, and he wasn't exactly a stranger to the chaotic-anarchist side of the law. Eek again! Dumb as the thought was, however, it kept nipping at the back of my mind, drawing the shadows closer.

I spent the next two hours scouring the control room and computers for Gideon's handiwork, then I made my way to the factory's front doors. At least I didn't have to scramble over metallic dinosaur skeletons on the way; the GenM support team, ambulance guys, and sheriffs had cleared most of the mess in that direction. Only a few of the most die-hard reporters still lingered in the dark parking lot, watching the mixture of FBI personnel and deputies securing the crime scene. I spotted Dave across the pavement and caught his attention as he saw Von Towe into one of the field agents' tinted-window vehicles. The profiler's studiously masklike face regarded us both enigmatically as the car pulled away.

"Dave, have you seen Loren?" I asked quietly.

My obviously over-stressed boss glanced around, as if expecting his missing hacker to suddenly appear out of the pavement. Then he brightened as his memory came to his rescue. "I saw him getting into a sheriff's truck about an hour ago. Said he wanted to get started on analyzing the factory system."

"Thanks," I said. *See?* the nasty little voice in the back of my head whispered. *He's made his getaway—and in a cop car, no less. A very bold, revolutionary touch there. Very Loren.* "Dave, what did G.D. Davis say?"

"He said that Gideon is a dangerous psychopath and begged the Mounties to promise to keep him safe." Dave kept his voice low on the off chance that one of the lingering media hounds was equipped with a directional mike.

"And you believe that enough—or Shawnie's boss does—to send a specialist out here." I sighed. "Dave, he had to say something to save his skin, so he's trying to convince everybody he's the innocent victim here. Oldest game in the book. I'm surprised D.C. fell for it."

Dave looked at me, managerial concern seeping into his deliberately vague expression. "You look beat, Sue. Don't worry about Von Towe. Go home, sleep in—come in around noon tomorrow. You're doing a good job."

Oh, great—as I drove home alone, I had two uncomfortable thought-phantoms to keep me company. As if I didn't have enough to bother myself about with this irrational suspicion of Loren, now I had to worry why Dave had told me not to worry about Von Towe. The logical next thought in the chain hit me hard enough that I had to jam on the brakes to keep from sailing right through a red light. They thought Loren was Gideon too—and probably figured I was in on it with him! Dave didn't want me to think that he believed it too, and he probably didn't, but—

"Enough," I told myself aloud as I turned onto the freeway. "You've been up for about thirty-six hours straight. That nap you took when your head hit the desk didn't count. You're overtired, and you need to go home and sleep. Your boss just gave you permission to come in late. What more excuse do you need?"

Much to my surprise, I actually did sleep—in fact, I crashed like a rock the moment I got home, barely managing to kick out of my work clothes and kneel for a short but heartfelt prayer—for Cortez, for his family, and for our own efforts.

A lightweight bounce on the mattress near my knee half woke me, but then I let the rhythm of four paws slinking along my body lull me back toward sleep. Just the cat. A cold nose attached to a warm, purring body poked into my ear.

Wait a minute—I didn't have a cat.

"Loren?" I called drowsily. "Did you bring a cat home?"

No answer. Odd. I sat up, rubbing my eyes and then gently shoving the kitten away. His brothers and sisters pounced among the wispy curtains trailing from the elaborate canopy of my bed. I slipped through the curtains and brushed past the pair of ghosts waiting for me in the hallway, holding up a hand against their standard moaning complaints. "Not now. Have you seen Loren?"

They hadn't, but the cat that morphed into Jaylee from my Primary class indicated that she had. She took my clawed hand, chewing the ends of her dress sashes as she indistinctly asked, "What are we learning about today?"

"Megalomania," said Von Towe, stroking his goatee as he stood before the blaze roaring in the lion's-mouth fireplace. "It manifests itself in irrational confidence and desire for external reinforcement — particularly from small children. Is there anything you wish to tell us, Miss Jones?"

"No," I snarled, furious at him for invading my home. As if the ghosts weren't bad enough! And to invade when I had my Primary class here made it even worse. They raced around the room, shouting and laughing.

"Don't let him scare you," Loren said from the other side of the hearth.

I turned toward him, relieved. "Oh, there you are. Loren, did you bring a bunch of cats home?" My question trailed off. "Why do you have wings?"

He gave me a bright, angelic smile. "Wings represent the speed of thought. All angels have them. Servants of God have wings to indicate their swiftness in dealing justice."

Von Towe glided forward, his cape flapping around him as he held a silver Rorschach square toward Loren. A stream of diagnoses flowed from his motionless lips: "Antisocial personality disorder. Borderline attention-deficit syndrome. Narcissism — "

The floor shivered and lumped up under the carpet. I caught as many of my Sunbeams as I could, pulling them away to an alcove containing a short table covered with papers and crayons. They fought over colors as I hurriedly closed the curtains. Loren still smiled, but his face had flattened into bland, standard beauty under the seraphic glow. He tossed a disk into the fire, which flared into binary smoke that filled the room with hazy number ones and zeros. Von Towe's psychological mantra rose to a scream as the bumps under the carpet ripped through, their mechanical tendrils flailing madly toward him. The metal pillars supporting the hall ceiling twisted, their programming spinning out of control. One caught Von Towe, smashing him into the maw of the fireplace; he flailed, a bug on a pin, as the ceiling collapsed, raining blocks of stone down toward us.

"Come with us," the avatar wearing Loren's face called, extending a hand to me. Gsmith and G.D. Davis stood behind him in the V-Net portal, anxiously waiting.

"Miss Jones," Cortez whispered, held against the wall by a broken pillar. "Help me."

I reached toward him, but the floor twisted and collapsed. I sprang away, but too late; I fell into the dark with the blocks of stone from the walls, my house falling around me.

"Oh, jeez," I groaned into my pillow, then rolled over and rubbed my eyes. Talk about taking your work home with you. Sure, Lehi had dreams that showed him the entire Plan of Salvation in one surrealist landscape. Me? I just played out my constant feelings of inadequacy as a Primary teacher and created imaginary scenarios that starred Loren as my arch nemesis.

I knew better than to actually ask for divine revelation about Gideon's identity and whereabouts as I knelt beside my bed for morning prayer; it's a wicked and adulterous generation that asks for a sign, after all — though I fit only one of those two criteria by any stretch of the imagination. Besides, I already knew the answer: work it out for yourself, then ask if you've got it right. That's the way it had always worked in my life, and in a way I appreciated the vote of confidence.

I got up, stretched, and pulled on my workout clothes. The newscasters reiterated Gideon's statement twice just during my round of stretches and punches. GenM's spokesman, looking genuinely upset, assured viewers of the company's deep regret for their employee's sad fate and of their commitment to the continued safety and driving satisfaction of the general public.

The next sound-bite segment featured Dave, caught in the camera lights just after I left, stating that the FBI and NIPC were continuing their investigations and making progress in tracking the responsible cyberterrorists. He did not get to spread the good news of yesterday's victory, however; the shot shifted to FBI headquarters in Washington, where the FBI spokeswoman assigned to the case, Special Agent Shawndell Lincoln — *hi, Shawnie* — informed us that one of the band of crackers responsible for the GenM attack as well as the invasion of Sunshine Foods and StarWest Bank had been apprehended in Vancouver. Canadian police had taken Chad Glock, alias G.D. Davis, into custody, and he was cooperating with the FBI.

Shawnie refused to reveal the details, giving the camera a cool, official look and informing the reporter that she did not wish to compromise a continuing investigation. That didn't stop the media mavens from speculating widely — and wildly, given that they had relatively few facts. Gideon was a Canadian nationalist! No, he was a radical ex-member of the Guerilla Christian Militia! Over shots of the factory, both last night's dark bulk and this morning's gray industrial block, Michelle recapped the story for those of us who had come in late. They had finally gotten some of their facts straight—the factory had not been bombed, and Mr. Cortez was a programming supervisor instead of a night watchman.

I managed to keep an objective emotional distance from the whole thing until Mrs. Cortez appeared onscreen, walking through the shouting crowd outside the hospital. She looked stunned but dignified, brushing through the reporters without saying a word, softly thanking the police officer who held the door of her car open for her before she drove away. Another woman and man accompanied her, equally somber and quiet in the glare of the cameras; Michelle identified them as a brother and sister-in-law of the victim.

The victim. The word seemed to drain the reality away from the man I had seen in the ID photo, flattening him into a one-dimensional image yellowing in an old newspaper after the public's voyeuristic, secondhand grief ebbed. But he had been this woman's husband, a daddy to his kids, a brother, friend, coworker—a person with a soul, who had meant something to other souls. I hoped that Mrs. Cortez knew that he still existed, that he still cared, that she and her kids could be with their husband and daddy again. I couldn't imagine facing a death not knowing that; even with the firm belief that death was just a door, not an ending, life felt very lonely for those who had to stay.

I slowly straightened from a stretch and clicked off the stupidly loud commercial that replaced the newscast, tears gathering behind my eyes, lumping up in my throat. Letting them run down my face with the hot, soapy shower water, I felt fiercely proud of Mrs. Cortez and her quiet, classy dignity.

When my parents were killed, there had been cameras and shouted questions at the airport too, reporters asking how it felt to lose loved ones in a plane crash. Some of the tearstained families had sobbed anew for the cameras; my sister Penny and I had held each others' hands tightly and kept our eyes down as we left. Death should not be proud, but it did deserve dignity and privacy. So did our parents, who had never drawn attention to themselves in their quiet, generous lives—they merited an affectionate goodbye, not a circus. I hoped Mrs. Cortez and her children could do the same for their husband and father.

The dream image of Elian Cortez filled my mind's eye, asking me to help him. And I hadn't. Rationally, I knew that I couldn't have prevented his death; I wasn't even there when the accident happened, and I had no forewarning, no way to guess where Gideon would strike next or that he would cause such horrible consequences. Emotionally, however, I had to fight the guilt that insisted if I had only caught Gideon sooner, cracked his code when he broke into Sunshine Foods and sent Stark to apprehend him, Mr. Cortez would have come home to his family this morning, and they would not have had to face the curious stares and a future without him.

I looked at myself in the steamy mirror, red-eyed and twig-haired — not exactly a heroic image. "So you didn't stop it from happening," I said to myself. "That's too bad, but you can't make it up to them by mentally flogging yourself and bawling. So include them in your prayers, send a sympathy card, and catch this slime mold before he hurts somebody else!"

That made me feel a bit better, put some vehemence into my fingers as I rubbed my hair semidry and marched into the bedroom, where I buttoned my shirt as if I was strapping on the armor of God. Expiating guilt by transforming it into righteous anger. What would a psychologist say about that? I didn't actually ask even when I had the chance.

It felt strange to walk into work at eleven-fifteen in the first place, but finding our usually mausoleum-like cubicle farm buzzing with activity made the experience even weirder. Ed had pulled a makeshift cardboard ceiling and door across his cubicle, shutting out the unwelcome crowd. Chattering bodies occupied fully half of the customarily empty seats — which only made Loren's absence more blatant.

"Hey, Sue," Pinky called, rolling her chair over.

"Hey, Pinky," I said, pulling a smile I didn't feel. Pinky usually worked from home, investigating fraud in the sprawling online marketplaces. She had a real nose for ferreting out corruption and dishonesty. Unfortunately, she also had a voracious taste for gossip and a compulsive tendency to share whatever dirt she dug up. No wonder she decided to come in today, I thought, catching a glimpse of Von Towe's scarecrow shape in Dave's office. In this case it looked like several of our colleagues shared her curiosity. They casually sauntered by Dave's office on their way to get too many cups of coffee or pretended to talk to each other as they stood in the aisle.

Pinky took the direct route, openly watching the scene through the window in the office door. "You're coming in late," she observed.

"I was up late." I flicked on my console. Sekhmet woke and stretched, looking curiously over the top border of my e-mail browser.

"So, where's Loren?" Pinky asked.

"He was up late too," I replied, irritated at her fishing but not above doing some of my own. "Why? Do you need him for something?"

She laughed throatily, shaking her curly halo of hair. "Me? I don't need him for anything. Darlin', I like more meat on a fella's bones. It's this new shrink that's got the hots for our skinny ex-cracker buddy. He's already asked us about Loren, what we've noticed, our professional opinions and all. Dave's pulled out his court files and personnel folder. Looks like somebody upstairs thinks Blue Eyes has been up to something." She leaned forward confidentially. "Is it this Gideon case you've been working on, or has he been hacking into Aireon again?"

Oh, right—like I'd confide anything to her! As Loren said, there are several efficient methods of widely disseminating information: telephone, television, tell-a-Pinky. Darn Von Towe's hide, and Dave's too, for being so indiscreet. If Pinky knew they were investigating Loren, then everyone else in the office did—and everyone outside the office too.

"Haven't the slightest," I told Pinky, opening an e-mail as if I were too busy to talk right now. Actually, this particular message thoroughly captured my attention—it contained a transcript of Chad Glock's statement. I skimmed over the biographical facts—he was a doctoral student, single, originally from the Seattle area, et cetera—and got to the meat of the matter. As Von Towe had hinted, the cracker I still thought of as G.D. Davis claimed that he'd met someone named Gideon in a hacker's club on the V-Net. Gideon had suckered him into crime, fixing it for him to go to work at Sunshine as an intern, then convincing him to help plant some extra code in the drone trucks' program as a prank. He hadn't known that Gideon meant to steal the groceries and was horrified when he saw the reports on the news and realized what a nasty customer he'd gotten mixed up with. He'd already gone on to graduate school in Vancouver, building a completely blameless life, though he did still see Gideon on the V-Net occasionally—just socially, of course.

He explained his attack on our computer as misguided self-defense; he'd worried that we were getting too close to Gideon and that Gideon would sell him out, so he'd hit our computers in a panic, hoping to eliminate the evidence that implicated him in Gideon's activities. He didn't explain how he thought a denial-of-service attack and an e-mail blizzard would eliminate evidence, or why he'd bragged about shutting down NIPC, or why he'd called to Gideon for help when I caught him. He did offer to tell everything he knew and testify against Gideon — in exchange for immunity, which meant he wouldn't give us anything until his deal came through. I suspected he wouldn't be able to give us much. Gideon had clearly kept G.D. Davis at arm's length. Once again, good for him, bad for us.

"You may want to find out what Hunter's up to for your own good," Pinky advised cattily, irritated at my inattention. "Because they pulled your file too."

Dave interrupted before I had a chance to think of a response to that. "Sue, glad you're here. Have you got a minute?" Pinky gave me a knowing smirk and retired to her seldom-used cubicle.

No, Dave, I don't, I wanted to say. *And don't act like you've caught me sneaking into work late, either. You told me to sleep in!* Instead I just smiled at Pinky again and said, "Sure."

Nothing like the fish-eyed stare of an FBI psychological specialist to make me want to start talking about the time I met a Martian in the backyard, but I managed to restrain myself. It wasn't fair to take my pique at Pinky and Dave out on this guy, even if Shawnie did send him because she didn't think I could handle it. Whoa. Calm.

"How long have you worked for the National Infrastructure Protection Center?" Von Towe asked, gesturing for me to take one of the visitor's seats in front of Dave's desk. Dave himself took the other; Von Towe had appropriated the faux-leather boss's chair.

"Five years now. I started just after I got my master's degree," I told him. He didn't write it down, but that didn't surprise me; he already knew that from my personnel folder.

"And to what cases have you been assigned?"

"Several," I said impatiently. I didn't have time or patience for this. Dr. Mifune had helped both Penny and me when we'd gone to him for grief counseling, and I knew that forensic psychology actually could yield valid results — but this guy's vampire routine rubbed all my fur the wrong way. Either he'd watched one too many V-Net documentaries on FBI profilers, or he'd been the guinea pig in a secret government experiment on eliminating all natural personality.

I decided to see if he responded to direct communication. "Dr. Von Towe, what do you want to know? Don't try to get into my head through a back door, and don't worry about dancing around my sensitive feelings. I've done the whole counseling thing already, and I'm just fine. You've already seen my file, so you know my record. Need more personal info? I'm single, have no living family besides a sister and her husband, and have been a devout Mormon all my life. Now, let's get to the real reason you're doing this."

Dave shot me an admonishing look, but Von Towe just leaned back, steepling his fingers. "As a Mormon, you consider yourself Christian, do you not?"

"Yes, I do." I leaned back myself. Nope—he wasn't going to drop the mask. Dang.

"And are you familiar with the Bible?" he continued.

"Yes, I am. In fact, I'm more than familiar with it—I've read it several times. Well, the New Testament part of it, anyway—the Old Testament gets too over-the-top for me. I'm even better with the Book of Mormon, and I've got a passing acquaintance with the Koran, Lotus Sutra, Bhagavad-Gita, and Shinto origin tales too. Comparative religion class in college." I leaned forward. "In fact, I'm familiar enough with various versions of scripture to know that there's a special place in hell for people who use God's name to justify their own agendas. I'm trying to catch Gideon, not help him."

"But you do admit you've corresponded with him," Dave said, earning a cold look from Von Towe and a hot one from me.

"Corresponded with him!" I snapped. "That's a way to put it. He got my ID from Sunshine's system and sent me a mash note to get me off his back. Crackers do that, Dave—they like playing cat and mouse with the cops. You know that. Since you've been tracking my e-mails, you also know I told him I wasn't going for his excuses and I wasn't interested in joining his band of wrong-headed cyber-revolutionaries."

"Despite your sympathy for Gideon's stated goals?" Von Towe shot back.

"I have sympathy for Mrs. Cortez and her kids. And for the poor farmers Sunshine gouges with extra delivery fees. And for the people who have gotten hurt in car crashes or lost money to StarWest's financial shenanigans. I have no sympathy for criminals and cowards who hide behind computers and set themselves up as agents of divine justice."

"What about your partner, Mr. Hunter? Does he share your distaste for Gideon's methods?" This time the profiler kept the question clinically neutral, as if he didn't really care either way.

I didn't even answer him—I just turned to Dave and said, "You're kidding, right? Pinky said you've been asking questions about Loren. Are you out of your mind?"

Dave looked at the psychological specialist instead of answering me. "Have you got everything you need, Dr. Von Towe? I can handle this."

Von Towe nodded judicially. "Certainly. I shall expect your report."

"You do that," Dave said, escorting Von Towe the four steps to the door of the office. The profiler swept out, ignoring the fascinated stares that covertly followed him.

"Look, it's nothing personal. It's just that Loren's got the background for it." Dave flopped into his chair. "Listen, Sue, they didn't send Von Towe here specifically to look for Gideon."

"He's here to check up on Loren," I announced more than asked.

Dave nodded, looking pained. "I know it's hard for you, but look at it logically. He and Gideon may not be the same person after all, but we've been getting pressure from the higher-ups to check out a possible rogue programmer—specifically, Loren. If you don't know him like we do, he fits all the criteria. We picked him up for trying to even up social injustices by hacking into other systems. He still tries to break into Aireon on a regular basis. He's a member of half a dozen hacker groups all over the V-Net. There's precedent for him taking extreme action. That outfit he was with, Sherris and her goons, didn't hesitate to cause some mayhem, either."

"They didn't, but he did. When he found out what they really were, he helped us stop them. As for frequenting hacker lairs, of course he does. I do too. So did you, before you got sucked into management. So do we all. You've got to know what people are up to out there! As for Aireon, they're just the biggest target out there, and he's—" I stopped abruptly. The whole situation was too silly. I laughed at myself for even entertaining the idea, however briefly, and for giving myself such an emotional upheaval over it.

"Dave," I gasped. "Listen to yourself! Are you actually thinking that Loren is Gideon? Oh, sure, Loren technically could be

Gideon—they'd never been seen in the same room, after all, and Loren has long since beaten the system as far as having multiple avatars. I wouldn't put it past him to use the Seventh Angel as an alias, either, come to that. But can you seriously picture our sarcastic, agnostic, bleeding heart as a pompous, humorless, Jesus-freak fascist? Can you see him as the general of a motley mob of crackers? Loren, whose report card never read *plays well with others*?" I took a deep breath and let it out slowly. "Seriously, Dave, with all due respect to Shawnie and Dr. Von Towe and the experts back at national headquarters, Loren Hunter is not Gideon."

Dave sighed again. "Then where is he? Von Towe's already asked."

"Who? Gideon or Loren?"

"Mr. Hunter," Dave said, adding a reproving look.

"I have no idea," I told him. Then I added, just as honestly, "But I'll bet he's intentionally avoiding you. You haven't exactly given him a lot of incentive to cooperate. Instead, you've made it clear you've already decided he's under suspicion of something without even talking to him."

I glared at Dave, more upset with him than with the walking-cliché profiler. "Huge tactical mistake, there," I continued, "alienating a guy just when he was starting to feel like he was part of the team. If you weren't willing to trust him, Dave, you never should've brought him on." I stood up, too angry to worry about the eventual consequences of chewing out my boss. In fact, thinking about Loren made me ask without thinking, "So, is it Paul Stanton trying to get Loren tossed off the case? Putting pressure on the bureau's funding, like Zevon was?"

The second that came out, I realized how loopy it sounded. Good thing Von Towe had already left. I covered my embarrassment by fixing Dave with another glare. "Now, I have a nasty cracker to find. Excuse me."

He didn't try to stop me as I left.

I didn't slam the door. Despite that show of restraint, I was in no mood for the message that popped up on my monitor. *Dearest Sekhmet: Though Judas's kiss could not betray us into your hands, the betrayal shall be punished. The time grows short before the harvest, when the wheat shall be gathered into the barns while the tares burn in the fields. As the sunrise in the east lights the world, none shall deny the coming of justice. Every knee shall bow and every tongue confess its secret transgressions. Hope for mercy, for you are in the iron grip of justice.*

Justice, huh? I'd give him justice. I slapped the Forward button to save Dave the trouble of having Jacques hack into my e-mail account, added a note suggesting they put G.D. Davis into protective custody just in case Gideon did mean to do him physical damage, and stormed out without giving Gideon's drivel the dignity of a reply. I did pause just long enough to grab Loren's duffle bag from under his desk to prevent them from digging through his possessions, if they hadn't already done so yet. It was pitifully light on my shoulder.

To be honest, I had to restrain myself from poking into the bag when I got home. I showed remarkable self-control by putting it securely in my hall closet without so much as testing the zipper.

Pace, pace, pace. Fifteen steps right, turn. Fifteen steps left, turn. At this rate I was going to wear a trail in my entrance-hallway vinyl. Playing guitar hadn't helped; I'd just kept forgetting the words as my fingers got lost and tangled in the strings.

My thoughts had already started to leave skid marks on the inside of my skull, but in a circle rather than a straight line. We didn't know where Gideon was. However, Gideon knew that the big guns were after him now, because he'd hit three high-profile targets in a week. A week! Had it really been just since Monday that we'd been chasing him?

He also knew that the Mounties had apprehended G.D. Davis and that his ex-comrade was going to spill everything—however little—he knew about the operation. Gideon's apocalyptic fixation with punishing the wicked was getting worse with each message, and this latest one obviously meant that Judgment Day wasn't a long time off, which in turn meant that we had to catch him before he pulled what he obviously considered the ultimate attack. I had to trust his taste in disasters; whatever it was, it was going to be huge.

But we didn't know where Gideon was. . . . There we were again, right back at the top of the circle! Arrgghh! The more I thought about it, the less headway I made.

Switching my train of thought onto the other available track didn't help either; that one led in an even tighter circle. If anybody could figure it out, Loren and I could—with enough time, which Gideon probably wasn't going to give us. Even if he did, we had Dave and Von Towe and Shawnie breathing down our necks. I wondered if Loren would even agree to keep working on the case, after Dave had showed the world he wouldn't defend us when other people started looking sideways at Loren and me. We needed to bring in Gideon to save our own sanity, as well as throw Dave's mistrust back in his face. And I needed Loren to help me figure it out. . . .

I stopped dead, balled up my fists in the coat I'd snatched off its hook in the hall, and screamed into the fabric with everything I could muster. Finally I stopped, dizzy but starting to think in straight lines again. I had to step back and let my brain cool off, or I'd be no good for anything. Yes, this was a stressful situation, but going to pieces wasn't the answer. Deep breath.

"Heavenly Father," I whispered, "please take care of Loren and Mr. Cortez's family. Don't let him do anything stupid, and please be with them right now, when they need thy comforting spirit so much. And please help me see what we're missing with Gideon or where we should look next." I paused, keeping my mind clear and quiet, but nothing more came, either from inside or out. "I do thank thee for thy help with G.D. Davis and for all the ways thou hast helped me in other ways too. Please help me to do right and to do good. In the name of thy son, Jesus Christ, amen."

I took another deep breath. It did help—with the calmness, at any rate. *Keep that serenity going,* I told myself. *Let your subconscious work on the problem.* I knew that Freud and his followers had envisioned the subconscious as the dwelling place of humanity's ultimate animal nature, but I'd always pictured it more as the conduit to extra processing power, the part of the soul that doesn't have to use logical or rational methods to find answers. It was the part of my brain that went deeper than the monkey mind chattering away on top and the part that could hear and understand God's Spirit, if I put myself in the right attitude and stayed quiet enough to really listen. Usually my subconscious came up with simple ideas so obviously right that the only possible reaction was, "Duh! Why didn't I see that sooner?" I just figured that if feeding all the information I could find into my subconscious and asking for divine help in sorting it out had worked for understanding Isaiah, it'd work for anything. Including Gideon.

I keyed on my home console, wrote a short but heartfelt note to Mrs. Cortez—just *My deepest sympathy for your loss,* nothing pushy or intrusive—sent a contribution to the charity set up for her kids, then turned off the e-mail. Copycat, sleeping happily in a corner of the screen, caught my attention. I thought about her as I wandered into the kitchen to pull an apple and hunk of cheese out of the fridge—dang, I was short on everything. Better go grocery shopping soon. I added a handful of crackers but then ruined my appearance of virtue by dumping a big handful of chocolate candies onto the plate before I flopped down in front of my computer again.

Copycat obediently upchucked the WormMaster's captured program into the secure cell on my computer. Crunching my apple, I sent Sekhmet after it. The worm tried to get away from me, dodging in and out, but the minimal structure I'd set up provided very little cover. I already knew all its evasive maneuvers anyway, the techniques it used to insinuate itself into secured areas, its insatiable hunger for e-mail résumés. I chased it around just for fun, launching from wall to ceiling to floor as it flashed around barriers. It couldn't resist the programmers' résumés I scattered in its path, however—it stopped to graze, and I pounced, pinning it in my claws.

Once caught, the worm writhed wetly but didn't fight back; it wasn't a warrior, it was a spy. I neatly disabled it and began the real work of taking it apart. Programmers use a decompiler much like a skinning knife, reducing an exie to its component bits, and I always keep my tools sharp. I activated the program, pointed it toward its quarry, and sat back as it went to work. Code promptly unspooled from the worm's sliced flanks in gouts of greenish ichor—I tried not to see or smell it as worm guts, but I gacked slightly anyway before I got my imagination reined in.

Next, I pulled out the decrypter for the finer butchering. There were some advantages to working for the feds, and this was one of them—trust the NSA to come up with a sneaky application for pure mathematics. I ran the decrypter over the worm's twitching corpse, revealing the lines of commands that created and motivated the résumé-stealing digital critter.

Most hackers couldn't help putting their personal touches into their creations, which was very useful for people like me who made a living tracking them down. I skimmed along the keyboarded lines, looking for telltale signs the WormMaster had left in his worm's innards: girlfriends' names, quotes from favorite vid programs, V-Net names, scripture quotes, anything the guy who built the worm might have added as a joke or reference. In this case, though, it was like fishing in a swimming pool. The lines scrolling past were neat, tightly written, completely logical, totally elegant, and utterly without personality.

I did find the set of criteria the worm used to determine whether a résumé smelled good enough to eat. To my surprise, the instructions were downright mundane. Far from details about snatching carelessly revealed passwords, addresses of potential robbery victims, phone numbers to use for phreaking bills, or other illicit information, the worm's instructions were not only mundane but completely harmless. The search cues all matched the customized characteristics OmniMental posted on their V-Net site and used to sort résumés in their employment database: *123* meant engineer, *B* specified four to six years of experience, *86B* indicated Steve Jobs University, and so on. Along with those codes, the WormMaster had included the membership lists of several underground hacker cliques for cross-referencing. From the looks of it, the WormMaster had a very specific idea of his ideal victim: software programmers with distinct cracker tendencies who'd recently graduated from the middle tier of computer science schools.

Doing a bit of his own recruiting for free in OmniMental's databases, was he? Why not just put an ad in the schools' post-graduation employment sites or tuck an invitation into any of the couple-hundred online magazines that catered to up-and-coming hackers? Creating a sophisticated worm just to scam a few résumés from OmniMental without paying their standard headhunter fee seemed like complete overkill—unless the WormMaster didn't want anybody to know he was looking for programmers . . .

I practically heard the click and buzz inside my skull. Amazing how things can come into focus so abruptly. This elegant thief program looked eerily like the programs Gideon had used—all written in the same accomplished digital hand. So Gideon was hiring programmers to help him.

I hooked into OmniMental's network with the supervisor's account they had given me last week—it was still active, which was convenient for me, though stupid of them—and tossed the worm's search criteria into their database, including available and currently employed possibilities. It obediently spit out a list of seventeen potential matches. I flicked through them impatiently, scanning unfamiliar faces and names. Number nine, however, sprang to life with the thin, bespectacled face of none other than G.D. Davis. He had even updated his résumé to include Sunshine Foods! Then, at number twelve, the face of Gideon Johnson of GenM fame—I sent a quick e-mail to Stark, telling him to track down one Mervyn Hoskins and attaching the résumé. At number fourteen, the blond, bland, pudgy face of Gsmith stared from the digital page.

"Ah ha, Gsmith—or should I say, Albert Anderson—we meet again!" I laughed aloud, leapt from my chair, and did a dance of joy around my living-room rug, then threw my hands in the air. "Thank you! Thank you!" As a prayer it was more enthusiastic than strictly proper, but it was definitely heartfelt.

No wonder Gideon already knew my avatar and V-Net address and sent me taunting e-mails—he'd been doing this for months, ever since I started tracking him as the WormMaster! He'd told G.D. Davis about me, too—"Curiosity killed the cat," eh, nerd boy?—and probably Gsmith as well. But I knew him now—Gideon, WormMaster, whatever he wanted to call himself, whether he appeared as a fallen-angel worm wrangler or a blank-faced messiah staring out of a message window. All I had to do was find him, track him down, and tie him up in his own digital webs.

"Thank you again," I whispered, stopping midspin. "Heavenly Father, thank you so much. Now, please help us find him before he hurts somebody else." A scratching noise from the door made me add a hasty, "Including me!"

Good heavens, somebody was messing with the lock! I lunged forward, smacking off the lights as the doorknob began to turn. I dove for the kitchen as the front door opened, light from the hall spilling into the tiny entranceway. I felt inside the drawers in the dark, cursing my dislike of organized sports and thus the pitiful lack of golf clubs or baseball bats in my apartment. I settled for a rolling pin instead. I hefted the culinary tool, trying to get a feel for its weight and balance. I had the sinking feeling that it presented more of a danger to pie dough than to prowlers.

Someone in dark clothes, carrying a suspicious-looking box, had moved into the living room toward the glow of my monitor, closing the front door behind him and not even glancing into the kitchen to see the glint reflecting off my eyes. I leapt out silently and whacked him with the rolling pin, substituting self-defense enthusiasm for finesse.

Unlike on all the vids, he didn't drop to the floor, out stone cold. Instead he staggered, yelled something incoherent—and turned out to be Loren. He grabbed my wrist, holding the rolling pin far away from both of us. The box hit the floor, spilling the fragged hard drive from StarWest and the GenM data disks onto my rug. Then Loren tripped over the box, and we both joined the hardware on the floor.

At least my response was vid-worthy. I yelped the obvious

identification as the monitor screen illuminated his face about three inches from mine. "Loren! What are you doing here?"

"Getting hit in the head with a two-by-four," he growled, gingerly feeling the back of his head with both hands.

"Oof. Get off, would you?" I complained, resolutely not paying any attention to any sensations other than feeling squished. "You're heavy. And it's a rolling pin, not a two-by-four. Where have you been all day?"

"Oh, well, that's okay then," he said sarcastically, but he did roll off and sit up. Then he hefted the rolling pin. "Nice domestic murder weapon."

"Better than a frozen leg of lamb," I agreed, scooping the disks and drive into the box before I switched on the lamp.

"I've been at the library all day," Loren belatedly answered, "working on restoring GenM's robot routine."

"The library's got heavy-duty disaster-recovery software?" I asked as I went into the kitchen for a hand towel and ice cubes.

"No. I just used their public V-Net connections to hack into the university and steal a few processor cycles to reconstruct the GenM data. I'll have to get them paid back, but I didn't want to show up at work. Dave's two-faced weasel act ticked me off, letting Van Helsing start that jabberwocky about me being dangerously unstable and prone to social violence. He ought to know better by now — if I wanted to cause him trouble, he'd know it."

"How do you know he did?" I asked, kneeling beside him and batting his hands away to inspect his head. Good thing he had such thick, glossy hair; a nasty bump was growing on the back of his head, but I didn't see any blood. Glossy? As if that contributed to the protection factor at all! I gently pressed the towel against the swelling.

"Thanks." He gave me a half-smile and took over holding the makeshift ice pack so I could move over to my computer. "They showed up at my ex-apartment around six-thirty this morning. About gave Sophie a heart attack — she dropped a note bawling me out. I figured they would. Van Helsing grabbed me when I left the factory and started asking me about my hostility toward everything from nuns to the FBI." His smile widened. "I told him to — well, let's just say he'll have a good time analyzing what I meant. So anyway, I decided to show them I could get away from them whenever I wanted."

"Yeah, and leave me to defend your sorry tail and answer all their dumb questions," I said, looking up from slotting the data disk into my computer. I didn't tell him that they'd been worried about him even before they started wondering if he were Gideon. That wouldn't help matters, and we'd soon prove those worries unfounded anyway.

"Sorry," he said. "I do feel bad about that, even if it is your own fault for being overly diligent and going in to work." Before I could get on him about that, he added, "But I feel worse about snapping at you. I know you're not naive or uncaring." He shrugged, looking at his hands instead of at me. "So, when I had to leave the library, I decided to come here and surprise you with the restored Gideon program."

"Sweet thought, but why didn't you just ring the doorbell or knock like a normal person? And how did you get in—are you a lock pick as well as an accomplished fugitive?" I had to admire his computer work—the GenM program blossomed on my monitor, every comma and period in place. It was Gideon, all right; the master cracker's elegant code scrolled right alongside the WormMaster's. Perfect fit.

"I figured you'd be at Personal Improvement Night or whatever you call it, so I didn't think anybody would answer," he explained. "And yes, I'm a pretty good lock pick, but I didn't have to. Remember? You gave me your extra keys last time you went to visit Penny—"

"Oh, I remember this conversation." I turned to look at him. "And you never did give them back, did you."

"Sorry. Jeez, you've got me saying that a lot tonight." He didn't look repentant. "Still, you didn't have to *hit* me."

I gave him a nice smile and didn't bother arguing. "All right, my dear Watson, you've done a wonderful job uncovering Gideon's tracks. Now, in the interest of the kind of total directness that prevents all kinds of miscommunication problems in a relationship, I have a question. Loren, are you Gideon or the WormMaster?"

"Gideon or the WormMaster," Loren repeated. The puzzlement in those big blue eyes lasted only a moment. He grabbed me, whirled me around, set me back down in my desk chair, and gave me a hearty kiss on the side of the head. "Show me."

I laughed and pulled up the display windows, pointing out the rhythms and quirks that flowed through the worm, Carmelita21, StarWest's account databases, and GenM's robot program. It wasn't as foolproof as fingerprints or DNA, but it was more of a lock than most of the theories by which evolutionary biologists live and die.

"Well, well, well, would ya lookee there," Loren said. "Your old nemesis and my alter ego, one and the same slimy creature. And you were thinking it was me." He lightly spatted the back of my head, then sighed. "I'd almost like to be. The guy's a psycho, but he's a slick one. And, my dear Murtaugh, I think I know what he's planning. Go back a bit in the StarWest hack."

The code scrolled by, so hypnotic in its smooth undulations that I jumped when Loren's finger stabbed toward the screen. "Right there. You see that? It has nothing to do with the rest of the program. It's a side routine that tests Aireon's secure connections to local intranets. All it does is just see if it can connect, then if the other network will accept a packet. That's it. It doesn't actually send the packet, just checks to see if it can." He grabbed my left hand and shook it out of the dataglove so he could take over half the navigation. "Now, Carmelita was doing the same thing when she snapped into Sunshine's main system to use their satellite connection. GenM's doesn't have it, because it was a stand-alone system anyway. But check this out—your worm's got the preliminary code right there. How do you like that?"

Actually, I quite liked it, but I thumped my shoulder against his chest anyway and reclaimed my dataglove. "Yeah, so what? And excuse me, Mister, but in my house, I drive."

"I just wanted an excuse to take you in my arms," he purred, then thoroughly broke the mood by shaking my chair vigorously. "My sweet Sue Anne, these little routines, properly exploited by somebody on the inside of a firewall, allow that person to completely crash the connected systems. To get right to the point, somebody inside Aireon's firewall could hook these routines into the download program for the NetSys update and take over everybody's V-Net connections."

"That totally fits," I said, my voice trailing off as the full impact hit me. I swallowed. "Loren, Gideon sent me a message this morning. He said that all secrets would be revealed. Every knee will bow and every tongue confess. He's already inside Aireon, and he knows the timetable for the release."

"And when they release tomorrow at midnight, Gideon's going to use his neat cracker program to bust everybody's systems wide open," Loren finished for me. "So we've got to get to him before that. Especially since he knows we've got two of his guys."

I reached for the phone. "I'll get Stark, tell him to get over to Aireon—"

Loren caught my hand. "No, wait, not yet. If we send Stark howling over there on another goose chase, we give away our game to Gideon and lose credibility with Dave. Crying wolf and all that. We've got to figure out who this guy is, which Aireon drone's sheepskin hides the wolf. Then we send Stark a name and a description, and he nails this guy to the wall."

"At least we've got a set of possibilities to check—plus we've got another name and description to hand him, too." I opened Gideon Johnson's résumé. "Meet our robo-corruption artist."

"Well, hello, Mr. Johnson—and all your potential anarchist buddies." Loren scanned through the list of possibilities. "All right, we check Aireon's employment rolls for anybody named Gideon and cross-check them against the résumés the WormMaster's exies might've looked at."

"Because so far, all three of them have used *Gideon* as part of their alias," I finished.

"Hey, you're not so dumb." He winked at me and reached for the datagloves again. "Employee info is listed right out on their V-Net site—we won't even have to hack in and evade Igor and his fellow night-shift goons."

"You just keep your hands to yourself," I informed him. "What is it with guys and datagloves? Or remotes, or game consoles, or whatever? I'm a big girl, and I can find Aireon's V-Net site even with one hand tied behind my back."

"Really?" Loren reached for one of my hands. "Let's see."

I laughed and evaded the ineffective snatch. "You'll have to take it on faith. Okay, here we are—*Introducing the Aireon Family*. Cute." I set their search engine looking for Gideon anything and sat back to watch. "So why do you think this guy got fixated on the name *Gideon*? Feeding his messiah complex out of Gideon Bibles, like the one we found in Gsmith's room?"

"The Bible's just an afterthought." Loren helped himself to a couple of candies from my dinner plate. "Come on, Primary teacher, you know the reference. It's Gideon's *army* we're dealing with. Remember them from the Old Testament? Gideon was the general who delivered Israel from the Midianites by tricking them into fighting each other—after God ordered him to go against the enemy with a pitifully small army." He nodded patronizingly with me. "Yes, now you remember. The pathetic thing is that he turned to idolatry at the end and wound up on the wrong side—just like this Gideon."

I wasn't sure this Gideon was ever actually on the *right* side, but I didn't argue. I had better things to do anyway, as the search displayed four names: Isaac Gideon, Gideon Paul, Jonathan Gideon Stachaski, and Gideon Thomas. The directory entries—in keeping with standard privacy practices—listed only their e-mail addresses.

"All right, so now we check these guys out," I said. "Find out what they've been working on and how long they've been with the company. And no, you don't get to try hacking into Aireon again. There are other ways to skin this particular cat. How about we just call Aireon, explain the situation, and *ask* them!"

The support tech who answered my phone call, however, seemed determined to justify Loren's skeptical *humph* at my optimistic attempt to go through proper channels. "Well, I don't know if I can give out that kind of information," she said. "You should check back later, during regular work hours."

"As I said, this is an FBI investigation," I told her. "It's not something that can wait for regular work hours—by that time, it may be too late. May I speak to your supervisor? That way he can make the decision and you're off the hook."

She reluctantly agreed, which precipitated a long delay and runaround. Apparently the supervisor was out getting coffee or in the bathroom or something. When he finally came on the line, he in turn referred me to *his* superior. I ended up talking to two more support techs, each one slightly higher up the ladder. At last I was on hold to talk to the shift supervisor, Daniel Hancock.

"Well, this is going nicely." Loren stretched and yawned. "They keep this up, we're both going to zonk out, and then you won't be able to teach Primary anymore after we've slept together."

"Don't tempt me," I told him.

"What?" Of course, the supervisor had chosen that moment to pick up.

"Hello," I said. "This is Sue Jones from the National Infrastructure Protection Center office here in town—"

"Who?" This guy was definitely not a night-shift regular; he sounded as tired as I felt, and he didn't even have the extra jolt of adrenaline. He would soon, though.

"FBI," I told him. "You know, the cyber-crimes division? We're investigating the series of cyberterrorist attacks that have happened this week, and we have reason to believe that one or more of the perpetrators may be working for Aireon."

That got his attention. "Aireon doesn't have anything to do with that Gideon character!"

"You might shortly," I said, my patience wearing thin. "Mr. Hancock, we need to crosscheck your employee database against our list of suspects, because Gideon is planning to hijack the NetSys 11.4 release! Now, will you please give us authorization so we can stop him? I'm connected to your system now, as Sekhmet, and requesting further rights."

I could almost hear him sweating over the line, but he didn't let anxiety railroad him into thinking sensibly. "All right, I see you. But you're coming from a domestic console, not from the FBI. I can't authorize that!"

Loren took the receiver. "This is Agent Hunter. Can you authorize it if we do connect through an official FBI computer?"

"Well, yes, I can—" He didn't get a chance to finish.

"Good. Reconnecting now." Loren handed the phone back to me, took over the terminal, and snapped off the stalled connection. This time I didn't give him any trouble about surrendering the virtual driver's seat.

After putting the Aireon supervisor on hold—which served him right—I couldn't resist giving Loren a bit of a hard time. "Agent Hunter?"

"List of suspects?" he shot back, diving into the V-Net streams and coming up at the authorization gate for his own workstation at the NIPC office, completely bypassing the usual set of firewalls and password authentications that a remote connection usually required. A blare of beat-rock music crashed out of the speakers.

I turned them down quickly. "Let me guess—masking those aural cues, right? You know Dave would have kittens if he knew you'd put a backdoor into the network."

"What he doesn't know won't hurt him." Loren shrugged. "There. Connecting to Aireon now, as Sam, and requesting access to their employee database. Let dither-man know we're coming in."

This time Mr. Hancock didn't give me any trouble, relieved to see us—in incontrovertible pixel letters—connecting from an authorized, encrypted, utterly official FBI computer. He granted Sam the necessary access permission without hesitation. "What should I do?" he asked anxiously as Loren fed our search criteria into the database, adding the list of names Gideon had stolen from Omni-Mental's résumé cache.

"Wait for us to contact you," I told him. "That's very important. Just wait. And don't worry, Mr. Hancock. If you cooperate, I'm sure we'll be able to resolve this whole business before anything nasty happens."

"Talk about a limp noodle," Loren said after I hung up. "We come in, flash a badge, and he rolls right over. If we weren't so good at keeping our terminals secure, anybody could've done the same thing."

"That's why Dave doesn't like backdoors," I reminded him. "Whoa—look at that! Gideon Thomas, hired only six months ago, working in the NetSys Admin group, and there's his résumé, kifed right out of OmniMental's database. Pleasant looking kid, for a cracker terrorist." My thrill of elation dimmed somewhat, however, as SEARCH COMPLETE flashed across the screen. "He can't be Gideon. Where's his boss?"

"Joshua G. Billians—team leader, Aireon Connections Technologies. And he's looking at us," Loren said softly. At the bottom of the screen, the teleconference icon had turned on. "We've got company in the link."

He waved open the CONNECTIONS window, setting a trace on our uninvited company. The whirling earth-and-stars logo blossomed on the screen, the golden glowing line of the teleconference link arrowing down toward the globe. It highlighted a representation of my apartment as home base and then shot away, tracing the V-Net link to show us our eavesdropper's location. We'd done that once before, tracing G.D. Davis's attack to the satellite transmitter he'd used to attack NIPC's computers. This time, however, the trace stayed at ground level instead of lunging skyward. Oddly, it split in half, each glowing tendril going its separate way.

"All kinds of spies out tonight," I said.

"Not for long," Loren assured me. "They're about to meet their master." He added an evil-villain laugh—"bwaa-haa-haa-haa!"—and flashed off the stolen Aireon boomerang even before the trace settled onto its final destinations.

With a soundless flare, the trace highlighted NIPC headquarters. A split second later, my monitor displayed the white-water background of Dave's computer. His avatar, a blow-dried Elvis icon, glowed into view beside the cigarette-wielding bombshell Pinky used as her online persona.

"Pinky's helping Dave stake out your console!" I said indignantly. "Disloyal wench."

"We've got worse problems than Pinky." Loren pointed at the CONNECTIONS window. The second arm of that golden tracer tendril got as far as Aireon's firewall, but then someone on the other side saw it coming—a brilliant cyber-sonar pulse lit the screen for a split second, breaking the connection. Loren ducked the rebounding boomerang, but the monitor wavered under the program's ricochet.

A message, written in fiery letters, burned its way across the screen: *And when he had opened the seventh seal, there was silence in heaven about the space of half an hour.*

"He's at Aireon," I said, "and he knows we know. He must've been monitoring the employment databases and everything else at Aireon, waiting for us to show up. He's paranoid, for an angel."

"So let's get out there," Loren suggested, springing out of my office chair and grabbing at my jacket on his way to the door.

I avoided his grab and flopped into my chair. "Whoa—just a sec. He's got to reset the Aireon deployment software, and he just told us that'd take a half-hour."

"Like he'd tell the truth on that," Loren objected.

"He's taunting me, as usual. If anything, he's optimistic. These things always take longer than you want them to." I sent a *Gotcha!* message to Dave and Pinky, along with a dump of what we'd found in the Aireon personnel database, and then I dialed the office number. "Dave, stop spying on us and start paying attention to what the *real* villain's doing!" I barked, when Dave's guilty voice came on the line. "Get Stark and Ieyasu and everybody else you can to the Aireon main campus yesterday—but do it discreetly, because he's there." Dave asked me who. "Gideon, what do you—Dave, just get them out there! We don't have a lot of time here. Loren and I will find our own way."

We found our own way, all right—Loren's Buck Rogers driving style comes in handy occasionally. I didn't even manage to pry my fingers loose from their death grip on the edges of my seat to change the radio station. I'm sure the distinguished couple in the late-model sedan that we passed at Warp 8 looked at each other, shook their heads sadly, and asked each other why there was never a cop around when you needed one.

Even so, we hit Aireon's front parking lot only a couple of minutes before Stark and Ieyasu arrived in one of the agency's sinister, black four-wheel drives, with a mob of their fellow field agents pouring out of the short convoy that followed. The headlights lit a small collection of slightly shabby buildings huddled amid nicely landscaped lawns and flowerbeds. Aireon's success had come so quickly that they hadn't moved into better quarters yet; they still used the cheap-rent buildings Paul Stanton had practically lived in when he started the company, though they did own the lots now rather than just renting them.

"All they're missing is lights and sirens," Loren growled. He grabbed my hand and ran across the lawns with fine disregard for the fact that Aireon's sprinklers were running at the time.

We splashed across the dark grass, Stark and his colleagues following us—complaining about the sprinklers—as we bypassed the main building and galloped toward the installation housing Aireon's primary V-Net service installation. Our dramatic entrance ran into a major snag as we bounced off the electronically locked front doors.

Behind us, however, doors opened all through the complex, accompanied by the deeply annoying buzzing of dozens of fire alarms. The hordes of Aireon serfs, diligently manning the ramparts of the world's premiere V-Net technology on the eve of their about-to-be-hijacked major triumph, poured out of the buildings. The growing mob milled in confusion, spreading into the parking lot, yelling questions at each other—about the alarm, about what was going on, about the half-dozen official-looking undercover vehicles parked haphazardly on the ornamental walkway in front of the carved granite AIREON UNLIMITED sign.

Stark screeched to a halt and extended the enquiring-minds theme. "What's going on?"

"Duh—classic distraction," Loren informed him sarcastically, hitting the glass doors with a fist.

"Gideon's in one of these buildings, and he's going to mess up Aireon's NetSys 11.4 release, using a modified worm—" I began, then stopped. "Listen, Stark, we're looking for a guy named Joshua Billians. He's probably in this building. He's set off the fire alarms to clear the rest of the buildings, and he's locked this door. We've got to find somebody to open these doors."

Waving several of the agents toward the crowd, Stark commanded, "Don't let anybody leave," then treated us to one of those G-man smirks. "Out of the way, geeks. We'll unlock the door." He pulled his sidearm and sent four shots through the glass doors. They shattered inward.

"Unlock, right," Loren said, but he didn't hesitate. The glass bits crunched under our feet as we ran through the small, functional lobby and down the stairs to the heavy doors marked COMPUTER CENTRAL. Two more bullets took care of the ID-scanner and the door lock.

Loren and I dove for two engineers' chairs in front of the bank of monitors. Stark, Ieyasu, and two other agents — merely suit-clad shadows on the edges of my attention — infiltrated the room in classic FBI style, front-and-back cover in two-by-two formation. All their caution was for nothing — the room contained only us and the six huge, humming V-Net computers that supported Aireon's millions of users.

"There it is," Loren said. "Auto-deployment program for Net-Sys 11.4. And here's the worm." Commands sprang into life, the lines of code all too familiar by now. The worm was poised to snatch the system passwords the deployment program used to automatically update the operating system, store them in its guts, and then retransmit them to Gideon, along with the keys to every database, computer, list, and site on the V-Net. No secrets, indeed — and all of them under Gideon's righteous control, ready for Judgment Day.

Loren and I exchanged a look. "Dang," I said. He just nodded and tried to delete the worm code from the deployment program. Of course, it didn't work — the program was already compiled and the source code was beyond our reach in one of the development buildings — but it was a good try anyway.

Stark reappeared, slipping out from behind the huge cabinets, and glanced at the displays scrolling across the screens in front of us. "Nobody here. Who are we looking for?"

"This guy," I said, bringing up Billians's ID photo. A square-jawed, shockingly young face topped with sandy red hair stared intensely out of the bland background. I pulled up Gideon Thomas's image as well — another youngster, this one with a dubious half-smile and a cowlick.

"He's got to be in this building," Loren announced. "He's cut off all outside access from the rest of Aireon's network so nobody can stop him. Probably upstairs in the offices. Try the front desk — see if you can find a floor plan." He didn't turn around, staring at the screen as he searched through the user list for an account to snatch.

Stark grunted and motioned to the door with the barrel of his gun. "All right, back upstairs. Fan out. When you find them, keep those jokers away from the datagloves." He glanced at me.

I nodded. "We'll handle things here." I didn't bother to watch them leave, instead slapping Sekhmet's disk into the drive and plunging into the world of Aireon's internal systems.

The virtual walls sprang up around me, smoothly seamless. A blank-faced authentication robot blocked Sekhmet's path. "User name and password," it demanded tonelessly.

"Have you got it?" I demanded of Loren.

"Yes! Got a password," he exclaimed, satisfied. Onscreen, Gilliam blazed into polished-ebony life beside me and tossed a key at the robot. It caught the key, swallowed it, and disappeared.

Gilliam and I ran through the *Welcome to Aireon Unlimited, Ziggy Trina* that scrolled before us like a translucent curtain. The hallways stretched before us, a labyrinth of possibilities and portals that we passed without a second glance in our race for the V-Net portals that linked Aireon — and thus Gideon — to the unwitting victims of the outside world. We had to stop him from triggering the auto-deployment program; if it copied the altered version of NetSys 11.4 throughout the network of Aireon's users, Gideon would have full access to and control of everyone's systems.

Mistake. A huge, clawed paw flashed out of one of those neglected side passages, narrowly missing my furry back. I flipped forward, evading its code-freezing infiltration virus, and tossed a logic bomb at it as I landed. The claw convulsed and disintegrated as the ambush program crumbled. A rending crash blew through the speakers as another attack smashed into Gilliam's tightly coded armor and splintered on the anti-possession programs Loren had built into the black knight.

"Too easy," Gilliam boomed. "Automated booby traps. Delaying us."

"Yes," I hissed back, pulling a detector out of my handy tool pouch.

The detector alerted us to another set of snatchers, which Gilliam dispatched with two heavy blows from his gauntleted fists. This time, however, they had reinforcements — a tide of digital spiders swarmed out of the rotting remains of one massive claw. The tiny bugs covered Gilliam's brilliant casing, burrowing into its joints and spreading their poison through the knight's electronic system. The cascade of nonsense messages worked like a denial-of-service attack, disrupting Gilliam's logic cycles from inside his defenses.

"Go!" he roared at me, activating the receptors that sucked in the rest of the spiders.

I felt the pull myself as I sprinted away — only to come up against another stone-faced authentication bot demanding a user name and password. Ziggy Trina's key simply bounced off its impassive facade. "Failed authentication," it said flatly.

"Great," I growled.

"Move it, Fuzzy." Trixie appeared, her whip flicking. She planted one stiletto-heeled boot against the robot's gleaming front and smacked the whip into its intake slot. "Open, says me."

How could it resist such a persuasive argument? After a moment's hesitation, steam poured from its joints. "Welcome to Aireon's V-Net deployment interface," it droned to our backs.

The rush of the V-Net portals grew in our ears, their glow lighting the drab walls with the shivering patterns of the fast-flowing electronic current. The blazing, ruddy glow of an opening conduit added an air of menace to the familiar sight. Gideon had managed to stick to his thirty-minute schedule after all. I'd have to congratulate him — after we tied him up in his own network cables, of course. He was in the link with us now, casting his own digital spells to stop us from stopping him.

"Incoming connection!" I yelped. "Internal!"

Trixie executed an impossibly athletic high kick, delivering a solid No Access command to the potential data flow. Only a couple of packets escaped before the opening slammed shut. I pounced and snatched them up, ripping them open. Then I pulled the data string from its casing. The scaly face of Gideon's modified invader worm writhed behind the neatly packed ones and zeros.

"Got it yet, Kitty?" Trixie called, delivering another Quit order to slam Gideon's doorway into the V-Net. The door closed much more slowly this time, as Gideon read her permissions and compensated for them. "I'm getting tired of this!"

"Got it!" I exclaimed, throwing the list of doors we had to block to Trixie.

She had no chance to catch them. A shutdown command fell from the ceiling like a net, covering her. For a moment, her internal protections prevailed. Then she sank to the ground, out cold.

Another similar but not identical net flew out of the yawning mouth that Gideon opened in front of me, wrapping my arms in its sticky webs as it tried to shut me down too. I slashed at the fibers with my fore and hind claws, ripping away the strands as fast as I could, but I could feel myself slowing down.

Packets flashed above my head, the first few outriders of

Gideon's program, seeking to connect with the mainframe V-Net computers that would let Gideon's poison spread throughout Aireon's customer networks. I ripped free, batting the packets out of the air. They bounced from the walls and floor, reorienting themselves and arrowing toward the rushing flow of the V-Net connection. They hissed and sizzled in the roaring firewall that sprang up, blocking their access.

Sam shot me a film noir glance from beside the flickering barrier. I scrambled up, taking my place at the other side. Packets flew toward us in an ever-thickening stream, burning in the firewall at first and then suddenly changing color as Gideon compensated. I snatched the first mutated packet and pulled its new instructions from its glowing insides. Sam incorporated the new information into the firewall, which flamed with renewed vigor, devouring the second transmission — until it morphed again, squirming away from the firewall toward yet another path to freedom.

"Can't keep it up," I gasped. We were slamming portals and launching counter-programs as fast as we could, and Gideon was gaining the edge. He had all the system's error-detection and correction software on his side, and the system, blindly loyal to its programming, was fighting us too, using random-connection generation to overcome what it thought was simply network congestion or routing errors.

"No," Sam agreed, and he disappeared.

This time, however, no new avatar appeared to reinforce me. I frantically deployed my own random-static generator, hoping to at least slow Gideon's data stream enough to adapt to the cascading changes he used to slide into the link. I batted furiously at the stream, diverting as much of the current as I could with false information, but I watched in horror as the flow split, running along two paths, one blasting past me and sending its connection through the ineffective firewall and into the accommodating computers beyond.

I reached into my pouch and threw Copycat into one of the streams. She wailed like only cats do, swelling to three times her size as her program nearly overloaded. Duplicated packets exploded out of her, flying everywhere, clogging the second data path with an incredible broadcast storm. Gideon's software struggled to process the barrage, but there were simply too many of the packets; they began to stack up like drifting snow against the portal.

Just one more data stream to stop! I whirled to face it, only to see the sparkling curtain part in a moonlight glow as the WormMaster's angelic avatar rose out of the hotly contested tide. No soul-string trailed from his golden hair this time; we both had direct connections to the battlefield.

"Sekhmet," he bellowed. "We meet at last for the final battle."

Well, hello, Gideon. I didn't have time for this. I pulled a logic bomb from my toolkit and used it to temporarily paralyze the computer sending the NetSys upgrade program into the link. The backed-up packets were getting deep—I could feel my own motions getting slower as the computers struggled with the overload of data running through them.

He wasn't giving up on banter, however. "Look behind you."

Oldest trick in the book—but I did. Good thing too, because another one of his worms loomed out of the packet-drift and lunged toward me, its sharp teeth clashing in its sphincter-like mouth. I froze, watching its attack, then I leapt out of the way at the last possible second. The worm crashed into the data slush, its slimy scales losing purchase. The nasty thing recovered too quickly, though, twisting around on itself for another go. This time I wasn't fast enough. The thing's sticky head smashed into me, holding me in place as its body wrapped around my arm.

The WormMaster's laugh rang through the rush of packets as my logic bomb failed. The avalanche of instructions barreled toward us, on its way to infect the computer systems of Aireon and other users everywhere. I pulled all the power I could and leapt into the stream. It swept me up, worm and all, throwing me into the portal—and into the WormMaster's angelic face. We crashed together, our avatars' programming trying to switch into personal-interaction mode, my tools scattering, as the worm sucked information and digital life out of both of us. I saw the WormMaster's expression twist into horror as he lost control of his avatar, his consol, and the data stream. I managed to send one of Sekhmet's sharp grins before I lost control of her as well.

Abruptly the scene blanked out, glowing streams of data replaced with velvety blackness. For a split second I thought that Gideon had succeeded, despite the system corruption Sekhmet's randomly freed bits had caused. Then simple lines of white letters appeared in the dark: *No access. No activity. Connection lost.*

I sprang from my chair, reorienting myself to the real world. "Loren!"

"Got him!" Loren reappeared from behind the mainframe

cabinets, holding the disconnected ends of the cables that ran from the huge computers to the lines beyond.

"Satellite link!" I yelped. "He can still send it! He has to reconfigure the stream, but he may be able to use another console!"

Loren spat something that definitely didn't appear on my approved swearing list, tossing the cables aside and glaring at the computer cabinets with murder in his eyes. Their stainless-steel boxes hid both their delicate innards and the connections to the cables that led to the satellite transmitters on the roof. Those cases would withstand anything we could throw at them without power tools.

"Power," I said.

This time I was the one who caught Loren's hand and tore off, following the conduits in the ceiling. (Thank heavens for the years-old architecture fad that included exposed plumbing and wiring pipes as a design feature—and thank them again that Aireon hadn't moved into new, modern buildings with carbon-dioxide fire-suppression systems!) The conduits led to a door equipped with a keypad and card reader set into the reinforced metal doorframe. Looking down at my smooth-soled pumps, I nearly used an inappropriate exclamation myself, but then I stifled it as I turned to look at Loren's shoes. Ha! Rubber-soled sneakers—as usual.

"Loren, scuff across the rug," I ordered. "Then touch the doorframe right above the lock."

He did, building up enough of a static charge that the lock obediently clicked. I caught it before it had a chance to relock. Punch-down blocks and cable boxes lined the walls, across from rows of unlabeled circuit-breaker cabinets. Loren started flicking off each switch, working down the line without knowing which one corresponded to either Gideon's workstation or the mainframe controlling the satellite link.

No time for a surgical strike. I ran to the end of the circuit-breaker display grabbed the handle of the power switch marked MAIN, and pulling it down with all my might. It didn't spark, but the moment the switch closed the lights wavered, gasped, and went out, leaving us in total darkness and knocking all Aireon's computers completely off the V-Net.

"There goes V-Net access for half the civilized world," I said.

"That's the problem with centralization," Loren noted from somewhere in the ebony visual velvet. "I've always wanted to do that—completely K.O. Stanton with one flick of the switch. Rome burned in a day, an entire monopoly goes up in a flash."

"You'd think they'd be better prepared," I said with a laugh, but the relief froze in my chest as a sulfur-yellow ambience grew around us.

"Attention—there has been a power interruption. Emergency systems are on. Emergency power outage will occur in thirty minutes," an automated voice calmly informed us through the intercom.

"They *are* better prepared—they've got UPS set up to keep the computers going!" Loren finished for me. "We've gotta knock out those mainframes!"

We tore off again, back toward the computer room through the half-lit hallways.

"Grab all the papers you pass," Loren yelled to me.

I obediently grabbed a wad of printout from the maintenance station and dropped them to spread in a fluttering flock over the floor. "The recycle bin!"

We dragged the big blue container into the middle of the computer room and loosely crumpled as many papers as we could lay our hands on. "Got a light?" I asked.

Loren actually felt his pockets for one irrational moment, but then an arsonist gleam lit his eyes. He ripped a double handful of power cords out of the terminals' backs, their ends spitting as they touched each other, and tossed the mass into the pillow of paper. It seemed to take absolutely forever, but at last the inevitable happened—a spark caught on exactly the right flammable edge and sired a flame that moved hungrily along the pile as Loren and I eagerly fanned it along. *Fahrenheit 451*, I thought illogically, the flashpoint of paper. The heat rose as more sheets surrendered to the fire's appetite, driving us back, blistering the tiles, and triggering the fire-control system.

An instant monsoon poured from the ceiling, drowning the blaze, soaking the chairs, contributing to a growing puddle on the floor—and shorting the computers in a secondary rain of sparks. One by one the terminals lost the battle against the water. The mainframes withstood the water's onslaught a few seconds longer, but the power and status lights decorating their impassive fronts first flickered uncertainly and then blanked out one by one as the rain worked into their ventilation slots and the tide washed over their bases.

That same tide rose quickly toward us as well, buzzing cables sinking under its surface—eep! I grabbed Loren and threw myself backward onto the hip-high console desk, sending a monitor crashing into the flood and bringing Loren down on top of me, our shoes lifting out of the way of potential water-assisted electrocution as the UPS embedded in the mainframes gave up the ghost in a hiss of final sparks.

"Whew," I breathed as the last circuits died, leaving only the red glow of the sprinkler system's own emergency light. Loren's eyes looked violet-black so close to mine. "How romantic," I whispered.

"Yes." He kissed the word against my lips.

I kissed him back, surprising both of us again.

We broke it off less quickly than we could've. He rolled off me; I sat up. Neither of us knew where to look.

"Well, that's extraordinarily uncomfortable," I said inanely.

The distant sound of gunshots saved us from having to continue the conversation. We sloshed our way upstairs, where we found a gunshot-accessed lock. "Stark's been here," Loren noted.

"He's still here," I said, hearing shouts of "Don't move! FBI!" echoing from the room beyond.

The frantic pounding of running feet filled the room, along with a crash and skittering as something — probably a spool of disks — fell to the floor. A shadowy figure ran toward us, saw us silhouetted in the hall's emergency light, and reversed itself, nearly falling down as it tried to change course with no traction on the slick floor. Loren, proving forever that he's an impulsive creature, promptly tore after it. I didn't do much better in the common-sense area, pulling a big recycle bin and two chairs over to block the door and heading into the dark confusion myself.

Loren's comment about the old Keystone Kops movies applied even better here than they had in Gsmith's case. We tore around the hamster cages, sending printouts flying, slipping on the wet floor, and slamming into things. I rounded a corner and nearly got shot as Ieyasu sprang out at the other end of the hallway, sidearm right out front and ready.

"Sue!" I yelled, "I'm Sue!" I didn't wait to see if he recognized me before throwing myself backward into a podful of printers — only to hit something soft, warm, and much too animated.

"Yikes!" I yelled again, springing away, grabbing the gimbaled chair I nearly tripped over, and thrusting it toward whoever I had bumped into. My eyes had adjusted pretty well by now, and I realized this couldn't be one of our guys — not tall enough for Loren, not wearing a white shirt like the Special Agents. Ieyasu stood silhouetted against the comparatively lighter windows for an instant before he came *over* the cube wall, smashing his quarry to the floor. I jumped out of the way, flailed wildly before I landed in the chair, and slid across the corridor into the wall of the next set of cubes.

From somewhere toward the windows, Stark bellowed, "If you move, I will shoot you!" The next thing I knew, a series of gunshots blasted through the comparative silence.

Another figure loomed, lurching out of the hamster warren toward the semiblocked door. Stark, frantically slamming a new clip into his gun, charged from one direction, and Loren ran toward the stumbling fugitive. Stark hit a puddle and went into a semicontrolled skid rendered more difficult by the soggy paper on the floor. Loren skidded to a stop as the figure brandished what looked like a knife in the offset emergency lights.

Gideon—it must be Gideon—threw the chairs out of the way, struggling one-handed with the heavy recycling bin. Loren grabbed a small monitor off the nearest desk.

"Look out behind you!" I yelled, just as Loren heaved it at Gideon.

Gideon looked, all right—in the wrong direction, toward Stark, as I'd hoped. The monitor hit him from the side, crumpling him to the wet floor. The Special Agents pounced instantly. I made my way over to Loren, rubbing my bruises as Stark and the other agents cuffed the rogue programmers.

"This is way more painful than cyber battles," I observed. "You all right?"

"Fine," Loren said.

It took me a second before I realized that he was feeling me over for bullet holes. I wanted to hug him as I slapped his hands away. "I said I was fine. Did you strain anything, tossing that monitor?"

He laughed. "Oh, right—I can pick *you* up, but tossing a monitor's going to give me a hernia. Come on, let's get out of here."

We wandered after our Special Agent hounds to the shattered entrance, where we met the media head on. Stark and the boys, looking like something out of a disaster film, herded a pair of very soggy, battered computer programmers through the lobby and into the klieg-light atmosphere outside the building. Reporters, police, and even a SWAT team had joined the crowd of Aireon employees gathered in the open spaces between the buildings.

Joshua Billians, proudly flaunting his gun-shot arm, met the shining camera eyes with his head up and a ready statement. "Yes," he cried in response to a reporter's indistinct question and forward-thrust microphone. "I am General Gideon, the Seventh Angel, the right hand of righteousness. Evil shall not prevail, despite the treacherous efforts of the Beast! I will rise again!"

Loren nudged me. "You going over to introduce yourself, Beast?"

"Nah," I sniffed, shivering slightly in the cold air. "I've had quite enough of Gideon for tonight. Besides, he seems perfectly happy laying the foundation for an insanity plea without me."

The press, alerted as usual to a major cyber-terrorist event, seemed as satisfied to document Gideon's defeat as they had been to publicize his triumphs. Ratings are ratings, after all. With a fine disregard for the public's right to have their surrogates shout loopy inquiries at a notorious proto-celebrity, Stark hustled Gideon into the waiting ambulance, climbed in after him, and slammed the door firmly against further questions—and answers. Ieyasu ushered a pale, subdued Gideon Thomas toward an FBI truck with much less interference or interest.

"Mr. Hunter? Miss Jones?" We turned to find a tall, thin, delicately handsome man standing behind us. Paul Stanton himself had come to witness his empire's plunge into darkness and its dramatic rescue. He didn't seem overly concerned about it, however, as he shook our hands.

"Thank you," he told us sincerely, pumping Loren's hand. Loren just stared at him, stunned, making no effort to reclaim his hand. "You have saved not only thousands of V-Net users' privacy, but Aireon Unlimited as well. Exemplary work. Thank you again." He smiled at us both as a harried-looking woman pushed her way through the crowd, reporters in tow. "Please excuse me."

He turned away, facing the reporters' cameras and questions with his hands deep in his jacket pockets, the famous Stanton half-smile on his face. "It appears that we are going to be down for a couple of hours," he told them. "Of course, all of us here at Aireon apologize to our loyal customers for the inconvenience. However, we are working closely with the FBI on this matter, and with their expert help we have isolated and corrected a problem that could have deeply affected all V-Net users, not only Aireon's legions of customers. The V-Net is a safer place tonight than ever, thanks to the efforts of dedicated Aireon programmers and the National Infrastructure Protection Center. As Dave Connor, Special Agent in

Charge, will explain, the apprehension of the cyberterrorist calling himself Gideon came about with the assistance and cooperation of—" His explanation faded behind us, expertly smoothing ruffled feathers and scandal-hungry wolves as he appropriated at least half the credit and evaded responsibility for the whole thing.

I punched Loren's arm as we slipped away from the crowd, crossing the trampled lawn to my car. "Gee, you're Paul Stanton's hero!"

He snorted. "We better get you home and dried off. All that water's seeped through your hair and into your brain."

"You're not exactly up to recommended aridity standards yourself."

"I'm all wet with admiration for Stanton," Loren said. "Do you believe that guy? He's going to have them telling everybody that Aireon managed to catch Gideon practically single-handed, instead of breaking the news that Aireon was actually *paying* Gideon!"

"Stanton does know his way around public relations," I agreed. "Hey, don't look so down. We'll spread it around the Kaos Komputer Klub, post it in a few discussion forums. Joe User might not know, but the real V-Net heads will know."

"Oh, great—like they don't already know that Stanton is slicker than ectoplasmic residue anyway. Speaking of which, here comes Dave." Loren sighed.

"Well, at least he's lost Van Helsing," I pointed out. "Looks like you're vindicated. Hey, Dave. Come to admit you were wrong and tell us we're wonderful?"

"I was wrong, and you were wonderful," Dave said, but then he tarnished the moment by adding, "even though you did take down Aireon's entire network and service-provider linkage."

Loren smirked. "We also managed to drown a couple million dollars' worth of mainframes."

Dave groaned. "I don't want to know until I see it in your report." He straightened his tie as the outlying media hounds noticed us and charged forward, wanting confirmation and adoration of Stanton's story. "In the meantime, though, consider yourselves commended. Go home, get some sleep, and don't answer *any* questions!" He strode forward to meet the pack, smiling confidently. "Yes, the FBI is investigating what happened here. We have apprehended a suspect—"

I got into the car and slammed the door. Loren settled into the passenger side and pulled out his portable. "Careful—we don't want any more electronic fireworks," I said. "Is that thing water-proof?"

"Yup," Loren said. "Well, look at this—you've got mail, Gideon again, but short and to the point this time. *'The last shall be first, and the first shall be last.'* Hmm—dated after the power went off."

I looked at him, my eyes wide. "You don't think—"

"No, I don't." Loren shrugged. "You know how easy it is to fake a timestamp. Besides, Stanton's guys will close the hole the worm was using, now that we know where it is. You're the one who knows spoofing when she sees it, remember?"

I believed him, but I still had to pull over, take the portable, and use Truth or Die to check the time stamp for myself. "All right, smart aleck," I said, handing it back before I pulled out of the parking lot, weaving through the mess of cars, trucks, and mobile satellite units. "Whew. I hope they put him in a box with no V-Net access for a very long time."

"Waste of excellent programming talent," Loren noted, and I agreed. "Too bad he succumbed to idol worship, just like his name-sake—ego, the ultimate modern idol."

I smiled nastily. "Yes, you should take a lesson there—stay on the straight and narrow. As for Gideon, if he ever does manage to snake his way out, Sekhmet's all ready to hunt him again, 'a snare unto Gideon, and unto his house.' See? I do remember a bit about it."

Loren groaned. "Maybe you should get a cat after all—especially since Copycat isn't going to be around much longer. It's not been a good night for kitties, between her and Sekhmet's brave demise." He brightened visibly. "But hey, it's Saturday night. What's the lesson in Primary tomorrow?"

This time it was my turn to groan. "We're going to be grateful for hands. I have no idea what I'm going to say about that."

He nodded thoughtfully. "Well, without hands, you can't use datagloves as well."

Just then, the radio caught our attention. "We're live at the headquarters of Aireon Unlimited," Ayesha the radio goddess informed us, "where David Connor, head of the regional NIPC department, confirms that FBI agents have taken a suspect into custody. Unconfirmed reports indicate the suspect may be the notorious cyberterrorist known as Gideon. The apprehension resulted in the interruption of vital V-Net services to several million Aireon customers tonight, but Aireon owner and CEO Paul Stanton has issued a statement assuring all Aireon customers that their service will be restored promptly, with the outage reflected on their monthly statements. A press release purporting to be from Gideon that arrived at our station shortly before the outage indicates that he had targeted Aireon, referring to the company as the 'handmaid of the whore of Babylon,' despite the company's sterling record of customer service—"

"Or change radio stations," I agreed, suiting action to words. A chugging beat filled the car.

"So," Loren said after a moment, "what do you bet Stanton planned the whole thing?"

"Trashing his own mainframes? Knocking his own customers off the V-Net for hours?" I asked incredulously. "Please. He paid Gideon—or rather, Billians—but for legitimate coding work!"

"Grabbing the chance to let the wired world know that Aireon's way beyond messing with?" Loren shot back. "Getting even more interest for his open operating system, more eyes combing through the code for possible holes, equaling more bug fixes? Maybe even cadging insurance money to upgrade his buildings and computer hardware, probably to a set of wetware boxes? And his company's the only one of the lot that didn't really lose anything."

Taking my hand, Loren met my skeptical stare with a raised eyebrow of his own. "All right, maybe not," he said. "But it makes you think, doesn't it?"

About the Author

Jessica Draper is the author of the Last Days adventure trilogy: *Seventh Seal, Rising Storm,* and *Final Hour*. A bibliophile and wannabe librarian, she landed unexpectedly in the wired world. After several years of writing software documentation — which sometimes qualifies as speculative fiction — she left the tech industry to become an instructional designer creating multimedia courseware. Her latest novel *Hunting Gideon* and its upcoming prequel, *Dancing with Eddie D'Eath*, represent additional forays into a not-so-distant future, simultaneously fantastic and believable.

Additional Titles Published by Zarahemla Books

Brother Brigham—In this novel by D. Michael Martindale, C.H. Young has sacrificed his dreams to earn a living for his family—until one day he receives an amazing supernatural visitation. As Brother Brigham's appearances and instructions grow increasingly bold, C.H. struggles to hold together his faith, his marriage, and his sanity.

Hooligans: A Mormon Boyhood—Detailing the author's years growing up in Provo, Utah, during the Depression and World War Two, Douglas Thayer's memoir shares literary DNA in common with Frank McCourt's *Angela's Ashes*, Mark Twain's *The Adventures of Huckleberry Finn*, and William Golding's *Lord of the Flies*.

Kindred Spirits—In this novel by Christopher Kimball Bigelow, Utah-bred Eliza Spainhower has carved out an independent life for herself in Boston. After she makes a love connection with a local native on the subway, she's forced to reckon in new ways with her Mormon identity and her sometimes-overactive religious imagination.

Long After Dark—In these award-winning stories and a new novella, Todd Robert Petersen takes the reader on expeditions to Utah, Arizona, Brazil, Rwanda, and into the souls of twenty-first-century Mormons caught between their humanity, faith, and church. "It is a wonderful book!" says Richard H. Cracroft, emeritus BYU English professor.

On the Road to Heaven—From the author of *Latter Days: A Guided Tour Through Six Billion Years of Mormonism* comes this exuberant and groundbreaking autobiographical novel about the modern Mormon convert experience. Revealing author Coke Newell's hard-won path to meaning, faith, and forgiveness, *On the Road to Heaven* is a love story about a girl and a guy and their search for heaven—a lotta love, a little heaven, and one heck of a ride in between.

ZarahemlaBooks.com • info@zarahemlabooks.com

Also available at Amazon.com and other booksellers

* 9 7 8 0 9 7 8 7 9 7 1 4 0 *